"Nice to see you again, Countess."

For an instant she froze. After what she'd told Clint Lonigan last night, the first response that came to her mind was, *How dare you?* But people were watching. The last thing she wanted was to make a scene.

"It's Mrs. Townsend," she said in a chilly voice. "And it's nice to see you too, Mr. Lonigan. Now, if you don't mind, I have some purchases to pay for." She turned toward the clerk. "I'll have two peppermint sticks for the children, please."

"Coming right up, Countess."

She frowned. "As I just told the gentleman, it's Mrs. Townsend. This isn't England and I'm certainly not royalty."

"But still a very proper lady." Clint Lonigan's voice had taken on a teasing tone.

Ignoring him, Eve signed for her purchases, gave each of the children a peppermint stick and reached for her basket. "I'll be taking leave of you now, M

AUTHOR NOTE

As a little girl I loved playing cowgirls and cowboys. My cousins and I would cut willows from the canal bank and ride them like horses, whooping and chasing all over the neighbourhood. In the small mountain town where I grew up we couldn't get a TV signal until I was in high school. But we didn't need TV. We had our imaginations—and the movies we looked forward to every weekend.

My favourite movies were Westerns, with great stars like John Wayne, Alan Ladd, Roy Rogers, Dale Evans, and wonderful Maureen O'Hara. And I loved Western books, too. By the time I was thirteen I'd read every Zane Grey book on the shelf at the town library. No wonder that when I became a published author I turned to writing Western romance. For me, writing a Western is like going home.

The Countess and the Cowboy is an old-fashioned, rip-roaring Western with a little spice thrown in. Clint is all cowboy and all man, fighting for the rights of small ranchers against the evil cattle baron who burned his ranch and killed his wife and unborn child. Eve is everything Clint isn't—a gently reared English lady who wants nothing more than to raise her sister's children in peace. Instead she finds herself in the middle of a range war, torn between her beloved children on the one side and her irresistible cowboy on the other.

I love hearing from my readers. You can contact me through my website elizabethlaneauthor.com

THE COUNTESS
AND THE COWBOY

Elizabeth Lane

Published in Great Britain 2015
by Mills & Boon, an imprint of Harlequin (UK) Limited,
Eton House, 18-24 Paradise Road, Richmond, Surrey, TW9 1SR

© 2015 Elizabeth Lane

ISBN: 978-0-263-24806-7

Harlequin (UK) Limited's policy is to use papers that are natural, renewable and recyclable products and made from wood grown in sustainable forests. The logging and manufacturing processes conform to the legal environmental regulations of the country of origin.

Printed and bound in Spain
by CPI, Barcelona

Elizabeth Lane has lived and travelled in many parts of the world, including Europe, Latin America and the Far East, but her heart remains in the American West, where she was born and raised. Her idea of heaven is hiking a mountain trail on a clear autumn day. She also enjoys music, animals and dancing. You can learn more about Elizabeth by visiting her website at elizabethlaneauthor.com

Books by Elizabeth Lane

Mills & Boon® Historical Romance

Visit the author profile page at millsandboon.co.uk for more titles

For Walter and Sadie, who wake me up laughing.

Chapter One

Northern Wyoming, August 1888

The stagecoach, a canvas-covered mud wagon that had seen better days, rattled over the washboard road. The final leg of the run from Casper to Lodgepole was blessedly short, but the horses were already lathered from the afternoon heat. Dust billowed from under the wheels to settle like fine brown velvet on the driver, the guard and the three passengers inside—two women and a man.

Clint Lonigan sat directly across from the veiled woman. Pretending to doze, he studied her through slitted eyes. He'd already guessed who—and what—she was. Ten days ago, when he'd left Lodgepole to sit with a dying friend, the town had been abuzz with the news that an honest-to-God countess, the widow of an English earl, was coming to live with her sister, Margaret Hanford.

Clint had paid scant attention to the gossip. Mrs. Hanford seemed like a nice enough woman, but her husband, Roderick, was the most arrogant, pretentious piece of cow manure in the whole county. Clint wouldn't have been impressed to hear that Queen Victoria herself planned on dropping by the Hanford ranch for a damned spot of tea.

But here was the countess in the flesh. And now that he'd seen her, damned if he wasn't intrigued. The Dowager Countess of Manderfield—Hanford had made sure folks knew her full title. No question that this woman was the real thing. Who but an upper-class foreigner would travel on a sweltering day dressed head to toe in widow's weeds? She had to be sweating like a mule under that heavy black silk.

If the woman's costume left any question of her status, the engraved signet ring on her left hand erased all doubt. It was heavy gold with a ruby the size of a black-eyed pea. He couldn't help but marvel that some plug-ugly hadn't hacked off her finger to steal it.

A widow's bonnet, black with a dusty silk veil, concealed her hair and face. Apart from her slender frame, Clint couldn't tell whether she was young or old, plain or pretty. Even her lace-mitted hands gave no clue. The "Dowager" in her title suggested a woman past middle age. But that didn't make a bean's worth of difference, because there was one thing Clint knew for sure.

If the countess was planning to move in with Roderick Hanford, she was already one of the enemy.

Eve Townsend, Dowager Countess of Manderfield, braced her boots against the floor of the coach, shifting on the seat in an attempt to ease her tortured buttocks. She'd lowered her veil against the dust, but there was nothing to be done for the constant jarring.

Or the heat. Eve felt as if her body was being baked in treacle. She'd worn her mourning clothes to prompt some deference on the journey and discourage any strange men who might otherwise accost her. To that extent the costume had worked. But she was not at all certain that the benefits outweighed the unending discomfort. Traveling in black silk bombazine was like sitting in a Turkish bath.

But enough complaints! This was the American West, and Margaret had warned her to expect some rough conditions. The stormy, sickness-fraught ocean voyage, followed by the jostling train ride from New York to the railhead at Casper, had drained Eve in body and spirit. But this was the last leg of a journey that would soon be over. With Margaret and her children she would have a roof over her head and family around her. She could hardly wait to hold Margaret's baby, due to be born this very month.

"Will your sister's family be meeting the stage, Countess?" Plump, middle-aged and chatty, Mrs. Etta Simpkins had already introduced herself. She ran a bakery in Lodgepole and appeared to know the business of everyone in town.

"I certainly hope so," Eve answered politely. "And you needn't call me Countess. This is America, after all. Mrs. Townsend will do."

"Very well." The woman sounded a trifle disappointed. "But don't count on Margaret being there when you arrive. When I saw her two weeks ago, she was as big around the waist as a fifty-pound pumpkin. I'd wager she's had that baby by now. From the look of her, it could even be twins."

"Twins! Goodness, wouldn't that be wonderful? That's why I've come, you know, to help Margaret with the children."

It was enough truth for now, Eve reasoned. There was no need to spread the word that, upon her husband's death, her grown stepson, Albert, had burned his father's updated will—which would have left her generously provided for—and booted her off the Manderfield estate with little more than her title and her wedding ring. If not for her sister's invitation, she could be languishing in the poorhouse.

Eve brushed a blowfly off her skirt, its movement drawing her eye to the man who sat on the opposite bench, his knees almost touching hers. At the moment, he appeared to be sleeping. But the glimmer beneath his lowered eyelids told her he was fully alert, like a dozing panther.

He'd muttered an introduction before taking his seat. Lonigan—that was the surname, she remembered. Irish, of course, having the name and the look of that wretched race, though his speech sounded American. She'd acknowledged him with an icy nod. He'd seemed not to care or even to notice her disdain. Perversely, his utter indifference piqued her interest.

She studied him through her veil—a lanky

frame, long denim-covered legs, dusty Mexican-style riding boots, a faded shirt and a well-worn leather vest. His sun-burnished hands were callused—a workingman's hands. His proud bearing suggested he might be a landholder. But he didn't appear to be wealthy like Margaret's husband, Roderick, who, according to her letters, owned more than twenty thousand head of cattle and a house as big as an English manor.

Eve's eyes lingered on the man's face. He had features like chiseled granite, framed by unruly chestnut hair that curled over the tops of his ears. The scar that slashed across his cleft chin lent him a subtle aura of danger. He struck her as the sort of man no proper lady should have anything to do with.

Still, she caught herself trying to imagine the color of his mostly closed eyes.

A sudden pistol shot whanged from behind the coach. The bullet pierced the canvas cover, splintering the wooden framework overhead. Eve jerked upright, paralyzed by disbelief. Why would anybody be shooting at them?

"Damn it, get down!" Lonigan was out of his seat in an instant, shoving both women onto the floor and flattening himself on top of them. Eve struggled under his weight, eating dust as the coach lurched and picked up speed. He refused to move, his solid chest pressing down on her back. Beneath his leather vest, she could feel the distinct outline of a small, holstered pistol.

The coach swayed crazily as it thundered along the rutted road. Bullets sang overhead like angry wasps. Mrs. Simpkins was shrieking in terror.

A hump in the road launched the coach into an instant's flight, then dropped it with a sickening crunch. The vehicle careened to one side, shuddered and came to rest on one broken wheel. Eve bit back a whimper. Clearly, they'd been run down by highwaymen and their lives were in grave danger. But her late father, who'd served his country during the great Indian mutiny, had schooled her to hide her fear.

"Everybody outside!" The male voice sounded young and nervous. "Do as you're told and nobody gets hurt."

Lonigan muttered a string of curses. Eve gulped dusty air as his rock-hard weight eased off her. "Give me your ring!" he growled in her ear.

"And why, pray tell, should I do that?"

"They'll take it if they see it. Might even cut

your finger off to get at it if you don't cooperate. Give me the damned ring!" Without waiting for a reply, he seized Eve's hand and yanked
the ring off her finger. It vanished into a vest
pocket as he rose to his knees and unlatched
the door of the coach.

"We're coming out," he shouted. "But mind
your manners. There are ladies in here."

Eve scrambled onto the seat as he opened the
door and stepped out. Mrs. Simpkins appeared
to have fainted. Eve found her smelling salts in
her reticule and waved the vial under the woman's nose. She flinched, snorted and opened her
eyes. "What's happened?" she gasped.

"We're being robbed. They want us to get
out."

"Oh, dear!" She looked as if she were going
to faint again.

"Come on—and keep still. The less we say
the better." Eve helped the woman rise. Passing
her ahead to Lonigan, Eve took a breath to collect herself and then climbed out of the coach
and into the sunbaked air. Her legs felt as unsteady as a newborn lamb's, but she straightened her spine to hide her nerves and anxiety.

Through the haze of settling dust she sur-
veyed the chaos—the lathered horses and the

coach sagging onto its shattered wheel. The grizzled driver's hands were in the air. The guard clutched his bleeding arm but didn't appear badly hurt. Eve saw no sign of the double-barreled shotgun he'd carried.

There were just two robbers, their hats pulled low and their faces masked with bandannas. Slim and erect on their mounts, they could've been schoolboys. But there was nothing childish about their weapons—heavy pistols, cocked and aimed.

"Is everybody out?" Eve recognized the nervous voice of the robber who'd ordered them from the coach.

"We are." Lonigan faced him boldly. Eve remembered the gun under his vest. Did he plan to use it? "As you see, boys, it's just me and these two good widow ladies. None of us has anything worth stealing. So pack your pistols and go home before somebody else gets hurt." His eyes flickered toward the wounded guard. "Damned lucky you didn't kill that man. You could end up swinging by your fool necks."

Eve glanced at him from beneath her veil. Something didn't seem right, and suddenly she knew what it was. Lonigan didn't seem the least bit afraid. He was lecturing the robbers like a stern uncle.

He knew them!

Lonigan swore silently. He'd told the Potter brothers to lie low and keep things quiet while he was away. What in Sam Hill were they doing holding up the stage, especially in broad daylight? The bandannas couldn't hide their builds and it sounded as if they hadn't even tried to disguise their voices. Didn't the young fools understand what could happen if they were recognized?

When he got them alone, he'd give them the tongue-lashing of their lives. Meanwhile, he needed to get them out of this mess before things went from bad to worse.

"It's the strongbox we come for," Newt, the older of the brothers, said. "Throw it down, and we'll go."

The driver shook his shaggy head. "Man, there's no strongbox on this stage."

"That ain't what we was told." This time it was Gideon who spoke. "A box of cash from the Cattlemen's Association in Cheyenne. They was sendin' it to hire gunfighters."

Lonigan suppressed a groan. He'd been in

Cheyenne with his ears open, but he'd heard nothing about any cash, nor had he seen any signs of a strongbox when they'd loaded the coach. It had to be a mistake or, more likely, a trap.

A bead of sweat trickled down the side of his face. The Potter boys had become part of his secret operation two years ago, after their father was framed and hanged for cattle rustling. They'd long since proved their courage, but they were young and reckless. If someone had planted the rumor about the cash to draw them out, the sheriff's men could already be on their way to arrest them.

He had to get the boys away from here. But how could he do it without showing his own hand?

The driver shrugged. "There's no cash on this stage. Look for yourself."

Newt nodded toward his younger brother. "Go on. I'll keep 'em covered."

Gideon dismounted and checked the front boot, where the strongbox was usually kept. He shook his head and moved on to search the rest of the stage. Clint glanced at the two women beside him. Mrs. Simpkins seemed ready to collapse. The countess stood ramrod straight, supporting the terrified woman with one arm.

Looking over, Clint noticed that Newt was staring at the countess, as well. He was the volatile one of the brothers, with a nervous tic and a jumpy trigger finger. Anything could set him off. "I don't like it when I can't see folks' faces," he snapped. "Lift that veil, lady."

Hesitating, she glanced toward Clint.

"Do it," he growled.

Her free hand caught the veil's lace edge and swept it back.

Clint had resolved not to gape at the woman, but he couldn't help himself. He'd expected a grim widow approaching middle age. But the countess couldn't have been much past thirty. Raven hair framed a porcelain face with classic features. Her full, almost sensual mouth was accented by a tiny mole at one corner. When she glanced toward him, the eyes that met his were a startling shade of blue, framed by dark-winged brows and lush black lashes.

Clint bit back a curse. The countess was, without doubt, the most stunning woman he'd ever seen.

Not that her beauty mattered to him either way. He wasn't looking for a woman, especially not one going to live in the enemy camp. Everything she saw and heard today would go straight back to her brother-in-law, Roderick Hanford. And Hanford was no fool. If he managed to piece things together and realized that Clint recognized the men responsible for nearly shooting up the man's sister-in-law, they'd all be in trouble.

"The strongbox ain't here," Gideon announced. "I looked everyplace, even underneath."

"Damnation!" Newt spat a stream of tobacco into the dust.

"I'd say you've been fooled, boys." Clint spoke calmly. "If you know what's good for you, you'll swing those ponies around and head for the tall timber."

Gideon was back in the saddle. Half turning his horse, he glanced at his brother. "Let's go," he said.

But Newt was building to an explosion. Clint knew the signs—the twitching eyes, the shaking hands. The boy could be unpredictable when he was out of control, and the law could be here any minute.

Newt's pistol quivered in his hand. "We come this far. We ain't leavin' empty-handed."

Clint struggled to curb his anxiety. There was only one thing left to do, and the countess wasn't going to like it. He fished in his pocket and came up with the ruby ring. "This will make it worth your trouble. Take it and get the hell out of here."

The countess gasped as Newt leaned down and snatched the ring. Clint exhaled as the two would-be stage robbers wheeled their mounts, spurred them to a gallop and thundered over the crest of a nearby hill. They were safe for now. But those young hooligans had put his whole operation at risk. When he saw them again, he was going to give them Jesse, and he wouldn't let up till he had some solid answers about who had told them such a damn fool story, and why they'd been thick enough to believe it.

Right now he had other problems—not the least of them a riled woman who wanted a piece of his hide.

"How *could* you?" The countess's eyes blazed blue fire. She looked as if she wanted to fly at him and claw his face to bloody ribbons. "First you take my ring so it won't get stolen! Then you give it to the thieves! That ring was in my late husband's family for generations. It was all I had left of him! Now it's gone!"

As she glared up at him, Clint saw tears brimming in her azure eyes. He forced himself to turn aside. Pity for Hanford's sister-in-law, who probably had more money than all the county's poor ranch families combined, was an emotion he could ill afford.

"Look at me!" She caught his sleeve. "Don't you have anything to say for yourself?"

Clint hardened his gaze. "I did what I had to, lady. Would you rather have been shot, or maybe raped? Would you rather they'd hurt someone else?"

"Of course not. But if you think I'm going to let those robbers ride off with my most precious possession you're sorely mistaken. I'm holding you responsible, Mr. Lonigan. And if I don't get that ring back, my brother-in-law, Mr. Hanford, has the power to make you pay!"

The mention of Roderick Hanford triggered a surge of bitter fury. Clint fought it back. "Fine," he snapped, "but that will have to wait. For now, stop caterwauling and make yourself useful. You can look after Mrs. Simpkins while I check the guard and help the driver replace that broken wheel."

Without waiting for her response, he turned his back on her and strode toward the front of the stage.

* * *

Seething, Eve watched him walk away. It wasn't so much his argument that had offended her—on the contrary, it made sense that something had been needed to mollify the robbers. But his manner was insufferable. She was the widow of a nobleman, but he'd spoken to her as if she were a backward child. In England, no commoner would have dared address her with such insolence.

True, she was no longer in England. Everyone was a commoner here. But some were more common than others, and rudeness was rudeness. Mr. Lonigan was clearly no gentleman. For all she knew, he could be in league with the pair who'd held up the coach. He'd certainly appeared to know them. Perhaps he'd planned all along to give them her ring.

The ring was a devastating loss. But for the time being, there was nothing she could do to recover it, so Eve tried not to think about it. Instead, she guided Mrs. Simpkins to a nearby flat boulder, then hurried back to the stage for parasols, her reticule and a canteen of water. The sun was blistering, and there was no shade to be found.

"Are you all right?" Eve raised the woman's parasol and pressed the canteen to her lips.

"I will be." Mrs. Simpkins took several dainty swallows and wiped her mouth with the back of her hand. "My stars, what a fright! I'm so sorry about your ring, my dear."

The familiar term was oddly comforting, even coming from a stranger. Eve let it pass. "Did you recognize those two robbers, Mrs. Simpkins?" she asked.

The woman shook her graying head. "One of the voices might have sounded familiar, but I can't be certain. Given the state I was in, I wouldn't have recognized my own children."

"And do you know that wretched Mr. Lonigan?" Eve glanced toward the stage, where Lonigan was wrapping the guard's wounded arm with a red bandanna.

"I know him, but not well. He's got a small ranch north of Lodgepole. Paid cash for the land, I hear tell. He was widowed two years ago, but I never did meet his wife. They kept to themselves and she didn't come into town. Not even for church. I've heard rumors of a scandalous past, but nothing I can tell you for sure. Mercy, but it's hot!"

"Here, this should help." Eve reached into her

reticule, withdrew a black lace fan and snapped it open. Mrs. Simpkins accepted it with a grateful sigh.

"My, but this is lovely!" she exclaimed.

"Then it's yours. Keep it as a remembrance." Eve would have no need for it soon. She had long since resolved to set her mourning aside at the journey's end. She'd agreed to marry Arthur Townsend, Sixth Earl of Manderfield, after he'd offered to pay off her father's debts. Arthur had been a kindly man, and he'd treated her like a queen; but he'd been more than twice her age. She'd liked and respected him, but they certainly had not been in love. Three years prior to his death a stroke had left him an invalid. Eve had cared for him faithfully until the end—when his son, Albert, had stepped in, taken over the estate and cast her out like a common strumpet. But never mind. The past was behind her now. She was ready to make a new start.

And in such a wild place! Her gaze swept upward to the mountains, so tall and rugged that they seemed to pierce the sky. Even under the August sun, their rocky peaks bore glistening patches of snow. Below the timberline, forests of dark green pine carpeted the slopes, giving way to the green-gold of aspens and the grassy hills that fed thousands of white-faced Hereford cattle, the wealth of this untamed land.

From the train Eve had seen buffalo herds and wide-eyed pronghorn antelope that could out-race the wind. And she'd heard tales of the predators that prowled the forest shadows—wolves, bears and the fierce golden cat of many names: puma, cougar, catamount, panther, mountain lion.

But she'd come to believe that the most savage creatures in the untamed frontier of this country were the men. It was as if the fight for survival had beaten all the civility out of them. They were like snarling beasts, jumpy and alert, ready to reach for a weapon at the slightest provocation. When they met they sized each other up like bristling hounds, measuring size and speed, testing their power.

Foolish posturing, that's all it was.

Her gaze returned to Lonigan. He'd finished tending to the wounded guard and was helping lift the stage off its broken wheel, raising the axle inch by inch while the aging driver braced it up with rocks. It was hard work. His leather vest and holstered pistol lay in the grass at the roadside. His shirt was dripping with sweat. The faded fabric clung like a second skin to his muscular body—not an unpleasant sight, Eve conceded. His eyes, she now recalled, were like sharp gray flint, deepening in hue around their black centers. If he were to submit to a bath, a barber and a suit of decent clothes, he could be quite attractive. Yet maybe it was better that he stayed as he was. His appearance now made no effort to hide the harshness of his true nature.

Lonigan was no different from other men she'd observed. At best, he was arrogant and ill-mannered. Short of that, he could be a thief or at least a friend of thieves. Worse, if anything, he was Irish. She would do nothing to rile him for now. Until their journey ended, she was uncomfortably at his mercy. However, once the stage reached Lodgepole and she was safely ensconced with her sister's family, she would turn the matter of the ring over to Roderick and have nothing more to do with him.

With the spare wheel in place, the stage lumbered the last few miles toward Lodgepole. Clint had given the wounded guard his seat inside. Riding shotgun with the driver, he scanned the brushy hills. At any minute, he'd expected to see Sheriff Harv Womack and his deputies come galloping into sight, but it hadn't happened. Maybe the rumor about the cash shipment hadn't been a trap, after all. Or maybe Clint was just jumping at shadows. The truth might have to wait till he caught up with Newt and Gideon.

"Did you have any plans to carry cash?" he asked the driver. "I'm just wondering where those two galoots got the idea there'd be a strongbox."

The driver spat a stream of tobacco off the side of the stage. "Not from me. If I'd been carryin' a strongbox, I would've had a second guard up here. Lucky for us nobody got hurt worse'n that hen scratch on Zeke's arm."

"Are you planning to report the holdup?"

He shook his head. "I'll let the sheriff know if I see him—or you can tell him yourself if you want to. But it's not worth takin' time to file a report. We're runnin' late as it is. And them two kids didn't strike me as hardened criminals. I don't expect they'll bother us again."

Clint's fears eased some, but Newt and Gideon weren't out of the woods yet. Damn it, he should've asked somebody to ride herd on those boys. They'd earned the right to be part of his operation—a handful of small ranchers who'd banded together to protect each other and their neighbors from the cattle barons who wanted their land. But the brothers were always pushing the limits. If they got themselves caught thieving and were scared enough to name names to avoid a noose, all hell could break loose.

The young fools were well-known and easy to recognize. Now four people besides Clint had seen them holding up the stage. The driver and guard were from Casper. They could describe the robbers but didn't likely know them. Mrs. Simpkins knew the brothers, but she'd been frightened out of her wits. Clint could only hope she hadn't guessed who they were. At least she hadn't shown any signs of recognizing them. As for the countess…

The image of that Madonna-like face glimmered like a phantom in his mind. Yes, she was the dangerous one. She'd lost a priceless heirloom and she was determined to get it back at any cost. Worse, she'd have the ear of Roderick Hanford, the most powerful and ruthless rancher in the county.

Clint cursed his own shortsightedness. He'd only wanted to get Newt and Gideon out of harm's way. But he'd stepped in it this time, up to his well-meaning chin.

This couldn't wait. He had to find the boys and get that damned ring back.

The driver had let Lonigan off at the livery stable on the edge of town. As the coach rolled into Lodgepole, Eve raised the edge of the canvas cover for a look at her new home.

She stifled a groan.

Lodgepole's main street was a long strip of dirt. Ugly clapboard buildings, most of them wanting paint, lined both sides, fronted by a sagging boardwalk. Eve recognized a saloon, a general store, a bank of sorts and a gaudy-looking structure that might have been a brothel. A farm wagon, drawn by a plodding, mismatched team, rolled down the opposite side of the street. A horse tied outside the saloon raised its tail and dropped a steaming pile of manure in the dust.

Tucked between the general store and the bank was a neat little shop with a Closed sign in the window. That would be Mrs. Simpkins's bakery. At least it had curtains and a flowerpot on the sill. As for the rest of the town…

But never mind, Eve lectured herself. Soon she would be with Margaret and the children. That was the only thing that mattered.

Though they'd been apart for nearly eleven

years, the two sisters had remained close. They'd written to each other every few weeks, sharing secrets, sorrows and small victories. Anyplace with Margaret would be home. And Eve would so enjoy the children—Thomas, who was eight, Rose, who was six, and the new baby. It would be almost as good as having children of her own.

True, she'd never cared for Margaret's husband, Roderick, whom she'd known since childhood. The second son of a neighboring farmer, he'd always been something of a braggart and a bully. But that hadn't kept Margaret from marrying him and following him to the wilds of America. Eve had never tried to mask her dislike for her brother-in-law. But at least he'd agreed to take her in. For her sister's sake, and for harmony in the household, she would make every effort to tolerate the man.

The stage was slowing down. Eve's pulse raced with anticipation as it pulled up to the covered porch of a two-story building that appeared to be a hotel. She glimpsed three figures on the porch—a tall man and two children.

It had to be Roderick. Eve hadn't seen him in more than a decade, but she'd know that gaunt scarecrow figure anywhere. There was no sign of his wife. Did that mean Margaret had already given birth? Was she home with the baby?

Mrs. Simpkins motioned her toward the door. "Go ahead and get out first, my dear. You've come such a long way. You must be exhausted."

With a murmur of thanks, Eve swept back her veil, unlatched the door and stepped out onto the boardwalk.

It was indeed Roderick on the porch with the children—such beautiful children. Thomas was dark and solemn like his maternal grandfather. And Rose was like her name, a dainty little fair-haired flower. Wondering what she should say first, Eve hurried toward them.

Their stricken faces stopped her cold.

Eve's hand crept to her throat. Even before she heard it, she guessed the truth.

Roderick broke the silence. "It's good you've come, Eve. Margaret died in childbirth ten days ago."

"And the baby?" Her question emerged as a choked whisper.

Roderick shook his head. "The baby, too."

Chapter Two

"You mule-headed bunglers! Don't you know what could've happened if you'd been caught?" Clint had found the Potter brothers hiding in his barn. He could only hope his tongue-lashing would scare some sense into them. "What in hell's name did you think you were doing, holding up that stage?"

"We heard tell there was money on it." Newt cringed against the side of the milking stall. "Money for hired guns, to drive us off our land. Don't be mad, Clint. We'd've told you but you wasn't here. We had to do somethin'."

"Where did you hear about the money? Who told you?"

"Smitty passed it on," Gideon replied. "Said some of Hanford's men was talkin' about it at the bar."

Clint scowled, weighing what he'd heard. Smitty, the one-legged bartender at the Red Dog Saloon, had always been a reliable source. If he said he'd heard about the money, it was likely true.

Had the cattlemen discovered that Smitty was passing information to the small ranchers? Could they have fed him a lie to set a trap?

The failure of the sheriff's men to appear and spring that trap would argue against it.

So what if the information about the money had been true? What if the cash had been on board the stage, after all—not in a strongbox, but hidden on one of the passengers?

Which one? He could probably rule out Etta Simpkins, who was little more than a harmless chatterbox. That left the mysterious beauty draped from head to toe in sweltering black silk.

What had the countess been wearing under those widow's weeds? He'd bet the farm it wasn't just lace-trimmed petticoats and silk drawers—unless she'd hidden the stash in her trunk.

"That ring you took—where is it?" he demanded.

Newt fished the ruby ring out of his pocket,

spat on the stone and rubbed it on his shirt. "Purty thing. Looks like it might be worth a piece. How much d'you reckon we could get for it?"

"Here in Lodgepole, all you'd get is a necktie party from Roderick Hanford. That widow on the stage was Hanford's sister-in-law. The ring's hers."

"The countess?" Apparently Gideon had heard the rumors. "Didn't count on her bein' such a looker. What were you doin' with her ring?"

Clint hooked the ring with his forefinger and dropped it into his vest pocket. "I took it for safekeeping after the shooting started. When I gave it up to get rid of you boys, she was madder than a wet wildcat. If she doesn't get it back, she'll have our hides nailed to Hanford's barn."

"So how d'you figure on gettin' it to her? It's not like you can just march up Hanford's front steps and knock on the door."

"That's my problem. Your problem is staying out of jail. Lie low while I scout around and rustle you up some supplies so you can go hide out until this blows over. As soon as it's dark you can head up to that old herder's cabin below the peaks. You're not to show your faces around here till I send word that it's safe, hear?"

"What about our place?" Newt whined. "What about our stock?"

"Don't worry, I'll see to things." At that, the brothers subsided, looking like nothing so much as scolded schoolboys. Clint abandoned the rest of his lecture. Newt and Gideon weren't young enough to be his sons, but most of the time he felt like their father.

Warning them once more to stay hidden and quiet, Clint left the barn and made a slow circuit of his property. There was no sign of trouble, but a man couldn't be too careful. The countess, or even Etta Simpkins, could have described the stage robbers to Sheriff Womack in enough detail to identify the boys. The sheriff, or maybe some of Hanford's rowdies, could be watching on the chance that the Potter brothers might show up. Clint would need to behave as if nothing was amiss.

A neighbor's boy had been minding his place while he was in Cheyenne. Everything appeared fine, including the Herefords he grazed in an upper pasture; but Clint went through the motions of checking the hen coop, and the paddock where the milk cow and the horses grazed. His eyes swept the scrub-dotted foothills that rose behind the ranch, alert for the slightest movement or the flicker of reflected light on a gun barrel. Nothing. But that didn't mean he wasn't being watched.

He passed through the apple orchard he'd planted the year his wife died. The trees were still too young to bear fruit, but they were tall enough to shelter her grave. Maybe next spring they would shower the sad little mound of earth with soft white petals.

Clint paused, gazing down at the hand-chiseled marker. Corrie had died defending her home from the band of raiders that had raped her and burned the house and barn. At the time, she'd been seven months pregnant with his child.

Clint had been in town that night, summoned there by Roderick Hanford for a supposed meeting between the small ranchers and the members of the Cattlemen's Association. He'd arrived to find the meeting canceled and Hanford playing faro in the Three-legged Dog. When Hanford looked up at him, something in the man's cold eyes had chilled Clint to the marrow. Wild with dread, he'd galloped home to find his ranch ablaze and his wife's naked, bloodied body sprawled in the yard.

Despite the solid alibi, Clint had never stopped believing that Hanford was behind the raid. He'd buried Corrie and planted the trees as a promise that he would stay here, rebuild the ranch and seek justice for her murder. The second part of that promise had yet to be kept. But he hadn't given up.

Now there was a new player in the game— the mysterious beauty who'd be sharing Roderick Hanford's household. How much did the countess know about her brother-in-law's activities? How strong were her loyalties? Could she be swayed, even turned?

If she was already carrying money from the Cattlemen's Association, Clint would have to bet against the odds of winning her over to his side. But desperate times called for desperate measures. If the opportunity presented itself, he would use the woman any way he could.

Walking back toward the house, Clint felt the weight of the ring in his vest pocket. The setting sun cast his lengthening shadow across the ground—still his own ground, despite the cattlemen's attempts to drive him away.

He paused to watch the sky fade from flame

to the deep indigo hue of the countess's eyes. Soon it would be dark. He would see Newt and Gideon safely on the trail to the mountain hideout. Then, once things had settled down for the night, he'd drop by the Three-legged Dog to have a drink and catch up on the news. After that it might be time for a visit to the Hanford ranch.

Dinner that evening was a dismal affair. Alice, the aging cook, had gone to the trouble of making a nice meal. But the children had barely picked at their roast beef and potatoes. Eve had made an effort to eat, but could get only a few morsels down a throat swollen with unshed tears.

Margaret, her gentle, loving sister, was dead and the baby with her. The shock was too much for Eve to grasp.

Only Roderick seemed to have much appetite. He ate with relish, sopping his bread in the gravy and stuffing it into his mouth. Back in England, his lack of a gentleman's manners had been a handicap that had kept him from gaining acceptance in high society. Here, in the wild American West, the rules were different and Roderick was in his element.

Eve's gaze roamed the cavernous dining room with its high, beamed ceiling and deer-antler chandelier. Built of massive rough-hewn logs, the house was large enough to be impressive but looked as if it had been hastily thrown together with no regard for design or taste. She'd expected a welcoming warmth from her sister's home, not decorations that seemed designed to frighten or intimidate guests. The walls around the long table were adorned with mounted animal heads—buffalo, elk, deer, pronghorn antelope, a half-grown black bear and a snarling cougar with yellowed fangs as long as Eve's little finger. Its glass eyes stared down at her, a strange sadness in their empty depths. Or maybe the sadness she sensed was her own.

"I see you're admiring my trophy collection." Roderick had cleaned his plate and was watching her from under his thick, black brows. He was handsome in a long-jawed sort of way, but Eve had never found her brother-in-law attractive. "I treed that cat with the pack of hounds I keep out back," he said. "Got him with one shot straight through the heart."

"He must've been a beautiful animal in life." Eve, who was fond of cats, had no desire to hear about Roderick's hunting exploits and quickly changed the subject. "Who's looking after the children?" she asked.

"Alice has been seeing to their needs," Roderick answered. "But she's getting old and has all she can do with the cooking and cleaning. So I'm hoping you'll make yourself useful, Eve."

"Of course. That's why I've come. To help." She glanced across the table at her sister's children. The two sat in silence, their eyes downcast. This was far from the happy welcome she'd expected. But Thomas and Rose would need a great deal of mothering, and she was here to give it to them as well as she was able.

Roderick was leaning back in his chair, openly studying her. Not that she was any treat for the eye tonight. The news of Margaret's death had left her too stunned to deal with changing her dusty clothes or brushing out her sweat-dampened hair. As far as she was concerned, the last thing that mattered tonight was the way she looked.

"How was your trip, Eve?" he asked. "You haven't told us much about it."

The very question wearied her. She should probably tell him about the holdup and the loss of her ring, but her sister's death had shrunk those events to trivialities. Maybe tomorrow she would have the strength and patience to deal with them. But not tonight.

Eve rose from her chair. "The trip was long, and I'm exhausted. If you'll excuse me, Roderick, I'll take the children upstairs and help them to bed. Then I intend to get some rest myself. Please thank Alice for the lovely dinner."

He rose with her. "I was hoping we could talk."

"Tomorrow." Her smile was forced. "We'll talk then. Come and show me to your rooms, children."

Rose and Thomas took her outstretched hands and led her up the stairs. They shared adjoining nurseries down the hall from the room where Eve's luggage had been taken. Eve had felt nothing of her sister's presence downstairs, where the decor was dark, heavy and oppressively masculine. But the children's rooms spoke of Margaret—the bright chintz coverlets and curtains, the braided rugs, the fairy-tale pictures on the walls. It was as if here, with her little ones, Margaret's true nature had been allowed to blossom. But the rest of the house had clearly been ruled by Roderick.

Margaret's letters had never held a word of complaint against her husband. But how could a woman as sweet and gentle as her sister be happy in this house, and with such a man?

He'd probably read and approved every word she wrote.

Tonight the children were meek and quiet—too quiet. By the light of a flickering candle, Eve got them into their nightclothes, washed their faces and saw that they brushed their teeth. After mumbled prayers, they crawled into their beds and lay still. Poor, wounded little things, their stoicism made her want to weep. She already loved them.

Eve's own spacious room bore Margaret's touch, as well—the soft, flowered coverlet on the bed, the scattered cushions, the pretty little folding secretary against one wall and the upholstered bench by one window. Tears welled in Eve's eyes as she realized her sister had prepared this room just for her, likely within weeks of her death.

Eve used the candle to light the bedside lamp. Her trunk and her other bags sat in the middle of the floor where Roderick's hired men had left them. Back in England she'd have had a lady's maid to unpack her clothes and help ready her for bed. But that life was behind her now, and she was quite capable of doing for herself.

The room was stifling from the day's trapped heat. By the time she'd unpacked half her trunk, her face was damp with sweat. Crossing to the windows, she pulled back the drapes, unlatched the sashes and opened them wide. A draft of coolness swept over her face.

She closed her eyes, filling her lungs with the fresh Wyoming air—as cool in its way as English mist, but drier and sharper, with a light bouquet of pine needles, sagebrush, wood smoke and cattle. Her fingers plucked the pins from her tight bun, letting her hair fall loose as she leaned over the sill.

Heaven.

Savoring the soft breeze, she unbuttoned the high collar of her dress, opening it all the way down to her corset. She'd been miserable all day, so hot… What a blessed relief to feel cool air against her skin!

The moon was rising over the plain, waxing but not yet full. A distant speck of light glowed through the high window of the bunkhouse. Horses stirred and snorted in the corral. None of it was what she was used to—but it was all beautiful, in its way.

She would make the best of what she'd found here, Eve vowed. It wouldn't be easy, but somehow she would learn to tolerate Roderick, nurture her sister's motherless children and find her own small pleasures. Maybe one day she would even come to think of this strange, wild place as home.

But tonight she felt as lost and alone as a wanderer among the stars.

Clint swore under his breath as the countess leaned over the upstairs windowsill. Backlit by the lamp, with her bodice open and her hair streaming like ebony silk, she was a sight to heat the blood of any man—and Roderick Hanford's blood could be simmering already. Clint had heard in the saloon that Hanford's wife had died. No doubt the man would be looking for a replacement to warm his bed. Who better than the beautiful, widowed sister-in-law who'd come to look after his children? The fact that she was damn near royalty wouldn't hurt her chances of becoming the next Mrs. Roderick Hanford, either. If the bastard married her, Clint wouldn't put it past the pretentious ass to take on her title.

But he hadn't risked danger to ogle the woman or make guesses about her relationship with her brother-in-law, he reminded himself.

He hadn't even come to return her ring, though that was the reason he'd give, if she asked. In truth, he'd come to take stock of her situation, maybe even to warn her if he got the chance. He could always put the ring in the mail or wrap it in his bandanna and toss it onto the porch. But then he'd have no excuse to contact the countess—a contact that, if luck was in the cards, might prove useful.

Not that luck had ever shown him much favor.

Checking the shadows, he slipped around the side of the house. The ranch was a perilous place for a man like him. A hundred yards beyond the house, Roderick Hanford kept a kennel of hunting dogs, trained to be as vicious as possible. The scent of a stranger would set off a hellish baying. At a signal from the house, their handler—the master of hounds, Hanford called him—would turn the beasts loose to run down the intruder and tear him to pieces. That very thing had happened to a young cousin of the Potter brothers who'd been caught on Hanford's property. The next morning they'd found his mauled body, or what was left of it, where a night rider had flung it on their porch.

Tonight Clint was downwind from the dogs.

But the wind could change, and he was hair-trigger wary. His pistol was loaded, his horse tethered within sprinting distance. He was ready to leave at a moment's notice...but he hated the thought of going without doing what he'd come for—speaking with the countess.

So what now? The countess had left the window, but he glimpsed signs of her moving about in the lamp-lit room. The other windows in the house had gone dark. She appeared to be the only one still up and stirring. Should he toss a pebble at her pane on the chance that she'd hear? If he showed himself and held up the ring, would she come down to the porch and get it? Would she listen to what he had to say? Or would loyalty to her sister's family compel her to raise an alarm?

Clint forced himself to exhale, feeling the tension in every nerve. He would allow a little more time for the household to settle down, he resolved. Then he could decide whether to act or to leave.

Ever mindful of the wind and the dogs, he slipped into the shadows to wait.

Eve had finished unpacking. Her dresses and cloak hung in the wardrobe. Her brushes and toiletries lay on the mirrored dresser. Her underthings were folded into drawers. She still yearned for the books she'd been forced to leave behind at Manderfield—the volumes of poetry, science, history and literature that had sustained her through the years of Arthur's illness. They'd been hers, an inheritance from her father, who'd died two years after her marriage. But now, by law, in the absence of a will, they belonged to her late husband's estate. Her stepson's family had allowed her to take only a bible and a few precious volumes of Shakespeare's plays. They would have to do.

Eve was tired beyond exhaustion. Common sense told her she should finish undressing and get ready for bed. But something was tugging at her, some deep urge crying to be satisfied. And suddenly she knew what it was.

She had yet to say goodbye to her sister.

Earlier Roderick had mentioned that Margaret and the baby were laid to rest under a large cottonwood that grew a short distance from the house. He'd offered to show her the grave, but Eve had wanted to visit the spot alone. She'd put him off with an excuse and the evening had passed without another chance.

It wasn't too late to go. The moon was bright,

and the tree would make the mound of earth simple enough to find. Maybe some solitude beside her sister's grave would help her accept the news that still seemed no more than a terrible dream.

She took a moment to button her bodice. Then, leaving the lamp in her room, Eve moved out into the hall. Once her eyes became accustomed to the dark it wasn't too difficult to make her way down the stairs. Her senses prickled as she stepped out onto the front porch and closed the door behind her. A warning of danger lurking in the darkness? No, she told herself, it was just the strangeness of being in a new place at night. It would pass.

The wind lifted her hair as she descended the front steps and walked out into the yard. There was no lawn, only dry, gravelly earth that crunched beneath her shoes. Margaret had always loved flowers. Had she tried to plant them here, in this inhospitable place?

Eve could see the big cottonwood now, a stone's throw from the corner of the house. Its trunk was thick and twisted, with upward-reaching limbs as thick as a man's leg. Clouds of silvery leaves glimmered in the moonlight.

As she neared the tree, Eve felt the prickling

sensation again, like cold fingers brushing the back of her neck. She hesitated—but no, she was being silly. And now she was close enough that she could see the narrow mound of fresh earth below the tree. Bracing herself against a rush of emotions, she walked toward it.

The countess glided like a queen across the yard, hair and skirts fluttering behind her. Clint watched from the shadows, transfixed and puzzled. What the hell was she doing out here alone in the dark?

Hadn't she been warned about Hanford's dogs? She was new here. Her scent could set them off just as easily as his.

Whatever her silly reason for coming out alone at night, he couldn't deny that it suited his needs nicely. Now would be the perfect time to speak to her, without fear of drawing attention from the rest of the house. But caution and curiosity held him back. Where was she going?

He followed her at a short distance, keeping out of sight. On the far side of the big cottonwood, she dropped to her knees. Only as he moved forward did Clint notice the patch of heaped earth littered with the dried remains of flowers.

He was about to step into view when she spoke.

"Forgive me, Margaret, for arriving too late." Her voice was a choked whisper. "I should have been here for you, at least to hold you in my arms and say goodbye…"

Still in the shadows, Clint hesitated. He was wasting precious time, but this was a private moment and an emotional one. Discretion held him in check.

"I promise you, here on your grave, that I'll look after your children," the countess continued. "I'll care for them as my own, and they'll never want for love…" A sob cut off the rest of her words. Her shoulders shook as she pressed her hands to her face.

Clint took the ring from his pocket and stepped into sight. "I'm sorry about your sister, Countess," he said softly.

Her hands dropped from her face. She stared up at him with startled eyes. "You!" she whispered. "What are you doing here?"

"I came to return this." He held out the ring to her. "I'm hoping you'll accept it without asking too many questions."

"I'll certainly accept it." She rose, snatched the ring away from him and thrust it onto her middle finger. "But I have the right to ask as many questions as I choose, and you'd bloody well be prepared to answer them."

Clint found her mild profanity oddly sensual. She might be an elevated lady, but she was clearly a passionate woman. Though he'd prefer to see that passion directed at something other than ordering him around. It shouldn't surprise him that the lady was accustomed to giving orders, he reminded himself. Back in England, she'd probably had the servants quaking in their brogans. But she was about to learn that he wasn't one of her subjects.

"Listen here, Countess—" he began.

"This is America. I'm Mrs. Townsend. Eve."

The silkiness of the name, emerging between ripe lips, triggered a fleeting fantasy about being Adam. But Clint had come here for a far different reason.

"Well, as I was saying, *Eve*, you're new here and you need to understand a few things. First, since I know you're wondering, the answer is yes, I did know those young stage robbers. They're just a couple of fool boys. I gave them your ring to get them out of harm's way. When I caught up with them I demanded it back."

"Fine." Her eyes blazed up at him, moonlight

reflecting in their azure depths. "So why did you have to sneak up in the night to return it? Why couldn't you have called at the house during the day like a proper gentleman?"

"Because your brother-in-law would've set the dogs on me. He's my enemy, and the enemy of every decent, honest rancher in this valley."

It was a bold statement, meant to shock her. And he could see by the startled widening of her eyes that it had. Before she could reply he continued.

"Hanford and his cronies in the Cattlemen's Association want to drive the farmers and small ranchers off their land and leave the valleys open to graze their cattle. Their hirelings have burned houses and barns, ripped out fences, killed men, women, even children. Their favorite trick is to frame a man for cattle rustling, then string him up on the spot." He took a step closer, his face inches above hers. "You've landed in the middle of a range war, lady. And I've heard rumors it's about to get worse."

Clint paused for breath. He'd taken a dangerous plunge, revealing himself to a woman in his enemy's household. But even if she went running to Hanford to share everything later, he hadn't told her anything Hanford wouldn't already know. He'd only informed her that she was living with an evil man.

She drew herself up, meeting his gaze with her own steel. "So what's all this got to do with me?"

"You can close your eyes to what's happening or you can try to make a difference."

"Make a difference how? What are you suggesting?" she challenged him.

"In Hanford's house, you're bound to see things, hear things. If you're willing to pass on what you learn, you'll be helping to save innocent lives."

"You're asking me to be a spy."

"If that's what you want to call it, yes."

He heard the sharp intake of her breath before she spoke. "Listen to me, then, Mr. Lonigan. I know Roderick's no angel. But he's the father of my sister's children. Those precious little ones are in my care now. As long as they're under Roderick's roof, I'll do nothing—*nothing*—that might compromise my ability to protect them. Do I make myself clear?"

There was a note of ferocity in her voice, like the snarl of a tigress defending her cubs. Her stunning eyes glinted with defiance.

"I understand that the children are your priority and you don't want to get involved," Clint said. "But if you change your mind—"

"I have no intention of changing my mind. Now please get off this property and leave me alone. You won't be welcome again."

"Fine." Time to back off, Clint told himself. He'd planted a seed. That would have to be enough for now. But there was one more thing he had to know. "Before I leave I'm going to ask you a question," he said. "And I want an honest answer."

"Ask it," she said coldly. "I have nothing to hide."

"The boys who held up the stage were expecting to find money from the Cattlemen's Association in Cheyenne. They assumed it would be in a strongbox, but they didn't find it."

"Yes, I remember that. Go on."

"Were you carrying that money—either in your baggage or on your person?"

Her eyes widened. A gasp of indignation lifted her breasts. "Absolutely not," she snapped. "I don't know anything about the Cattlemen's Association or their money, nor do I wish to. My only concern is my sister's children. Are you satisfied, Mr. Lonigan? Do you believe me?"

"I have no reason not to—" Clint broke off,

sensing a sudden change. It was the breeze, he realized, finally identifying the feeling. It had shifted. "Lord, the wind…"

"What?" She stared up at him. "What is it?"

As if in answer, a sudden clamor rose from the kennel beyond the house—a burst of yelps and snarls that rose to a hideous, howling chorus.

Chapter Three

"Take your hands off me!" Eve sputtered as Clint Lonigan seized her shoulders. His grip was rough enough to hurt as he spun her in the direction of the front porch.

"Run!" he growled. "Get in the house!"

"Why should I? What is it?" She struggled, resisting.

"Hanford's dogs. They've scented us, and they're sounding the alarm. If he orders them set loose, they'll tear any stranger apart, including you. Now *run*, damn it!" He pushed her forward.

A light had flickered on in Roderick's window. It was moving back and forth, as if signaling. Suddenly the hellish baying grew louder, coming from around the far side of the house.

Eve broke into a sprint. For her, the safety

of the front door was mere seconds away. She could no longer see or hear Lonigan, but the dogs would be after him, too. And, unlike her, he'd have no safe place to go.

Tripping over her long skirts, she plunged up the front steps and raced across the porch to the door. Her fingers fumbled with the latch. It held fast. Had it somehow locked behind her when she'd left the house?

As she shrank into the doorway, a half dozen sleek forms came flying around the corner, baying and snarling as they plunged ahead.

Brindled coats flashed in the moonlight as the pack swung away from the house. She wasn't the one they were after. They were going for Lonigan. He might not be her friend, but that didn't mean she wanted him mauled to death. She had to stop what was about to happen.

Frantic, she flung herself against the door. "Roderick!" she screamed, shaking the latch and pounding on the heavy oak slab. "Roderick, it's me! Call them off! Call them off!"

With a sudden give, the latch released and the door swung open. Eve stumbled into the entry, then changed her mind and raced back onto the porch. She couldn't see Lonigan or the dogs, but the pack's chilling cry echoed across the moonlit yard.

"Roderick!" she screamed again. "For the love of heaven, call them back!"

For an instant time seemed to stop. Then three blasts of a steel whistle shattered the night. The baying dropped to a subdued chorus of yelps as the dogs wheeled and came loping back into sight. Eve shrank into the doorway as they skirted the corner of the house and vanished in the direction of the kennel.

There was no sign of Clint Lonigan. She could only hope he'd made a clean escape. Friend or enemy—whichever he might be— no man deserved to be ripped apart by those nightmarish creatures.

Knees sagging, she closed the door and slid the bolt into place. Roderick loomed at the top of the stairs, wearing a maroon velvet dressing gown and holding a lantern.

"Eve!" He addressed her as one might lecture a naughty child. "What were you doing outside after dark? Those hounds are trained to guard the property. They could've torn you to pieces."

She willed herself to speak calmly. "I wanted to visit my sister's grave. I didn't know about the dogs. You should've warned me."

He didn't even have the grace to look guilty, though her answer did seem to mollify him to an extent. "I would have, if I'd known you were going to wander around after dark." He glided down the stairs, pausing two steps short of the landing. "Were you alone out there? I thought I heard voices."

"I spoke a few fitting words over Margaret's grave. You may have heard me. I'm guessing the dogs did, too." It was a half-truth. A flicker of caution kept her from mentioning Clint Lonigan.

"Tomorrow I'll take you out and introduce you to the pack, let them get to know you. If you can spare an article of clothing, something that carries your scent, bring it along to leave with them."

"Can I assume the children will be safe around them?"

"Those hounds are like puppies with the children, as they were with Margaret. You might even want to wear one of her dresses when you visit the kennel for the first time. No need to wear mourning in this country. To be sure, there's plenty of cause for it, but with the dirt and the weather, women say black's too impractical here."

"I'm glad of that. Now, if you'll excuse me, I'm going up to bed."

She started for the stairs, expecting him to move aside and give her room to pass, but he stood fast, offering her the barest space against the wall. "I was hoping—" He broke off, staring down at her hand. "I didn't see that ring earlier."

Eve's pulse skittered. "It was my late husband's, one of the few things of his I was able to keep."

"But you weren't wearing it at supper. It's very impressive. What's a bauble like that worth?"

"It's late, Roderick," Eve said, cutting him off. "I've just had a fright, and I'm exhausted. All I want is to go upstairs and sleep. We'll talk in the morning."

"Very well. I'll bid you good-night then, Eve." He finally moved back against the railing, allowing her room to get by, but barely. His hand brushed the small of her back as she hurried past him.

By the time she reached the landing, Eve felt vaguely ill. She hadn't counted on this. With the earth barely settled on his wife's grave, Roderick was already acting as if he owned her. If it weren't for Margaret's children, she would pack up and leave on the next stage. But her promise to look after Thomas and Rose would bind her to this house, perhaps for years to come. And anyway, she had nowhere else to go, Eve reminded herself, shoulders slumping. So here she would stay, for better or for worse. She would just have to prepare for a reckoning with the man.

She took a moment to look in on the children. Both were slumbering, but Thomas's young face was streaked with salt where his tears had dried, and Rose was whimpering in her sleep. Eve adjusted their blankets and brushed a finger kiss across each silken head. These precious little ones would be a long time healing. She would be there for them every step of the way, Eve vowed—regardless of their father's behavior.

In her room, she bolted the door. Unsteady hands unbuttoned her black dress and let it fall to the rug. As she strained to unfasten her corset, she felt the burn where Clint Lonigan's strong hands had gripped her shoulders. A glance confirmed that he hadn't left bruises on her skin. But he'd shoved her toward the house with an urgent force that lingered, if only in her memory. What if he hadn't been there? What if she'd been caught off guard by Roderick's killer dogs?

The ruby ring felt cold and heavy on her finger. For now she would put it away in a safe place. Wearing it would only tempt possible thieves and set her apart from her neighbors. But she couldn't deny she was glad to have it back. Lonigan had risked his life to return it. But that was only half true, Eve reminded herself. The ring had masked the rascal's real intent—to recruit her as a spy.

She'd been right to refuse Lonigan's request, of course. Nothing he'd said about Roderick had surprised her. But this range war was neither her doing nor her business. Her only concern was for her sister's children.

Clint Lonigan had her answer—her final answer. The wise course now would be to turn her back and never speak to him again.

Still, as she walked to the open window to shut out the night chill, her eyes scanned the moonlit yard. Deny it though she might, the question haunted her.

Was he safe?

Out of the ranch's earshot, Clint spurred his tall buckskin to a gallop. The night wind cooled the sweat that had beaded on his face. It had been a damned narrow escape. Hanford's hounds had been so close on his heels that he could smell their foul breath. He'd been about to wheel and draw his pistol when their keeper's whistle had called them off.

It was the countess's screams that had saved his life. Since the dogs were chasing him, not her, he could only surmise she'd cried out to save *him*. It was a comforting thought. She may have refused to spy for him, but at least she'd been sympathetic enough to help him get away.

Or maybe she just couldn't stand the sight of blood. But no, he doubted she was the missish type. She had too much steel in her for that.

When she'd denied carrying money from the Cattlemen's Association, those azure eyes of hers could've melted stone. But how could he believe her, when logic told him that if anyone on that stage was hiding cash, it would've been the bewitching countess?

Eve. Her name was like a whisper of wind. He remembered how she'd looked leaning out the upstairs window, her loose black hair framing her face, her breasts pale half-moons above the lace edging of her camisole. The sight of her had stirred yearnings he hadn't felt since...

With a muttered curse, Clint forced her image from his mind. He was fighting a war, damn it; and if the countess wasn't with him, she was against him. As long as Eve lived under Roderick Hanford's roof and cared for his children, there could be no trusting her.

Right now Clint had other urgent concerns to deal with. One of his neighbors had lost half a dozen spring calves. A Dutch farmer, Yost had spotted the calves with a herd belonging to cattleman and county judge Seth McCutcheon. Yost was determined to get them back, even if he had to steal them.

Clint had seen this tactic too many times not to be wise to what would happen next. His neighbor would take his animals back—and McCutcheon's men would make no move to stop him. But once they were back in his possession, Yost would be accused of cattle rustling and strung up without a trial. His widow and children would be run off their farm and the cattle barons would move in like vultures to seize the land.

It was up to Clint to find the man and talk some sense into him—tonight, before it was too late. After that, assuming he was successful in talking Yost down, Clint might manage to grab a few hours sleep before his own morning chores and a visit to check on the Potter ranch. Blasted fool boys. Just when things were heating up, and he needed their guns and sharp eyes, they had to go and get in trouble.

Tomorrow, once the chores were done, he'd ride into town and nose around into the investigation on the stagecoach holdup. With luck, he'd be able to learn whether Sheriff Womack was looking for Newt and Gideon. If the coast was clear, it might be safe to bring the boys home.

Clint also needed to look into the rumors of money from the Cattlemen's Association. If they were true, and hired gun sharks were coming to Lodgepole, he would need to spread the word and come up with a plan.

But what plan? What could immigrant farmers and small ranchers do to protect themselves against seasoned killers? What chance would they have? He needed a way to learn more—how many, where and when they planned to strike.

Smitty in the Three-legged Dog and Etta Simpkins in the bakery might be good for passing on a bit of gossip. But gossip couldn't take the place of solid information.

For that he needed the countess on his side—

and the chance of winning her over was about as good as tying up a wildcat with a piece of string.

Eve sat at the dining room table helping Thomas with his multiplication tables. Rose sat across from them, practicing lines of alphabet letters in her notebook. The one-room school in Lodgepole was too far for a daily drive, especially in winter, so Margaret had schooled her children at home. She'd done an admirable job, which Eve hoped to continue.

It was only her second day here, but Eve had already made a number of discoveries. One was that Roderick had little interest in his children's upbringing or the running of his household. Those matters had been left to Margaret—and had now fallen to her. Another discovery was that Alice, the elderly housekeeper, was suffering from rheumatism. She could manage in the kitchen, but tasks like doing laundry and trudging up and down the stairs with mop buckets and chamber pots were becoming too much for the poor woman. Eve had resolved to find her some younger, stronger help, the sooner the better.

After the children's lessons she would take

the buggy into Lodgepole for some needed supplies. And while she was there, she would pay
a visit to Etta Simpkins at the bakery. Surely a
woman who knew the town so well could recommend a sturdy, trustworthy girl who needed
work.

Eve glanced at the children as they labored
over their lessons. She would ask Roderick to
let her take them into town. Maybe some peppermint sticks from the general store or a couple of small toys would bring a smile to their
sad little faces. The three of them might even
stop for a picnic on the way home.

As if the very thought of him could summon the man, Roderick strolled into the dining
room. He was dressed like the country gentleman he'd never been in England, in jodhpurs,
a tweed riding jacket and knee-high calfskin
boots polished to a gloss.

"Are you ready, Eve?" he asked. "I wanted
to take you out back to meet my hounds this
morning."

A knot tightened in the pit of her stomach. After last night she had no desire to meet
Roderick's baying, snarling dogs face-to-face.

"The children," she protested. "They're still
doing their lessons."

He did not spare Rose and Thomas even a glance. "They can finish alone. Bring something that has your scent on it."

Eve thought of the black silk bombazine she'd worn so long that it was stiff with sweat and dust. She'd had a mind to burn it on arrival, but literally throwing it to the dogs would work just as well. It was too far gone to survive washing, but maybe she could salvage a strip of it as a mourning band to wear for Margaret.

As she hurried upstairs to fetch the gown, the shock of her sister's death swept over her afresh. Dear, gentle, faithful Margaret. How Eve longed to hear her voice and see her patient smile again. Older by three years, Margaret had always been the solid, sensible sister. Growing up, it was Eve, the impulsive one, who was always finding ways to get into mischief. Yet it was Margaret who'd married a rough-edged adventurer bound for America, and Eve who, to save their father from financial ruin, had dutifully wed the middle-aged Earl of Manderfield.

While he lived, the earl had been the soul of kindness and generosity. Eve had never been in love with him, but he'd earned her gratitude and her lasting devotion, even in the latter years of his life, when her role toward him had been more nursemaid than wife. Margaret, who'd been so giddy with love for Roderick that she'd ignored warnings from friends and family, had paid dearly for following her heart. The thought of her sister enduring this uncivilized country and that pompous brute of a husband for eleven long years was enough to make Eve weep. If only she could have been here to give Margaret some love and support. Now she could only try to do as much for her sister's children.

In her room, she gathered up her mourning dress and tore out a strip from the inner seam of the skirt for an armband. Rolling the rest of the gown into a wad, she carried it back downstairs. Today she was dressed in sky-blue cotton voile with a dainty white lace collar. The frock was airy and cool. In England, it would have been considered plain and practical, but she sensed that even this might be too fine for Lodgepole. Most of the women she'd seen in town had been clad in faded calicos and sunbonnets. Eve had even seen one woman in overalls. But then, she supposed, her own style of dress would adapt over time until she fit right in.

Roderick was waiting at the bottom of the stairs. "Let's go and meet my pets," he said, offering his arm. Pretending not to see the gesture, Eve swept past him. Maybe he'd only meant to be polite, but if she didn't set boundaries now she could come to regret it later.

"You look right fetching today," he said. "Much better than in those widow's weeds. I hope that means you're done with mourning your husband and are ready to get on with your life."

She shot him a stern look over her shoulder. "I'm mourning my sister," she said. "I saved a strip of black from the skirt to make an armband. I'll make one for you, too, if you'd like."

"That would be very kind of you, Eve." His hand brushed her corseted waist as he ushered her around to the backyard.

The kennel, surrounded by a high wall of rough-sawn logs, was far enough from the house to keep odors from carrying, but close enough for the dogs to scent any strange presence. A grove of scraggly elms provided some shade. The creatures took up a hideous baying as Eve approached with Roderick. At a shrill blast on a whistle, like the one she'd heard last night, the baying subsided to whimpers.

Roderick opened the high wooden gate. Eve shrank back, expecting the dogs to rush out at her, but then saw they were inside a wire enclosure that formed part of the compound. There was also a closed storage shed and what looked to be a crude log cabin.

Standing outside the cabin was a shaggy giant of a man dressed in shapeless brown clothing and wearing a heavy silver police whistle on a leather thong around his neck.

"This is Hans, my master of hounds," Roderick said. "He hears well enough, but he doesn't speak. The dogs are trained to respond to the whistle."

"Hans, I'm pleased to meet you." Eve gave him a smile, which he returned with a shy nod. Half hidden by locks of matted gray-brown hair, his blue eyes were curiously gentle. Stepping aside, he gave Eve a full view of the dogs.

A shiver passed through her as she remembered the terror of seeing them run loose in the moonlight. There were six of them, all of a kind—huge, brindle-coated creatures with sleek, muscular bodies, long legs and heavy, drooling jaws, but of no definable breed. At the sight of Eve, they began snarling and lunging at the stout wire fence.

Roderick paid no heed. "I crossbred them myself," he boasted. "The speed of a coursing hound, the strength of a mastiff and the tenacity of a pit bull. They have it all—best game dogs in the country. They'll take on bear, cougar, wolf, buffalo, any creature you can name, except maybe a skunk." He chuckled at his own joke. "I've been offered a small fortune for them. Seth McCutcheon, for one, would take them off my hands in a minute. But I wouldn't part with them, or with Hans. They're much too useful—especially with so much common riffraff moving in on our open range."

Eve shuddered again, remembering last night. Roderick had bragged that his dogs would take on any prey. Evidently that included humans.

Taking the black silk dress from her, he passed it to Hans, who tossed it over the wire fence into the midst of the pack. There was a flurry of snarling, growling and tearing. Then they began snuffling at the fabric, filling their noses with the unfamiliar scent.

"We can go now." Roderick guided her toward the gate. "After they've spent a day or two with that dress, they'll be accustomed to your scent. Next time you won't smell like a stranger to them."

Next time.

Eve walked beside him in silence, struggling to forget the sight of those drooling jaws. She liked most dogs, even large hounds. But she'd never seen any as terrifying as these. Was their ferocity bred into them or had they been raised with the kind of brutality that drove them to attack?

And what was Hans's role as Roderick's "master of hounds"? Evidently he'd been there last night to set the dogs loose and blow a triple blast on his whistle to call them back. Did that odd giant of a man live right there in the compound with the dogs? It seemed that every hour spent here raised new questions—and a string of unpleasant answers.

Eve had been here less than a day and the dark miasma that hung over this place was already seeping into her bones. But never mind that, she was here for Margaret's children, and here she would stay, doing everything she could to give them love and brighten their lives.

"Alice needs a few things from the store," she said to Roderick. "I was hoping I could drive the buggy into town and take the children along for a treat."

"That's fine. I'll get one of the hands to drive you."

"I know how drive a buggy," Eve said, holding firm. "All I need is someone to hitch up the horse. The road's good, and it's not much more than an hour to town. Surely I can manage that."

Roderick frowned. "This isn't England, Eve. Wyoming's a dangerous place. You'll need a man with a gun along to protect you."

"My father taught me how to handle a rifle— and a team of horses. Just give me a weapon. I'll be fine. And so will the children."

His frown deepened. "Actually I have business in town today. I was planning to ride, but I can take you and the children in the buggy. We'll go after lunch."

Eve sighed in acquiescence. For now she would let him have his way. But she was not Margaret. She was not about to let this man control her life.

Clint had spent much of the morning looking for Anders Yost, the Dutch immigrant farmer who'd lost his calves to rancher Seth McCutcheon. Yost's wife, Berta, a tired looking woman with a swollen belly and two small children hanging on to her apron, told him that Yost had gone into town to speak to the sheriff. The expression on her weary face revealed that she knew her husband was wasting his time.

Clint agreed. But since he'd planned on heading into town anyway, and since he needed to dissuade Yost from going after the stolen calves, he swung his horse toward Lodgepole and nudged the leggy buckskin to a gallop.

Leaving the horse at the livery stable, he walked the two blocks to the sheriff's office. Yost wasn't there, but Sheriff Harv Womack, gruff and paunchy, admitted he had been earlier.

"I advised him that losing a few calves was better than getting strung up from a tree." Womack professed a neutral position between cattlemen and sodbusters, and generally avoided any involvement in their quarrels. But Clint suspected where his real loyalties lay, and had never quite trusted the man.

"I meant to tell him the same thing," Clint said. "Do you think he listened?"

The sheriff shook his balding head. "I'm hoping he thought it over. But he left here swearing he'd get those calves back with or without my help. Maybe he'll listen to you."

"If I can find him before he does something stupid." Clint turned toward the door, then remembered the other reason he'd stopped by. "Any luck tracking down those stage robbers?"

"Nope. Couple of fool kids, from what the

driver told me. Apart from winging the guard and running the stage off the road, they didn't do much harm—but you were there, weren't you?"

"I was. Like the driver said, a couple of fool kids up to no good. They were more nervous than the passengers. I can't imagine they'll try it again."

"Well, I've got better things to do than chase down those young galoots and slap their hands," the sheriff said. "But if you happen to see them in town and recognize them, let me know."

"I'll do that." Clint turned toward the door again, but the sheriff wasn't finished.

"Hear tell the countess was on that stage. The driver said she was a looker."

"She was pretty enough," Clint hedged. "But not too friendly with us common folk. She didn't say much."

"Don't suppose she'd have anything new to tell me about the robbery."

"Not unless you just want to get her in here for a look. Sorry, but I need to find Yost." Clint walked out before Womack could ask him anything else. He was just stepping onto the boardwalk when a black buggy passed him, going up the street. Roderick Hanford held the reins, his expression as smug as a self-satisfied cat's. Seated beside him, looking fresh as a lily in a blue dress and chic little straw bonnet, was the countess.

Eve.

Hanford pulled up long enough to let an elderly man with a cane hobble across the street in front of the horses. By chance, the countess glanced to her right and caught sight of Clint. For an instant their gazes locked. Her sky-colored eyes widened, holding his. Ignoring the electric jolt that ripped through his body, Clint raised his hand to the brim of his Stetson, tipped his hat and turned away. But as the buggy moved on up the street, with Hanford's children in the rear, Clint's gaze lingered on her rigid back and elegant head.

Had she told Hanford about last night's encounter? Clint hadn't been able to read anything in the look she gave him, but the only safe assumption was that she had. If the countess wasn't with him in his battle with the big ranchers—and she'd made that much clear last night—then she was against him. One of the enemy.

But right now he had other problems on his mind—like finding Anders Yost and checking out the alleged money shipment from the Cattlemen's Association. Etta Simpkins at the bakery was always good for a bit of town gossip. Maybe she had something to pass on.

The buggy had pulled up in front of the hotel. Hanford climbed out, helped the countess to the boardwalk and boosted his children out of the back. Walking away, they looked like any happy, prosperous family—a snappily attired man, a stunning woman and two pretty youngsters dressed for an outing.

If Corrie and our baby had lived… But this was no time for thoughts of what might have been. Tearing his gaze away, Clint turned and headed for the saloon. He had to find Yost before the man made a fatal mistake.

Chapter Four

"You said you had business in town," Eve reminded Roderick. Not that she cared a fig about his business, but she wanted to be free of his overpowering presence so she could enjoy the children.

"Yes, so I did." Roderick glanced at his gold pocket watch. "I'm meeting with some of the other ranchers in the hotel, at two o'clock. Looks like it's about time. You don't mind, do you?"

"Not in the least. We'll stroll around and pick up the odds and ends for Alice," Eve said. "How long do you expect to be?"

"Not more than an hour. If you and the children get tired you can wait on the bench in the hotel lobby."

"Fine, take your time." Eve made a quick

dash to retrieve the shopping basket from the buggy. At Manderfield, the servants had always done the shopping. This would be a brand-new experience. She was looking forward to it with mixed emotions.

"Have you got any money?" Roderick paused outside the hotel entrance and fished for his wallet. "We have an account at the general store, but for other shops, like the bakery, you'll need cash."

"Oh. Sorry, I'd quite forgotten." Color flooded Eve's face as she realized how close she'd come to making a fool of herself. She disliked the idea of accepting money from Roderick, but if she wanted to buy things she had little choice. Besides, most of what she'd be purchasing would be for the children. It was only proper that their father provide for them. With a mutter of thanks, she took the bills from his hand.

"You're very pretty when you blush, Eve," he said.

She turned away, pretending she hadn't heard. Tonight she would ask him to set up a household account so she wouldn't have to come begging to him every time she needed something. But maybe having her beg was what Roderick wanted.

The children were waiting, their little faces still pale and sad-looking. They walked on either side of her, Rose clasping her hand and Thomas carrying the empty basket.

Alice had given Eve a list of a half dozen small items she needed—salt, pepper, baking soda, cinnamon, sewing thread and a jar of the miniature pickles Roderick liked. There was nothing that couldn't be easily carried. "Just give the list and the basket to the clerk at the general store," Alice had instructed. "He'll fill the order for you."

That was easy enough to do. But as Eve waited with the children, her gaze roaming the well-stocked shelves, racks and barrels, she became conscious of eyes watching her—the women in faded calicos eyeing her fine clothes and stylish bonnet, the men casting her sidelong glances that skimmed over her figure. At least she'd decided not to wear her ruby ring. That would have drawn even more attention.

The store seemed inordinately busy—but after a few minutes she noticed that few of the customers were buying. It appeared that most of them had wandered in to look at *her*.

Eve fought the urge to flee out the door, where more curious looks would surely be awaiting her. How long would it take before she stopped feeling like a circus freak in this town?

Painfully self-conscious, she kept her gaze forward and her attention on the children, who were eyeing the glass candy jars on the counter. She didn't feel the tall, intensely masculine presence behind her until she heard his voice.

"Nice to see you again, Countess."

For an instant she froze. After what she'd told Clint Lonigan last night, the first response that came to mind was, *How dare you?* But people were watching. The last thing she wanted was to make a scene.

"It's Mrs. Townsend," she said in a chilly voice. "And it's nice to see you, too, Mr. Lonigan. Now if you don't mind, I have some purchases to pay for." She turned toward the clerk. "I'll have two peppermint sticks for the children, please."

"Coming right up, Countess."

She frowned. "As I just told the gentleman, it's Mrs. Townsend. This isn't England and I'm certainly not royalty."

"But still a very proper lady." Clint Lonigan's voice had taken on a teasing tone.

Ignoring him, Eve signed for her purchases, gave each of the children a peppermint stick and reached for her basket. "I'll be taking my leave of you now, Mr. Lonigan. Good day."

"I'll walk you to the street." He picked up the basket, giving her no choice except to stay with him. The children, sucking on their candy, paid little heed to their conversation.

"What in heaven's name do you think you're doing?" she hissed as they stepped onto the boardwalk.

"I'm taking the only chance I may get to ask you if you've changed your mind."

"I told you, I have no intention of becoming involved in your little war." She moved away from the store entrance and started down the boardwalk toward the bakery.

"Little war, is it?" His voice had taken on an edge. "You came into town with Hanford. Where is he now?"

"In the hotel. He said he had a meeting with some other ranchers."

"Did he tell you what the meeting was about?"

"I didn't ask. Just business, I suppose."

"Their so-called business is burning property and murdering every farmer and small rancher that won't leave the county."

His words triggered a clench in Eve's stomach. How could anything as awful as what Lonigan was suggesting be true? "I don't believe you," she said.

"Ask your precious brother-in-law on the way home. Not that he'll tell you the truth."

"And what is the truth, as you see it? That my brother-in-law goes skulking about in the night like a thief, personally eliminating anyone who gets in his way?"

"Of course not. Men like him don't get their hands dirty. They pay hired thugs to do their killing. But they're just as guilty as if they'd lit the torches, fired the guns and strung the nooses. If you could do something to stop it and you won't, you're guilty, too."

"No more of this!" Eve kept her voice low, aware of the curious looks from passersby, not to mention Thomas and Rose just a few steps away. "I told you, I'm here for my sister's children. My only concern is their welfare. They've had enough distress in their lives without my plotting against their father under his very roof. So go away and leave us alone!"

Clint Lonigan's mouth hardened into a grim line. After handing her the basket, he took a step away and touched the brim of his hat. "I understand. Have a pleasant day, *Countess*."

The title sizzled of his tongue, rife with unmistakable contempt. She watched him cross the street to the saloon and go inside without looking back at her. Shrugging off the unsettling encounter, she herded the children on down the street to the bakery.

Etta Simpkins greeted her with a warm smile. "What a pleasure to see you, Countess! And with those two sweet lambs! What can I do for you?"

"As I said, just Mrs. Townsend will do." How would she ever fit in here if people insisted on using that pompous-sounding title? "You have a lovely shop. It's the only place on the street that looks inviting."

"Call it a woman's touch." Mrs. Simpkins laughed. "I have some lovely cinnamon buns just out of the oven. And those oatmeal raisin cookies behind the glass were just made last night."

"I'll take a half dozen of each," Eve said. "Maybe I can persuade Mr. Hanford to stop for a little picnic on the way home. The children would enjoy that."

"What a dandy idea. I've got some cheese in the cool room out back. Would you like me to make you some sandwiches to take along?"

"Thank you. Just a few. The children can share." Eve had initially abandoned the picnic idea when Roderick had insisted on driving them to town. But maybe she could persuade him to take the time. He was the children's father, after all, and he seemed to have so little interaction with them.

Mrs. Simpkins bustled out the back, returned with a wedge of cheddar and began cutting off thin slices. Rose and Thomas had finished their candy and were looking at some iced sugar cookies. Eve curbed the impulse to buy them. It wouldn't do to spoil the children with too many sweets.

"So how are you getting on with Mr. Hanford?" Mrs. Simpson reached for a loaf of bread and began cutting it for sandwiches.

"Fine so far." The question struck Eve as too familiar, but she supposed it was the way of people in this frontier town. Gossip was, if nothing else, a way to combat loneliness.

"Treating you like a gentleman, is he?"

"Of course." Scrambling for a way to change the subject, Eve remembered her other reason for coming here. "Perhaps you can help me out with a suggestion. I'm looking for a strong young girl to help with the heavy work in the house. Alice is good in the kitchen, but with her rheumatism…"

"Oh, I know what you mean, dearie. The poor old soul can barely get around as it is. I do have a girl in mind. The family she worked for moved away, so she's looking for employment. Very willing and reliable. Her name is Beth Ann."

Dearie?

Eve drew in a startled breath. She disapproved of the formality of everyone calling her by her title, yet this seemed to go too far in the other direction. But this wasn't England, she reminded herself. If she wanted to belong, she would have to get used to Americans and their easygoing manners.

"I'm not sure what kind of salary I should offer her," she said. "Back in England, servants were tied to the family for generations."

"Room, board and three dollars a week should be plenty. If she's interested, can I just send her out to the ranch?"

"Certainly. On approval, of course—mine and Mr. Hanford's. Since she'll be around the children her language and behavior must be suitable."

"She'll do you fine." While Eve counted out

change, Mrs. Simpkins put the sandwiches, buns and cookies in a paper bag with a napkin. "Have a lovely picnic, dearie!" She waved them out the door.

Dearie. Eve bit back her instinctive frown and forced herself to smile and wave as she led her charges to the boardwalk.

By the time they'd walked up the other side of the street, peering in a few shop windows, the children were getting tired. They'd been far too quiet on this outing, Eve thought. If only she could lift their sadness and get them to laugh and play. But that, it seemed, would take some time.

Rose tugged at Eve's skirt. "My shoes hurt, Aunt Eve," she whined. "I want to go home now."

Thomas kicked a clod of mud off the boardwalk into the street. "Where's Papa? Why is he taking so long?"

Eve sighed. "Let's go into the hotel and find out. He said we could wait for him in there."

The Lodgepole Hotel was nothing like the fine places Eve had visited in England. The lobby was the size of a small parlor, with a wooden bench, two straight-backed chairs and a potbellied stove, unlit on this warm summer day. A badly mounted grizzly bear head, the mouth open in a snarl, hung above the desk. At the sight of it, Rose shrank against Eve's skirts.

"I'm not scared of it. It's dead, just like the ones in our house." Thomas pretended to shoot the beast with a make-believe rifle.

"Can I help you, ma'am?" The clerk, scarcely more than a boy, moved with a limp. A battle wound, perhaps, or just an accident?

"Yes, thank you," Eve said. "We're waiting for Mr. Roderick Hanford to drive us home. I don't suppose you know when his meeting will be finished."

"They're in the back room. Don't know when they'll be done, but I can check for you."

"Please don't disturb them. We can wait." Eve settled herself on the hard bench and pulled the children down on either side of her. But it soon became plain that the little ones were too restless to wait patiently. Rose was squirming, and Thomas kept finding excuses to jump up and race around the lobby. Unaccustomed to such behavior, Eve could feel her patience wearing thin. More than an hour had passed. What was taking Roderick so long?

Another ten minutes crawled by. Eve had given each of the children a cookie to quiet them, but it wasn't enough. Rose had begun to whine. Thomas was scuffing his heels against the end of the bench with maddening repetition.

Eve caught the young clerk's attention. "Perhaps you can just look in on that meeting. See if they're about to finish."

"Sure." He disappeared down a back hallway, returning a moment later. "I'm sorry, ma'am, it looks like they're still talking and…uh…playing cards."

With an impatient huff, Eve picked up her basket and reticule and rose from the bench. She could drive a buggy as well as any man, and she was tired of waiting here with these bored, cranky children while Roderick played cards. "When Mr. Hanford gets out of his meeting tell him we were here, but that we could not wait for him any longer. He can jolly well find his own way home."

The buggy was waiting where they'd left it, hitched to the rail in front of the hotel. Boosting the children into the back, Eve freed the reins, climbed onto the seat and clucked to the drowsing horse. As a girl, she'd learned to handle a buggy on outings with her father. Now she could put the lessons to good use.

* * *

Clint had hoped to find Yost in the saloon, but there was no sign of the big Dutchman. "You missed him by about twenty minutes," Smitty, the grizzled bartender, said. "He had a couple of whiskeys. Then he stomped out of here swearin' he'd get his calves back from McCutcheon if he had to kill the bastard."

Clint thought of Yost's pregnant wife and their two little children. He'd hoped for enough time to find the man and talk some sense into him before he did anything foolish. But if Yost was half-drunk and on the warpath, time had run out.

"Did he happen to say where he was headed?" Clint asked the old man.

Smitty scratched his ragged beard. "Somethin' about the calves bein' up Crow Hollow, above the road. But McCutcheon ain't there. I saw him go in the hotel, along with some of his cronies, and there's not a one of 'em come out yet."

That would be where Roderick Hanford had gone, too, in the meeting the countess had mentioned, Clint calculated. He'd give his teeth to know what was going on in that room. But there was no time for that. McCutcheon's men would

be guarding the cattle, waiting for the Dutchman to make a move. When he did, Yost would
be as good as dead.

Lengthening his stride, Clint left the saloon
and raced for the livery stable where he'd left
his horse. He wasn't much of a praying man, but
he'd need the help of heaven to get to Crow Hollow and find Anders Yost before tragedy struck.

Eve's spirits rose as the buggy rolled out of
town and into the open country. Grassy plains
swept away on one side, forested hills on the
other. The weather was clear, the sky a cloud-
less blaze of blue. With hours of summer daylight remaining, there would be plenty of time
to stop for their picnic.

Without Roderick's presence weighing down
her spirits, Eve felt an intoxicating sense of freedom. Accompanied by the steady clop-clop of
shod hooves on the road, she began to sing a
little nursery ditty that she and Margaret had
learned as children.

"'London Bridge is falling down, falling
down, falling down. London Bridge is falling
down, my fair lady!'"

When Rose and Thomas began singing
along, she realized Margaret must have taught

it to them. Laughing now, they finished the song and went on to "Row, Row Your Boat," and "Are You Sleeping?" It was the first time Eve had ever heard Margaret's sad little ones sound happy.

Minutes later Eve spotted the perfect picnic spot. A stone's throw above the road was a secluded bank where a crystal stream babbled out of a narrow canyon. Carpeted with grass, sheltered by willows and overhung by a stand of massive cottonwoods, it seemed made for enjoyment on a day like this.

After pulling up the horse, she climbed down from the buggy and looped the reins over a bush. With the basket, and a blanket she'd found under the seat, she led the way up the easy slope. The children trooped after her, their laughter pure music to her ears.

Eve spread the blanket on the grass and broke out the sandwiches. They were nothing but plain fresh bread and cheese, but the children, who'd only picked at Alice's delicious supper last night, savored them as if they were a feast fit for angels.

"Are you going to stay with us, Aunt Eve?" Rose's blue eyes, with their long, pale lashes, were heartbreakingly like Margaret's.

"Yes, dearest, I'm going to stay." Eve hugged her close.

"Forever?"

What did that word mean to a child? How could anyone promise forever? "I'll stay for as long as you need me," Eve said.

"How long is that?"

"Oh…maybe until you're a grown-up young lady, ready to get married and start a family of your own. Does that sound long enough?"

Rose pondered that idea for a moment. Then, as if filing it away for the future, she asked, "May I please have another cookie?"

If only satisfying every wish could be that easy. Laughing, Eve reached into the sack.

Thomas, ever the restless one, had left the blanket and was throwing pebbles into the creek that flowed below the bank. Eve was about to ask him if he wanted a cookie, too, when she felt a barely perceptible tremor pass through the ground beneath the blanket. For a heartbeat she thought she'd imagined it, but in the next instant she knew better. The rumble of pounding hooves shook the earth as a herd of white-faced cattle burst out of the canyon mouth, stampeding straight down the slope toward them.

There was no time to think, only to move.

Hooking one arm around Rose and grabbing Thomas with the other, Eve dived for the safest place in sight. With the children clasped close, she rolled over the edge of the steep bank, tumbling over and down, coming to rest in the creek bed just short of the water.

With the cattle racing along the top of the bank, they were far from safe. A steer could easily topple over the edge and crush them with its weight or, in its panic, attack them with deadly horns. Curving her body over and around the terrified children, Eve huddled against the tangled willow roots. If need be, she would die protecting them.

Nothing, or so she'd thought, could be more terrifying than that rumbling, lowing horde of cattle pouring down the slope past them. But now, coming fast behind the stampede, she heard the shouts of mounted riders, their horses thundering closer. Eve shrank deeper against the bank. Would the men be friendly herders, driving the cattle where they needed to go, or were they thieves and ruffians who wouldn't think twice about harming a lone woman with children?

And what about the blanket and basket left behind on the bank when she and the children had dived to safety? Would those objects give away their presence, leading someone to search for their hiding place, or had those items been trampled to pieces?

The cattle had thundered on past, but the riders seemed to have stopped near the cottonwood trees, a stone's throw from where she and the children were hiding. Eve could hear them laughing and cursing, hear the stamping and blowing of their horses. Dared she risk a look? The cattle had trampled the brush along the bank, but one stubborn clump of sage was still standing. It was just high enough and thick enough to screen the top part of her head.

Silently cautioning the children not to move, she unfolded her cramped body and crouched behind the bank. There was no sign of the blanket or basket. Most likely they'd been swept away in the stampede. But Eve could see the men gathered under the biggest cottonwood. There were five of them, all strangers and all mounted. But one looked out of place. Tall and husky, with pale blond hair, he was hatless; and he sat on his horse in an odd way, as if he couldn't use his arms.

Eve swallowed a gasp as she realized what she was seeing. The man's wrists were bound behind his back. One of the other riders was uncoiling a rope, looping one end into a noose.

Heaven save me, they're going to hang the poor fellow! Her first impulse was to cry out and try to stop them. But how could she make her presence known without endangering herself and the children? The best she could do was make sure Rose and Thomas didn't see the horror that was about to happen.

The man was whimpering, begging for his life. Eve knew she shouldn't look, but she couldn't tear her eyes away.

"Get down, Eve!" The rasping whisper came from just behind her ear. She froze. Even without turning she knew it was Clint Lonigan.

"I said *get down*!" Clint covered her mouth with one hand and yanked her down beside him. The children's eyes were huge in their frightened faces, but Clint had signaled them with a finger to his lips. They must've recognized the gesture and understood, because they hadn't made a peep.

Clint had crossed the back country at a gallop in the hope of reaching Crow Hollow before Yost tried to take back his calves. When he heard the stampede and saw McCutcheon's bald-faced Hereford cattle pouring out of the shallow canyon, he knew he'd arrived too late.

What he hadn't expected to find was Eve and Hanford's two children, right in the thick of things.

When he'd caught sight of the runaway horse, tearing up the road with the empty buggy, he'd realized they must be nearby and in trouble. It had taken precious minutes of dodging through the trees and crawling through the underbrush before he saw them from the far side of the creek. By then, McCutcheon's hired men had gathered under the big cottonwood with Anders Yost and a rope.

Clint knew what they were up to. Hanging Yost here, in plain sight of the road, would serve as a warning to any small ranchers who dared to defy the cattlemen. Clint was armed, and he was a good shot. But if he tried to get the drop on them he'd be facing four hardened gunfighters. He might get one or two before they shot him, but that wouldn't be enough to save Yost. And now he had a blasted woman and two kids to protect. How was he going to manage that?

Eve crouched beside him, with a protective arm around the children. "Now do you believe what I told you?" Clint asked her. "That man is a friend of mine. He has a pregnant wife and two little children at home. And all he wanted was to get his stolen property back."

"This is monstrous," she hissed. "Can't you do something to stop it?"

"Maybe…" Clint's resolve hardened as the plan came clear. "But you'll have to trust me, all right?"

She nodded, but he could see the fear in her blue eyes.

"Just play along with me," he said. "And you two—" he pointed to the children "—whatever happens, you stay right here. Don't look, and don't make a sound."

There was a tick of silence as one of the men tossed the rope over a sturdy limb of the biggest cottonwood tree and led Yost, still mounted, beneath it. Clint drew his pistol. "Now!" he whispered.

Leaping up onto the bank, he grabbed Eve's arm and jerked her up beside him with the gun barrel pressed against her temple. "Stop right there," he barked. "This is Hanford's sister-in-law, the countess. You make one more move to hang that man and she gets a bullet right through her pretty, royal head!"

Chapter Five

Eve was no actress. But she didn't need to be. She was genuinely terrified. Lonigan's grip was almost rough enough to yank her arm out of its socket, and she had little doubt that monster of a pistol, aimed right at her head, was loaded and cocked.

Trust me, he'd said, implying that he'd keep her safe. But right now she was ready to believe that if the hanging continued, he wouldn't hesitate to pull the trigger.

The men had turned to stare at him, leaving their captive astride his horse with the noose around his neck. If the animal shied, it would be all over for him.

"Hanford's taken quite a shine to this lady," Lonigan said. "If anything were to happen to her because you refused to cooperate, you'd have those dogs of his at your throats." He jammed the muzzle harder against Eve's head and thumbed back the hammer. "Now, slow and easy like, take the noose off that man and cut him loose. When he's safe, you can take her royal highness back to Hanford and hope he's in a mood to be generous."

Trust me, he'd said. Eve willed herself to remain perfectly still. What was the man thinking, offering to turn her over to those ruffians—if he didn't shoot her first? And what about the children hiding below the bank? What would become of them if she were taken away?

"Now!" Lonigan snapped. "Get that noose off his neck before the horse bucks. Then we'll talk."

The leader of the four men nodded. One of his lackeys was reaching for the rope when the sound of galloping hooves reached their ears, coming from town and getting closer.

"One of you, see who it is," Lonigan ordered the men. "Go on. And you—get that noose off."

One of the men lifted the loop from the prisoner's neck. Another trotted his horse down to the road. He peered into the distance. "Looks like Roderick Hanford," he called back over his shoulder. "An' he's ridin' like the devil was on his tail."

What now? Eve fought back a storm of warring emotions. The situation was complicated enough without Roderick riding into the middle of it. Anything could happen. She could only hope that, by the time the drama played out, everyone involved would still be alive.

Coming up on the scene, Roderick jerked his lathered horse to a rearing halt. "What the hell's going on here?" he demanded, yanking his pistol out of its holster. "Eve, are you all right?"

"Yes." She mouthed the word, fearful that any sudden move could send a bullet through her head.

"Where are the children? Damn it, if anything's happened to them—"

"Your children are fine, Hanford." Lonigan's voice was low and cold. "When my friend is free, I'll send them out to you."

Eve had half expected Rose and Thomas to break their silence and come running into the open to their papa. But Lonigan had warned them to keep still. Even with their father here, they were scared enough to obey.

"These are McCutcheon's men, but I'm betting they'll take orders from you," Lonigan said.

"Tell them to cut my friend loose and let him go. And put that gun away. You don't want to be the cause of this pretty lady getting hurt."

Holstering his pistol, Roderick turned toward the men clustered under the tree. "Do it," he snapped.

One of the riders untied the prisoner's hands. The big blond man looked dazed, as if uncertain what to do next.

"Get out of here, Yost," Lonigan said. "Go home to your family. I'll see about your calves."

Yost needed no more urging. Kicking his horse, he wheeled and galloped away through the trees. Lonigan eased off the pistol's hammer, but he kept the weapon pointed at Eve's head. His other hand was like an iron manacle around her arm. "Tell the children to come out," he said.

She struggled to find her voice. "Thomas, Rose, it's all right now. Come out and go to your father."

Like frightened little animals, the children crept out of the creek bed and into sight. Eve had expected them to run to their father's arms, but even after Roderick dismounted and ordered them to come to him, they dragged their feet, almost as if they were afraid of him.

Roderick waited till he had them in his clasp. "What about her?" he demanded, fixing his gaze on Eve.

Lonigan's grip tightened on her arm. "If I let her go right now, you'll just shoot me where I stand. No, the countess here is my insurance policy. When we're safely out of here, and when I get word those stolen calves are back where they belong, I'll send her home." He glanced toward the four men under the tree. "You boys get after those cows. Cut Yost's calves out of the herd and run them back onto his land—and I don't want to hear that you've bothered him or his family. And you, Hanford." Clint looked at Roderick again. "Take your youngsters home. Maybe with luck you can catch up with that runaway buggy. You'll get your woman back soon enough."

Your woman, he'd said. Heaven save her, was that what Lonigan believed?

For the space of a breath no one seemed to move. Lonigan jerked Eve upward, tight against his shoulder. "Get going, all of you, before I lose my patience!"

At an affirming nod from Roderick, the four men wheeled their horses and clattered down the slope after the cattle. Roderick boosted

Rose onto the front of the saddle, mounted, and pulled his son up behind him. "You should have waited for me, Eve." He spoke as if scolding a naughty child. "I told you the road was dangerous for a woman."

Eve thrust out her chin, meeting his gaze with her own steel. "As long as it prevents bloodshed, I'm willing to do whatever's needed. Just go. Get the children safely home."

Roderick's gaze shifted to Lonigan. His expression shriveled into a mask of hatred—or maybe the concerned look he'd given Eve was the real mask. "You'll pay for this, Lonigan. If I hear you've so much as touched her, I'll castrate you like a steer and throw you to my dogs!"

Without waiting for a reply he swung his mount homeward and headed up the road at a trot. Heartsick, Eve watched Thomas's forlorn little figure bouncing behind the saddle. The children would need comforting after today's ordeal, and a man like Roderick would have little consolation to offer. How could she not be there for them?

Lonigan had released her arm and holstered his pistol. Now that they were alone Eve's tightly reined terror exploded in fury. "How could you do that to me? I thought I was going to die!" Her hand flashed up to strike him. Lightning quick, he caught her wrist in midair.

"I said you could trust me, Eve." His gaze drilled into her, penetrating her defenses. "Did I hurt you? Did I hurt anybody?"

"No. But you could have." Eve pulled her hand away. She had willed herself to stay strong earlier, but now that the terror was over she began to crumble. Her body quivered as the tension flowed from her muscles. Her knees slackened beneath her. She stumbled, almost falling, as they gave way.

With a muttered curse, Lonigan caught her in his arms, supporting her as he might support a wounded comrade in battle. Nothing in his touch could have been construed as sensual. But Eve's response was a shimmering heat that rose from the core of her womanhood, to flow like warm honey into her thighs and burn her cheeks to a flush.

A virgin when she wed the earl, she'd submitted to her husband's feeble lust out of duty. Thankfully, it was a duty he'd seldom required her to perform. After his stroke there'd been nothing more; yet Eve had remained as faithful as a nun, not missing what little she'd known of the marriage bed. Now this reaction to a virile man near her own age caught her by surprise. Her lips parted in an unvoiced whimper as sensations she'd never known surged through her body. The iron-solid feel of him, the aroma of his skin—a blend of smoke and sage, horses and man-sweat—swam in her senses, as intoxicating as wine. She wanted to inhale him, to taste him…

His own breathing had deepened to a rasp. Could he be responding to her the way she was to him?

But what was she thinking? Decent women shouldn't have such wanton feelings. She was a respectable widow, not a whore. Her fearful experience had left her emotionally overwrought; that was all. Wherever this madness was leading her, she would stop it right now.

Twisting free of his arms, she drew herself up to face him. "That's quite enough. Let me go home to the children. They've had such a fright. They're going to need me."

His eyes were the color of a winter sky, and just as cold. "Is it the children who need you, Eve, or is it their father?"

Her chin went up. "How dare you imply—"

"What's to imply? Hanford made it clear that he considers you his property."

"But you didn't ask *me*, Clint Lonigan. I only just arrived in this ungodly country. And I'm not about to be parceled out like a cow or a piece of land. I'm *nobody's* property, least of all Roderick's—or *yours!*"

Silence hung between them, ripe with tension. Then a dangerous look flickered in his eyes. With no more warning than that, he jerked her close, his arms crushing her against his chest, his mouth grinding hers in a brutal kiss that ignited bonfires where the simmering warmth had been. She struggled against him, her resistance thrusting her against him in ways that heightening the secret, sinful pleasure of his male body pressing hers. In violation of all ladylike behavior her lips softened and parted, melting under the compelling heat of his kiss. Her arms twined around his neck, fingers raking his thick hair in wild abandon.

Eve's mind was a churning whirlpool; but one sensible thought struggled to the surface. The man wanted something, and it wasn't just her body. He was out to win her to his cause— *any way he could!*

Seduce her and use her as a spy against his enemies. That was his plan.

As the truth swept over her, she turned to ice

in his arms. Only anger gave her the strength to push away from him. They faced each other like dueling antagonists, both of them breathing hard.

"How dare you?" Once more her hand shot up to strike him. This time he made no move to stop her. Her palm caught his cheek with a stinging force that sent daggers shooting down her arm. She staggered backward, clutching her wrist as the pain subsided.

"Satisfied?" Lonigan hadn't flinched. His eyes revealed glints of laughter.

Eve's cheeks burned with humiliation. "You deserve worse than a slap, you conniving brute! If you're trying to win me to your cause, you've got some backwoods ideas about how to charm a woman!"

"You seemed to like it well enough." His mouth twitched in an ill-suppressed grin.

"Is this how you behave with American women?"

"Some. It depends."

Eve reined back the urge to slap him again. She'd only make an even bigger fool of herself. With a huff of dismissal, she turned toward the road. "Enough of this. Take me home."

He stood tall and rock-stubborn, refusing to

budge. "I'll do that with pleasure, Countess. But not till I know my friend is safe at home and has his calves back—and that your cattlemen friends aren't planning a reprisal for what happened today."

Your cattlemen friends. His choice of words had been deliberate. Eve chose to ignore them. "And how long can I plan on that taking?"

"A few hours. Maybe till morning. You'll be in no danger. But we can't stay here in the open. Especially not the way the weather's looking."

Eve followed his gaze. In the western sky angry black clouds, blown by a freshening wind, were boiling over the mountains. "So I'm to be your prisoner."

"If that's the way you want to put it, Countess. Come on. My horse is back in the trees."

With no other choice except to be left unprotected in the storm, she followed him up the slope and into a grove of aspens—slender trees, white as birch, with coin-shaped leaves that shimmered in the breeze. A handsome buckskin was tethered in a small clearing. It raised its head and nickered at their approach.

"Can you ride?" Lonigan asked.

"Well enough. But…" She eyed the Western

saddle with its prominent horn in front. "I've never ridden astride."

"There's a first time for everything. Up you go."

With no mounting block, the stirrup looked impossibly high. And even if she could get on the horse, straddling it would require lifting her narrow skirt and petticoat above her knees, exposing her unmentionables to a strange man.

A man who'd just kissed her.

But if it had to be done, it had to be done.

"Do you need any help?" he asked her.

"No. I'll be fine. Just turn around."

When she was sure he wasn't looking, Eve hiked up her skirts. Lifting her left foot high, she managed to slide it into the stirrup. But she wasn't a tall woman, and from that awkward position couldn't leverage herself off the ground.

Now what?

Lonigan's broad-shouldered back was toward her, but something in his attitude told her he knew what was going on—and was secretly laughing at her. Eve fumed as she gripped the saddle horn and struggled to hoist herself onto the nervous horse. What if the animal decided to bolt? Heaven save her, she could be dragged to death.

"Can I help you?" Lonigan's voice dripped amusement.

"I could use...a boost."

In a single motion, he turned, caught her waist and lifted her into the saddle as if she weighed no more than a feather. Eve had enjoyed riding in England, but the sensation of straddling the broad leather saddle was new and strange. Her legs hung down on either side, exposing her lace-edged drawers. Glancing down, she shook her head. Her high-class English neighbors would have been shocked. But this was America, and propriety bowed to necessity. And anyway, there was no one there to see but Clint Lonigan, who clearly already held her in contempt.

"Where are you going to...?"

The question died on her lips as he sprang onto the horse and shifted into place behind the cantle. His knees cradled hers, well-worn boots finding the stirrups that were too long for Eve's legs. Reaching around her on either side, he took the reins and nudged the horse into motion. They set off at a brisk uphill jog through the trees.

"Where are we...going?" The contact of her legs against his was disturbingly intimate. "Are we going to your ranch?"

"Not there." His breath tickled her ear as he spoke. "That's the first place Hanford would look for us. I've got somewhere else in mind. Just pray we can get there ahead of the rain."

"That's not the only thing I'll be praying for." Eve gripped the saddle horn as the buckskin lurched onto the top of a ridge. She hadn't asked for this wild adventure. All she'd wanted was to nurture Margaret's precious children. Now getting safely back to them would be her first concern—her only concern, she vowed. Whatever scheme Clint Lonigan might be plotting, she wasn't about to become involved in his accursed range war.

As they followed the ridgeline, Clint glanced back over his shoulder. Driven by the west wind, the storm was streaming across the sky. Still distant, sheet lightning danced from cloud to cloud. He counted five seconds between the flash and the growl of thunder. Five miles. Still a little time to spare, but the dark menace was moving fast. He'd hoped to make it to the Potter ranch before the rain struck. Since Newt and Gideon were on the mountain, the place would be empty and there'd be no danger of the countess recognizing the two young stage robbers. But with the storm bearing down, Clint would be cutting it close. He'd been rained on enough not to mind too much, but the countess wasn't accustomed to Wyoming's raw weather. Getting soaked and chilled could be dangerous to her health.

She sat balanced between his arms. Her head was up, her posture rigidly defiant. If she was distressed she seemed determined not to show it.

"Are you all right?" He broke the silence that had hung too long between them.

"For a woman who's been kidnapped I'm fine, thank you." Her voice was frigid. "Did you plan this?"

"No more than you planned being caught between a cattle stampede and a hanging."

"Even so, you took advantage of the situation."

"Seeing my friend with a noose around his neck, hell yes, I took advantage of the opportunity you represented. I'd have done anything to save his life."

"Did that include shooting me?"

He hesitated, then decided on an honest reply. "Not unless it became absolutely necessary."

"But you'd have done it." Her body quivered with tension.

"Yost has a wife and two little ones, with a third on the way. They wouldn't survive without him."

A quiver of outrage passed through the countess's slim body. "*Trust me*, you said! I'd have been safer trusting a viper! If you'd pulled that trigger, Roderick would have—"

A blinding flash and a deafening boom cut off her words as a bolt of lightning struck a scraggly pine at the top of the ridge. The horse shrieked and reared. The countess clung to the saddle as Clint sawed the reins to get the terrified animal under control. Only as he brought the tall buckskin to a shuddering halt did he realize she hadn't cried out. He had to give the lady credit for some courage. Maybe she wasn't as delicately reared as he'd believed.

Swinging to one side, he guided the horse off the ridge and down the far side into a grove of young pines that had sprouted after a fire. By now the clouds were roiling overhead. Wind whipped the small trees, bending their limber trunks almost flat. Clint felt the first drops of rain spatter his face like buckshot.

The countess's bonnet was gone. Her hair had blown loose from its pins and was streaming across her face. She raked long strands out of her eyes. "Now what? Do you have a plan?"

"I was headed for some friends' place in the hollow below the next ridge, but we'll be soaked if we try to make it that far."

She looked ahead, to where mature stands of pine darkened the slope. "Can't we ride under the trees?"

"Too dangerous. Lightning's apt to strike anything tall. Up the hill from here, there's some rimrock with overhanging ledges. It won't be comfortable, but at least we'll be safe from the storm."

Another lightning bolt cracked like a whip across the sky. This time Clint had the horse under tight rein. "If you don't mind walking, Countess, it'll be safer for you that way. The ledges aren't far."

Without waiting for her reply he shifted his weight behind her, slid off the horse and reached up to help her dismount. When, stiff from the unaccustomed riding, she struggled to get her right leg back over the saddle, he caught her waist, lifted her and, in one easy motion, swung her to the ground.

She stood facing him, her eyes wide, her midnight-black hair whipping in the wind, her wine-hued lips parting as she caught her breath. Lord, but she was beautiful. The insane desire to kiss that ripe, sensual mouth again blazed hot and sudden. Clint hesitated, torn. He knew better than to try, but so help him, the woman almost looked as if she *wanted* to be kissed.

He was saved from disaster by another thunderclap that split the churning clouds, releasing a torrent of heavy rain.

"Come on!" Guiding the horse with one hand, Clint curved an arm around the countess's shoulders, shielding her from the downpour as best he could. Already drenched, he trudged uphill through the blinding gray curtain of rain, relying more on instinct and memory than on vision.

The countess kept up without complaint, her lips pressed tight, her wet hair dripping down her back. For a pampered woman she was surprisingly tough. But the rain and the chill wind had to be taking their toll. If he didn't get her out of them, she could be in danger of pneumonia.

Clint pushed ahead, eyes scanning through the rain for the dark line that marked the ledges. He needed to get this woman to shelter—not just because she was beautiful, spirited and gentle, but because she could be the key to winning against Roderick Hanford and others like him. He couldn't afford to lose her.

Eve toiled upward, her fine kidskin boots sliding on the muddy ground. The wind tore at her wet clothes with icy fingers. She was soaked through, and her teeth were chattering like Spanish castanets. But miserable as she was, she had too much pride to let Clint Lonigan hear a peep of complaint.

With her thighs screaming from the unaccustomed stress of the saddle, every step was an act of will. She could ask her captor to put her back on the horse, but the added height could make her a target for lightning, which would kill not only her but the poor animal, as well. Besides, she was not about to ask Clint Lonigan for anything. She would keep slogging up the hill until she collapsed in a sodden heap.

The memory of his searing kiss and her wanton response was at least enough to warm her blood a little. Back in England the man could've been flogged for laying hands on her. But this was America, a land where, it seemed, men could take what they wanted from any woman, regardless of station. Not that station mattered in this wild, rough land where the rules of decent society seemed to have gone the way of the tea cozy.

"Up there!" Lonigan's voice roused her from her musings. Following his gaze she saw the line of rocky ledges jutting through the rain. They were so close she could have hit them with a stone. Time and weather had worn away the mineral layer at the base, creating hollows, like shallow caves.

Lonigan chose one with an entrance high enough to shelter the horse. Its sandy floor was littered with sticks, leaves and pine needles, probably blown inside by storms like this one.

Pausing outside, he picked up a limb from a nearby fallen tree. "Wait here," he said, handing her the reins to hold.

While Eve stood shivering in the downpour, he stepped into the opening and swept the brushy end of the limb over the rock at the back of the cave, then across the ceiling. What was he expecting to find? Bats? Snakes? Spiders? She stepped to one side, prepared for some creature to come rushing out at her, but the cave proved to be empty.

Only after he'd swept the detritus on the floor into a pile did he bring Eve inside, leaving the horse under the lip of the entrance, out of the rain. The cave was cold and dim, but at least it was dry. Too tired to stand, she sank to the ground, huddling with her arms wrapped around her, a sodden bundle of misery.

"Storms like this one don't last long." Lonigan's manner was much too cheerful to suit her. "For now, let's see what we can do to get you warm." He reached into his breast pocket and drew out a thin metal box. Matches, she realized, as he struck one against the wall of the cave. Shielding the tiny flame with one hand, he bent low and touched it to the pile of dry sweepings from the floor of the cave. They burst into a cozy blaze.

"Much better." Eve held her cold-numbed hands toward the warmth. The fire had been skillfully placed so that the smoke would be drawn out the entrance instead of filling the cave. It would be like Lonigan, she thought, to pay attention to that small detail.

But after what he'd done to her, how could

she entertain even a spark of admiration for the man?

"This bit of dry fuel won't last long." He settled with his back against the wall of rock and his boots stretched toward the small blaze. "But at least it should take the chill off while the storm passes."

Eve remained where she was, huddled on the floor of the cave with her dress dripping around her. Even with the fire nearby, her teeth were chattering.

"Come here, Eve." Lonigan spoke as if soothing a frightened animal. "You're still cold. Stretch your legs out next to me and let me warm you."

The man's invitation didn't fool her. He was out to win her any way he could—and that included seduction. But she was shivering beneath her gown and the fire wasn't enough. She could nestle against that warm, masculine body or she could stay here and freeze, raising her odds of catching cold or worse. She'd be of no use to the children if she was ill and bedridden.

Vowing to keep her guard up, she made the only sensible choice.

Chapter Six

Eve sat with her back against his arm, her feet toward the fire. A gray curtain of rain streamed off the lip of the cave, closing them in. The horse drowsed in the dim light, threads of vapor curling from its damp coat.

Apart from lending an arm to cushion her against the rock, Lonigan had made no familiar move toward her. Eve had been half prepared for the need to slap him again, but there'd been no call for it. Was she disappointed, even a little? But what a silly question.

Next to his body she was beginning to warm. But she was even more tired than she'd realized. The journey from Liverpool to Wyoming had been exhausting, and after the scare with the dogs, she'd hardly rested at all the previous night. Now the crackle of the fire and the drone of the rain were lulling her into drowsiness. She was losing her battle with the dark fog of sleep.

"You're a quiet one," Lonigan said, breaking the silence between them. "Are you hatching some kind of escape plot or is it just that you don't converse with low-class Irishmen?"

Eve pulled herself back to alertness. "If I were plotting an escape, I certainly wouldn't tell you. And I won't even comment on your low-class behavior. As for your being Irish... hearing you speak, I'd wager you never set foot on the Emerald Isle."

"You're right." He shifted his rump against the hard ground, stretching his legs. "I may have been conceived in Ireland, but I was born in New York, a few months after my parents got off the boat. They died in a typhoid epidemic when I was eight, along with my two sisters."

"I'm sorry," Eve said, meaning it. "So you were raised in an orphanage?"

He shook his head. "I grew up on the streets, hiding from the well-meaning folk who wanted to turn me over to the nuns and lock me up. I took odd jobs, stole when I had to, slept wherever I could find shelter. When I was sixteen, and big for my age, I got a job on a railroad crew and came west. By the time that was over, I'd had most of the Irish beat out of me."

He didn't need to explain that last remark. Back in England, and likely in America as well, the Irish were looked down on as slackers, drinkers and brawlers—handy targets for bullying. Poor Irish boys grew up tough or not at all.

"So what did you do after that?"

There was no answer.

"After the railroad, I mean." She clarified the question. "I hope you don't mind my asking. I rather enjoy finding out how people got to where they are."

Lonigan stared into the fire. His throat moved, but he didn't speak. Some doors weren't meant to be opened, Eve surmised. She might be wise to change the subject.

"Why did you kiss me?" The question, coming out of nowhere, left Eve shocked by her own boldness.

He glanced back toward her, sparks of amusement dancing in his storm-colored eyes. "Why did you let me?"

"I asked you first."

One dark eyebrow crinkled upward. "Maybe

I was just curious. Besides, you looked as if you needed kissing."

"I most certainly did not need kissing. And I didn't *let* you. You caught me off guard."

The twinkle deepened. "At least I know better than to try it again. Next time you could break my jaw—or maybe your wrist."

"You should have better manners than to trifle with a woman in mourning."

"In mourning?" He dropped his bantering air. "Sorry, I should've remembered that. You didn't look it today."

Eve rearranged her wet skirt to expose more surface to the heat of the fire. "Roderick says most widows don't wear black around here. And now that I've spent time in this place I can understand why. The heat, the dust and the mud would make mourning clothes unbearable."

"There's more to it than that—especially since, with this range war on, there are so many widows. Most of them are too poor to buy a new dress, let alone a whole new black wardrobe. And there's something else you need to understand. If a widow's poor, with children to feed, sometimes her only hope of survival is to find a new man and get remarried, the sooner the better. In this territory, women being as scarce as they are, that usually doesn't take long, especially if a widow's pretty. Time to mourn the loss of a husband is a precious luxury that few can afford."

Taken aback, Eve stared at him. "Shocking," she murmured.

"It's not shocking, Countess. It's life."

Eve's eyes traced his rugged profile. Physically, Lonigan was the sort of man who could easily turn a woman's head. His behavior led her to believe he must be single. But he had been married. Was there a new woman in his life? After the way he'd closed himself off earlier, she knew better than to ask.

She sniffed—the chill was making her nose run and her handkerchief was in her reticule, which could be anywhere. "Well, whatever the local custom, I intend to observe a proper mourning. I did save a strip of black fabric to make an armband in remembrance of my husband and my sister, but I've yet to finish it. You can be sure I'll be wearing it the next time I go out."

The mention of the armband pricked the memory of her black bombazine and what had befallen it earlier. Once more she changed the subject. "Roderick introduced me to his dogs this morning—and to the man who takes care of them. Such a strange person. Can you tell me anything about him?"

"Can't say as I know much. I've seen him from a distance with the dogs, but he doesn't venture into town. Rumor has it he was captured by the Pawnee years back. They tortured him and cut out his tongue before they left him for dead. I heard tell he's strange in the head, but after a nightmare like that, who wouldn't be?"

"He had a shy manner about him, almost childlike. And there was a cabin in the kennel compound, right by the dogs. I had the impression he lived there—though I can't imagine how he could stand the noise and the smell."

"Maybe the man's more comfortable around the dogs than around people. Hanford could likely tell you more if you ask him."

Lonigan looked away, as if the mention of Roderick and the reminder that she'd be going back to him had thrown up a wall between them. In the silence, Eve's eyelids began to droop again. She yawned.

"Get some rest," he said. "I'll wake you when the rain lets up."

"Fine." She should have come back with

some clever retort, Eve thought. But she was too tired for wit. Like a toddler past her bedtime she sagged toward him, until her head came to rest on his shoulder. By then her eyes were closed and her mind was spiraling into sleep.

Clint watched the fire burn down to smoldering coals. The rain was letting up, misting over the hills and drizzling off the lip of the cave. Soon the storm would clear and they could be on their way.

Eve's damp head rested in the hollow of his shoulder, as sweet and trusting as a child's. She hadn't planned the events this day; neither had he. Yet fate and the storm had brought them together here, two enemies in a necessary state of truce.

Had he made any progress in winning her to his side, or was she planning to go back to Roderick Hanford and tell him everything she'd learned? Even now, Clint knew he couldn't trust her. He'd be smart to limit what he let her see and hear before he sent her home.

She stirred, an aura of rosewater rising from her damp clothes to tease his nostrils. He glanced down at her sleeping face, soot-black lashes against a porcelain cheek, and that silky ripe plum of a mouth… Eve was a beautiful woman, spirited and sharp of wit, with the sort of sensual innocence that could drive a man wild. Being a widow, she'd be no virgin. But her hungry response to his kiss hinted that the marriage bed had left her wanting.

He'd deserved her slap for that impulsive kiss. But while she was in his arms, he'd felt her fire and sensed that behind that prim and proper facade the countess was as passionate as she was beautiful.

With a muttered oath, Clint tore his gaze away from her. Except for occasional visits to a backstreet house in Casper, just to blow off steam and settle his nerves, he'd had little to do with women since Corrie's death. And this woman was way out of bounds. Not just because she was in league with his bitterest enemy, but because of who he was—and what he'd been. If Eve Townsend, Dowager Countess of Manderfield, knew the truth about his past, she would spit on him and walk away without a backward glance.

In her eyes he wouldn't be fit to wipe her muddy boots. He'd be wise to remember that and to treat her accordingly.

The horse snorted in the stillness, alerting

him that the rain had stopped. Thin fingers of sunlight poked through the scattering clouds. Chickadees piped among the aspens below the cave. Eve was still asleep, curled sweetly against his shoulder. He weighed the idea of lingering, enjoying the moment a little longer. But they'd soon be losing daylight and this place wasn't safe. If Hanford was mad enough to put his hell hounds on their trail, the cave would be a nasty place to be tracked down and cornered.

She stirred, nestling closer, her hand settling on his upper thigh. Clint swore silently as his body responded to her touch. *None of that*, he warned himself. It was time to wake her up and clear out of here.

Shifting, he nudged her shoulder. "Rain's stopped. We need to get moving."

"Mmm?" She made a sleepy little cat sound and opened her eyes. For an instant she looked startled. "Is everything all right?" she muttered, sitting up.

"Fine. You had a nice nap, but the weather's clearing. We need to go." Clint stood and offered his hand. She clasped it and pulled herself to her feet. Her gown was rumpled and smeared with mud, her hair a damp mass of tangles, but she paid no heed to her appearance as she faced him.

"I'm begging you, Clint Lonigan, please let me go back to the children. They're so young, and they've had such a fright. They'll be needing me."

Those azure eyes, glimmering with tears, would have softened a heart of granite. But he couldn't forget the bastard who'd be waiting for her alongside those innocent children. And Clint hadn't brought her this far just to turn her loose again. "I'll send you home when I know that Yost, his family and his property are safe, and that your cattlemen friends haven't done any more mischief."

"I never said they were my friends!" Color heated her face. "My friends don't hang innocent people."

"Does that make me your friend?"

"I didn't say that, either." She began shaking out her sodden skirts. "After all, I've never had a friend hold a gun on me or take me hostage. I've only just arrived here. Why is everyone pushing me to choose sides? All I want is to be there for my sister's children!"

He turned away before her plea could move

him. "It'll be safe to ride now," he said, starting for the horse. "Let's go."

He helped her mount. She had to be sore from the ride and the cold, but she did no more than grimace as her legs settled over the saddle. She was quiet. Too quiet, he realized, an instant too late.

Before he could mount up behind her she seized the reins and set her heels into the horse's flanks. With a snort of surprise, the big buckskin shot out of the cave and rocketed down the slope.

Standing at the lip of the cave, Clint purpled the air with curses. The countess was leaning like a jockey over the horse's neck, her knees gripping the saddle. She appeared to be an able rider. But the hillside was slippery from the rain and crisscrossed with fallen trees. Her reckless plunge could easily cause the horse to fall, breaking the poor beast's legs and maybe her own neck in the bargain. And even if she made it to the hollow below, she was a stranger to the country. There was no way she knew how to get back to the road from here, let alone make it to Hanford's. The fool woman could end up deep in the back country, lost and in danger.

His heart stopped as horse and rider approached a deadfall that was blocking their path. The countess pressed forward in the saddle, clearly planning to jump the horse over the tangle of fallen trees and brush. Clint's curses became shouts of warning. This wasn't a damned English foxhunt. The big gelding was a superb cow pony, but not a trained jumper.

They were coming up on the obstacle—coming too fast. At the last split second, as if knowing its limits, the buckskin balked, skidding on wet leaves as it shuddered to a halt. Carried by forward momentum, the countess flew over the horse's head and plummeted earthward like a downed swan on the far side of the deadfall.

There was no cry from her, no movement, nothing. Clint flung himself down the slope, sliding on wet leaves, clambering over fallen limbs, muttering curses and prayers.

The horse stood next to the deadfall. It was quivering and rolling its eyes, but otherwise appeared all right. Steeling himself for what he might find, Clint climbed over the heap of twisted branches and clawing roots. People died from tumbles like the one Eve had just taken. Or they broke their spines and spent the rest of their days in a wheelchair.

He found her where she'd come to rest. Cushioned by rotting leaves and pine needles, she lay on her side with one arm crumpled beneath her. Her eyes were closed, her face pale except for an ugly red scratch along one cheek where something sharp must have caught her on the way down. If she was alive Clint could see no sign of it.

Sick with dread, he dropped to his knees and laid two fingers alongside her neck. His heart leaped as he detected a steady pulse. Now he could see the subtle rise and fall of her chest. She was alive, thank God. But after a fall like that, she could have a concussion, maybe broken bones, as well.

His fingers probed the roots of her damp hair, seeking any sign of swelling or blood. Finding none, he gave her shoulder a gentle squeeze. "Eve, can you hear me?"

Her eyelids fluttered, then jerked open. She gasped like a swimmer coming up for air.

Clint felt himself begin to breathe again. "Do you know me? Do you know where you are?"

"Yes." Her voice was spiderweb thin, barely a whisper.

"Can you remember what happened?"

She hesitated. "The horse balked."

"Careful now. Can you move your arms and legs? Tell me if it hurts anywhere."

She stirred, stretching her limbs cautiously, flexing her fingers and her feet. Little by little she eased herself to a sitting position. "I'm fine," she said, but her reassurance was contradicted by her next words. "Please help me stand." She was *not* fine, then—or she'd never have asked for his help, much less said please. Still, while she was undoubtedly bruised and battered by her fall, she didn't seem to have any serious injuries.

Rising, he clasped her elbows and pulled her to her feet. Clint had been frantic with worry. But now that he knew she was basically all right the anger blasted out of him like torched gunpowder.

"Damn it, woman, what did you think you were doing?" His grip tightened on her arms. "You could've killed my horse or killed yourself—maybe both! And even if you'd gotten away, where in hell's name did you think you were going?"

She glared up at him. "Home to the children. Surely somebody could have shown me the way."

"Somebody?" Clint muttered an ungentlemanly curse. "This isn't England, Countess. There are men in these hills who'd do anything to get their hands on a pretty woman like you, and once they had you they certainly wouldn't be sending you home. They wouldn't give a hang about your fancy title! Neither would wolves or bears or Indians if you happened to run into them! Damn fool thing you did, charging off like that. I ought to turn you over my knee and spank you!"

"You wouldn't dare!"

Wouldn't he? Clint fought the temptation to prove her wrong. The satisfaction wasn't worth the trouble, he told himself. Besides, she'd just been in a devil of an accident. If she had unseen injuries a careless spanking could make them worse.

"Let's go," he said, seizing her wrist and starting back toward the horse.

"Where are we going?" she demanded. "Are you taking me home now?"

"Not yet." Clint had been weighing the decision of where to take her. The Potter ranch was close, but he'd changed his mind about going there. It would be like Newt and Gideon to give up waiting on the mountain and come home. If the two brothers were there, Eve would recognize them as the stagecoach bandits. As for his own place, the road was likely to be watched by Hanford's men. Letting her go was the only choice that made sense. But first there was something he wanted her to see.

Reaching the horse, Clint swung into the saddle and stretched a hand down to her. "This time you ride behind," he said, locking his grip and pulling her up. Getting her on the horse was harder this way, but she hiked up her skirts and clambered on without complaint. Had she learned her lesson? That remained to be seen. Meanwhile, he had other things to teach her.

Eve clung to Lonigan's muscular back as the mountain trail bottomed out to join a well-worn wagon road. She was damp, sore and irritable. But complaining would only make things worse. Any sympathy the man might have felt for her had ended when she'd tried to escape on his horse. Now escape was out of the question. With dusk closing around them, she would not even try to get away, since it would only leave her alone and on foot, in the dark.

At least with the passing of the storm, the air had warmed. Her light cotton gown was far from dry, but she was no longer shivering.

Her hands gripped Lonigan's ribs. Through the damp fabric of his shirt, his body felt as solid, and as splendidly fashioned, as the Greek gods and athletes she'd seen in the Elgin Marbles collection at the British Museum. Lonigan naked would be a splendid sight—but merciful heaven, where had that wicked thought come from?

"You must know where we're going," she said. "I'd appreciate it if you'd share that with me."

His silence hinted that he was still angry with her. But after a moment he answered. "I need to make sure Yost is all right and that his calves are back where they belong. I'd also like to introduce you to the man and his family."

"Oh, please, I'm a fright!" The moment the words were out of her mouth, Eve realized how silly they sounded.

"It won't matter. They'll want a chance to thank you."

"Thank me for what? You had me at gunpoint! All I did was keep quiet!"

"If you hadn't been there, he would be dead. They're good people and proud people. I'm hoping you'll be kind enough to accept their gratitude."

Eve shook her head. Was this rough Wyoming cowboy giving her a lesson in manners? Who did he think he was talking to?

"I know how to behave properly, thank you," she said. "Just promise me you'll take me home when it's over."

Lonigan's silence was his only reply. He was promising her nothing.

The wagon road had cleared the woods. Now it meandered between rolling, grassy hills. In the distance Eve could make out the thin dark line of a wire fence. She remembered Roderick's passionate hatred of settlers and their fences. So this was what the range war was about.

The evening breeze was pleasantly warm. Eve's underclothes were still damp, but her dress was slowly drying as was Lonigan's shirt. She could feel the heat of his skin beneath the fabric. With every breath she took, the rain-freshened aromas of wood smoke, lye soap and clean sweat swam in her senses. She remembered the taste of his lips, the salty, whiskery burn of his rough kiss and her startling response—those deep, throbbing shimmers that had made her ache for something she couldn't even name. How could a decent woman feel such things? Perhaps, in the depths of her soul, she was more wicked than she'd ever believed.

Wandering late one night at Manderfield, she'd chanced to pass the closed door to a servant girl's room. Earlier the maid had been flirting with one of the footmen, so as the bed creaked and thumped, Eve could imagine what was going on. What had surprised her were the gasps and moans of pleasure that seemed to be coming from the girl. How could any female be so thrilled by the act that Eve herself endured only out of wifely duty?

The girl was common, that was all, with common tastes for baser pleasures, Eve had told herself as she moved on down the corridor. As time passed she'd forgotten the incident. Now, as she remembered how she'd felt in Lonigan's arms, the memory surfaced again, to be weighed and pondered.

Lonigan paused the horse where the fence skirted the road. "This is Yost's pasture," he said, peering into the twilight. "I'm hoping we'll see those stolen calves—" He caught his breath, then exhaled in relief. "There they are, off in that far corner by the willows. See them?"

Eve followed the line of his gaze to a cluster of bulky shapes, just visible in the gathering dusk. "Calves? But they're huge! I was thinking of babies."

"They're yearlings—but they still count as calves. Tomorrow I'll come over and help Yost put his brand on them so something like this will be less likely to happen again." He nudged the buckskin to a walk. "I wasn't sure they'd be here. Hanford must really want you back."

Eve stifled the urge to punch Lonigan. He was baiting her and she was tired of it. But why waste the energy? She had no romantic interest in Roderick, but his children were the world to her. If Lonigan hadn't figured that out by now, that was his problem.

They turned down a narrow lane. At the end of it was a log cabin, little more than a hut. Through the single front window Eve glimpsed the glow of lamplight. The smell of food drifted to her nostrils. Her empty belly emitted a most unladylike growl.

Lonigan chuckled. "Hungry, are you?"

"A little. But I'm certainly not expecting these poor people to feed me."

"They may offer. And if they do we'll accept. It would be rude not to."

Eve bridled, but held her tongue. Once more this rough-hewn Irish cowboy, who'd grown up brawling on the streets of New York, was teaching her manners as if she were a backward child. But the rules were different here, she reminded herself. And the people she was about to meet, poor as they might be, were her equals in a country with no aristocracy. She'd do well to remember that.

Seen in the twilight, the Yost farmyard had a certain charm. The ground was immaculately swept, the barn small but well built. A log corral held two horses and a mule. On one side of the cabin was a well-tended garden, on the other a hen coop and, farther to the back, an outhouse, screened by a row of spindly young apple trees.

On the porch, a scruffy shepherd-mix dog sprang up and began to bark. "Quiet, old boy, you know me," Clint said. With a wag of its shaggy tail the animal settled back into place.

At the sound of the dog's alarm, the door of the cabin opened and Yost stepped out, his shotgun at the ready. Recognizing his visitors, he lowered the weapon.

"I was hoping you would come by." He spoke with a thick Dutch accent.

"I saw the calves were back." Lonigan gave Eve a hand as she slid off the horse, then dismounted himself. "Did McCutcheon's men give you any trouble?"

"They might have. But the rain was coming too hard. All they did was shoot our good rooster. We're having him for supper—a treat for the children, at least." The Dutchman seemed to notice Eve for the first time. "But I forget my manners. Come inside. You are welcome at our table." Turning in the open doorway, he called, "Berta, two more places. Tonight we dine with friends."

Lonigan was right—it would have been rude to refuse the gracious hospitality of these humble people. Still, Eve was amazed that they would welcome her, knowing she was Roderick's sister-in-law.

Inside, the cabin was tiny. There was no parlor. The kitchen and dining table took up most of the living space, with a stone fireplace and two rockers on the far side. An open door revealed a single bedroom, with an overhead loft where the children likely slept. Crowded as it was, the place appeared clean and tidy.

Next to her husband, Berta Yost appeared small. She wore a ragged calico dress, the waist pulled high. Her belly bulged beneath the faded gingham apron that covered it. She gazed at Eve as if wondering whether she should curtsy.

Eve offered her hand. "Thank you for welcoming me to your home, Berta."

She responded with a tentative clasp and a murmured greeting. Berta was a pretty woman, still young, with lovely violet eyes; but hardship and worry had taken their toll. The word that would best describe her was careworn.

"Your husband mentioned that you have children," Eve said, trying to put her at ease.

"Yes, these two—Jan and Greta." She glanced down. Only then did Eve notice the two little faces peeking out from behind her skirts. They were younger than Rose and Thomas—perhaps three and four, with their father's wheaten hair and their mother's violet eyes. Such beautiful children, like little angels. Eve's heart turned to putty at the sight of them. Dropping to a crouch, she held out her hands. "Hello there," she whispered, smiling. "Would you like to come out and make friends?"

The children emerged slowly, timid at first, but growing bolder in response to her gentle coaxing. As she clasped their tiny hands, Eve sensed Lonigan's eyes watching her and she knew why he'd brought her here.

The man had tried every tactic, even seduction, to win her sympathy for his cause. Until now she'd remained defiantly neutral. But he had found her weakness. Clint Lonigan had set his trap with the one sweet bait she couldn't resist.

Chapter Seven

Clint stood in the doorway watching Eve make a pretty fuss over the Yost children. So far things were working just as he'd hoped. She might not care about him or his friends or their land and cattle. But if she grew to care about these precious youngsters, his experiences with her told him that she would fight like a tigress to keep them from harm.

As he stepped inside and closed the door behind him, she glanced up and met his eyes. The brief narrowing of her gaze told him everything. She knew how he'd manipulated her—bringing her here to meet this good couple and the innocent children who could do naught but capture her heart. But it was too late to back out of the trap. Clint had won this battle, and they both knew it. The questions was, would she be a gracious loser?

The family had been ready to eat when they'd arrived. Accommodating guests had been a matter of putting down two more tin plates with spoons and crowding to make room on the hand-hewn benches that flanked the sides of the table. The Yosts had to make do with little, but Berta was a fine cook. Tonight's meal consisted of a rich chicken stew with carrots and potatoes, some greens from the garden and fresh baking soda biscuits.

As they bowed their heads for grace, Clint studied Eve from beneath half-closed eyelids. She looked like a Madonna with her black hair falling in waves to frame the pale oval of her face, her lashes brushing her cheeks like dark silk fringe. She was without question the most beautiful woman he'd ever seen. Corrie, his wife, had been blonde and pretty in a sun-freckled way; lively and full of spunk. But why was he comparing the two? He had loved Corrie with his whole heart, as he would never love again. As for Eve, he admired her, but her beauty was as cold and remote as the moon—and to a man like him, just as far out of reach.

The pot with the chicken stew was placed in

the middle of the table. As the honored guest, Eve was invited to fill her plate first. Taking the ladle, she helped herself to carrots, potatoes and gravy, but left the meat for others. Remembering how Yost had mentioned that chicken was a rare treat, Clint couldn't help liking her for that.

They were all hungry, and the meal was delicious. The children filled their small bellies while the adults made polite conversation about the weather and the cattle. Clint knew that Yost would not want to discuss the near-hanging or other threats from the cattlemen in front of his family. With a baby on the way, Berta didn't need more worries.

When supper was finished Eve offered to help with the dishes. Berta wouldn't hear of it. "You are our guest," she insisted.

"Then please allow me to tell the children a bedtime story," Eve said. "I'll enjoy that, and it will keep them entertained while you work."

Clint leaned against the fireplace, looking on as she took a seat in one of the rockers and gathered the children onto her lap. He knew she was anxious to get home. But whether she wanted to repay Berta for the kindness of a meal, or just wanted an excuse to enjoy the children longer, who was he to rush her out the door?

Cradling the little ones close, Eve began the story of the Three Bears. If Clint had heard it at all, it must've been when he was very young, for it sounded new to him. When Eve spoke for the bears—the big, gruff Papa Bear, the treacle-voiced Mama Bear and the squeaky little Baby Bear—the children giggled with delight. Lord, the woman was an enchantress! The little ones were completely under her spell, and he was dangerously close to being mesmerized himself.

"The little girl was so frightened that she jumped out the window and ran home through the forest. And she never went to the Three Bears' house again." Eve ended the story with a double hug.

"What happened to Baby Bear's chair?" the little girl asked. "Did his papa fix it?"

"Oh, I'm sure he did! Papa Bear was a very good carpenter. After all, he'd built the house and everything in it." Laughing, Eve eased the children off her lap. "And now it's time for you to get ready for bed, and it's time for me to thank your parents and go."

"Will you come back?"

"Perhaps. I certainly hope so." She rose, sending Clint a stern glance. He returned a curt nod, understanding. Yes, he'd kept her long enough. It was time to take her home.

They thanked the Yosts for their hospitality and mounted up, with Eve riding behind. By now it was dark, with a fresh night breeze blowing off the peaks. In the east the moon was rising above the wooded hills. Platinum light, broken by flowing shadows of clouds, flooded the landscape.

Eve slumped against Lonigan's back, so tired she could barely hang on to him. What had started out as a pleasant outing with Margaret's children had come to this—she'd been kidnapped, kissed, rained on, thrown from a horse and now she was seriously considering taking on a role as a spy in a war she had no desire to fight. Her head ached. Her muscles screamed. She felt physically and emotionally drained. But something told her Lonigan wasn't in the mood for mercy.

Only after they'd cleared the farm and were headed along the wagon road did she straighten up and speak. "That was pure manipulation, Clint Lonigan. You knew exactly what you were doing, didn't you?"

Where her hands clasped his sides, she felt

the rise and fall of his ribs. "If you're waiting for an apology you're not going to get one. Things have been bad enough for the settlers with incidents like the one you saw today, where poor Yost was almost hanged. But if the cattlemen are bringing in hired guns, whole families will be slaughtered—women and children like the ones you met tonight."

"Don't." Eve blinked back a rush of tears. "Don't do this to me."

"Are you still insisting this isn't your war, *Countess*?" On his lips her title sounded like a curse.

She sagged against his back, feeling as if she'd been kicked into submission. An owl cried out in the stillness, a mournful, ghostly sound.

"What do you want from me?" she asked. "For the sake of my sister's children, I can't go against Roderick. He's their father, and I'm not strong enough to fight him. I could lose them."

"I'm not asking you to fight. I'm only asking you to listen. You're bound to hear things. He might even confide in you if you seem sympathetic. Just pass on what you learn. We may not be able to stop the gunfighters, but if we know when they're coming and where they plan to strike, at least we can try to get the women and children to a safe place. Can you do that much for us?"

What choice did she have? Given the innocent lives at stake, how, in the name of humanity, could she refuse?

He took her silence as a yes. "Right now our main concern is the money that the Cattlemen's Association supposedly sent to pay for hired guns. We need to know if it's real, and whether the money's been delivered. If it's still on its way, we might be able to intercept it."

Eve remembered the two inept young stage robbers. Had the money actually been on that coach? Could they have somehow missed it? Maybe that, at least, was something she could find out.

"If I learn anything, how will I get in touch with you?" she asked. "Is there anyone at the ranch I can trust to carry a message?"

"Nobody we can count on." Lonigan paused a moment, as if lost in thought. "On the boundary of the Hanford ranch, next to the road, there's an old log fence—a buck fence, they call it. It has plenty of nooks and crannies for leaving a note. When we pass there on the way to Hanford's we can pick a spot. I'll ride by and check every night. Maybe you can set up a signal to let me know that something's there."

Questions and doubts flew at Eve's mind like attacking crows. Could the hiding place be seen from the house? Was it close enough to walk or would she need to saddle a horse? What if there was no time to leave a message and have it picked up? So many things could go wrong.

"What do I do if there's an emergency that can't wait, and I need to find you?"

"I thought of that. In that case, come straight to me. The trail to my ranch cuts off from the main road to town. I'll show you where—we'll pass it on the way. It's not that far from Hanford's place."

They rode in silence for a time, both of them lost in thought. In the stillness Eve could hear the low rush of Lonigan's breathing. Trusting her was a dangerous gamble for him, she knew. She could easily betray him to Roderick or feed him false information that would leave him and his friends open to attack. And she was taking a chance, too. In letting herself be used as a spy, she'd be risking her safety and her access to Margaret's precious children.

Given the circumstances, it was a wonder they could trust each other at all.

A few minutes later he swung the horse onto a wider wagon road that Eve recognized as the one she'd taken into town. "That's the way to my ranch." He pointed to a worn track cutting off to the left. In the moonlight it was barely visible. "You follow it about a mile to where it ends at the mouth of a box canyon. Even at night you can't miss the place."

Eve scrutinized the landmarks, knowing the spot could look quite different by daylight. She would double-check it tomorrow. If she could remember the way back to the Yost farm as well, she might even pay them another visit. In the nursery room she'd found a trunk packed with Thomas's and Rose's outgrown clothes, as well as things for Margaret's baby. Surely Berta could use them for her children.

The road was looking more familiar now. Eve began to recognize things she'd passed on her way to town earlier—a time that now seemed like years ago. A tree, a fence, a watering tank. In the distance, to the right, she glimpsed a steady light. A chill went through her body as she realized it was Roderick's house.

"Here's the fence I was telling you about." Lonigan turned the horse off the road into a clump of willows that overhung a spring. The buck fence, as he'd called it, was an old one, most likely thrown up before wire was available, by some early settler who'd since moved on. It was made entirely of four-foot logs, braced one against another in a chain of Xs that reminded Eve of threads in a line of cross-stitch embroidery. Fashioned without nails, it had remained sturdy over the years.

Lonigan steadied Eve while she slid off the horse, then swung a leg over the saddle and dropped to the ground. It wasn't a bad spot for leaving a message—hidden by trees, yet close enough to reach from the house on foot. Probing between the logs, he found a hollow space that would conceal a folded note and hold it securely. It was high enough that he'd be able to lean down and reach the note without getting off his horse.

"Can you remember where this is?" he asked.

"I think so." She studied the small recess, memorizing the peculiar knot at the end of the log. From here on out, any manner of communication between them would be dangerous.

"We'll need some kind of signal that can be seen from the road," he said. "Something nobody else would notice."

"How about this?" Eve picked up a broken piece of branch, the length of her arm. "If there's a message, I put this in the fork of that big tree nearest the road. To others, it will look as if it's just fallen there. When you retrieve a message, you can take the branch out and drop it on the ground—all without leaving your saddle."

He frowned, then nodded. "That should work. And I can do the same if I've left a message for you. Don't take any chances getting out here— especially with the dogs."

"Roderick's in the process of getting them accustomed to me. They shouldn't—" She broke off at the sound of horses on the road, coming closer.

"Shh!" Lonigan pulled her into the trees, where they were hidden from sight, barely. "Don't move!" With his back to the road he wrapped his arms around her, his darker clothing covering as much of her light-colored dress as possible. His body was tense, primed for action. One hand held the pistol he'd drawn. The side of the weapon pressed cold against her spine. If they were discovered, would he fight to protect her or use her once more as a hostage to get away?

Eve froze, trembling against him as the

horses came closer—three, maybe four of them, moving at an easy pace. The riders seemed in good spirits, laughing, joking, bursting into bits of song. Cowboys, she judged, returning from an evening in town, probably drunk, certainly not paying attention to anything around them. All to the good.

She held her breath as they passed within an easy stone's toss. Lonigan's heart was a drumbeat in her ear as they waited. Down the road another fifty yards the cowboys took the turn-off to the Hanford ranch. So they were Roderick's men.

"Wait." Lonigan's whisper stirred her hair. His stubbled chin was rough against her forehead. She closed her eyes, filling her senses with the rocky contours of his body. As the cowboys moved out of hearing, headed for the bunkhouse, she felt the warm shimmer re-awaken in her loins. The sweet sensations crept down into her legs and up into her breasts. Her nipples shrank and hardened beneath her camisole. The feeling was so deliciously wicked she had to stifle a moan. It would be safe to pull away from him now, Eve told herself. But his arms were still holding her, and strangely enough, she didn't want him to let her go.

Lonigan didn't seem inclined to release her, either. His arms tightened around her, drawing her hips in close to his. A disturbing ridge rose against her belly, iron hard even through her skirts. She'd been the earl's bride long enough to know what it was; but that it could happen so easily, and in such a spectacular fashion, astonished her.

Her pounding heart sent a surge of reckless heat through her veins. Whatever this feeling was it couldn't lead to anything good. The man was far beneath her station. Worse, he was Irish. Worse than that, even, he was the sworn enemy of the man whose children she'd vowed to nurture and protect.

To do anything but turn and walk away would be foolish.

But never in her proper, dutiful, restricted life had Eve felt such a burning desire to play the fool.

Rising on tiptoe, she lifted her face to his. Her pulse rocketed as he bent toward her. His lips closed on hers, urgent and seeking as he nuzzled her; then, as if her response had kindled a blaze, the kiss deepened and became hungry, devouring her, filling her. Her mouth went molten, her lips clinging, nibbling, her tongue tasting salt and rain. Tasting him. Frenzied hands clasped his shoulders as he lifted her off her feet, pressing her pulsing heat against that compelling hardness. Even with layers of clothing between them she felt it—the hot coursing of need, the intense spasms of sensation that shook her like nothing she'd ever experienced in her life.

But then she felt something else—the side of his pistol against her spine. He was still holding it. The feel of that cold metal shocked her back to reality. Sensing the sudden tension in her, he dropped his arms, letting her go as he slid the weapon into its holster.

They faced each other, both of them breathing hard. "You need to go," he said. "Can I take you partway?"

Still warm jelly inside, she shook her head. "No, it isn't far. And if the dogs were out, we'd have heard them barking at the cowboys. I'll be fine walking."

"I'll stay here and watch till I know you're safe."

"That won't be necessary." But she knew he would. "For the sake of the families involved, I'll do what you want. But we mustn't see each other again. It wouldn't be wise."

"I understand, Countess." There was a frigid undertone in his voice.

"It's Mrs. Townsend." Tearing her gaze from him, she forced herself to turn around and walk away. As the urge to look back at him sharpened to an ache, she broke into a run that carried her as far as the turnoff to the ranch. With her heart slamming her ribs beneath her corset, she slowed to a determined walk.

She'd made a dangerous decision tonight. But now, of all times, she had to keep her head. Much as she might wish it, seeing Clint Lonigan again, and being in his arms, would risk both their lives—and trigger consequences that could touch off a bloodbath.

Mounted now, Clint watched the pale figure grow small with distance. His mouth still felt the burn of her kiss. He wouldn't mind picking up where they'd left off sometime soon. But Eve—*Mrs. Townsend*—was right. Except for accidental meetings in town, they couldn't risk being seen together. And there were other pitfalls, as well. There was no reason to believe he could trust her. She could lie to him, send him misleading messages, lure him into a trap or reveal everything she knew to Hanford.

And no matter how lovely she was, or how

vulnerable, he couldn't let his emotions get involved. If it came down to choosing between her life and the lives of his friends and their families, he had to be prepared to make the right choice, and to make it in an instant.

He could barely see her now, but she had already neared the house. When the front door opened, casting light across the porch, he reckoned she was safe.

Clint lingered a few more seconds, listening to the distant howl of a coyote. Then, turning his horse, he headed toward home.

Roderick had come outside and was waiting on the front porch with his arms folded over his chest. With his face in shadow, Eve couldn't be sure whether he was angry or relieved to see her.

"So the bastard finally let you go." Those were the first words out of his mouth. "Lord, you look like you've been rolling in the mud! And how did you get that scratch on your face? If the man so much as laid a hand on you, I'll—"

"Don't be silly, Roderick." Eve mounted the top step and stood facing him. "We got caught in the storm and the horse threw me. After the rain we went to make sure the calves had been returned. The family invited us to stay for supper, and then he brought me home." What she'd said was all true.

"So you went willingly."

"I tried once to escape. But in the end I didn't have a choice." She thrust her chin higher, in defiance. "Are the children all right?"

Roderick ignored her question. "You actually sat down and shared a meal with those... vermin?"

"I was hungry and it was good. Now, if you'll excuse me, I need to check on the children and get ready for bed."

He stood in her path, blocking the doorway. "This won't do, Eve. I can't have you ruining your reputation by gallivanting about the countryside, consorting with known criminals."

She'd been about to push past him when the last word caught her attention. "Criminals? What are you talking about?"

An ugly smirk crept over his face. "I take it Lonigan didn't tell you. I did some checking into his past. Before he came here, the man did seven years of hard labor in Lansing Penitentiary, Kansas...for train robbery."

Still reeling from what she'd learned, Eve climbed the stairs. Mounting each step was like lifting a leaden weight.

Roderick had meant to shock her. He'd succeeded, more profoundly than he would ever know. The discovery that the man whose kiss had thrilled her to the tips of her toes was an ex-convict, and a common criminal, had hit her like a blast of icy water. For the first few seconds she'd refused to believe it. But now that she remembered, Lonigan had been evasive when she'd asked him about his past. She'd sensed he was hiding a secret. Now she knew what it was.

How could she continue risking her safety to help such a man? But how could she not? Her concern wasn't for Lonigan. It was for innocent families like the Yosts, who would suffer if she turned her back on them. She had little choice except to pass on what she learned. But when it came to Clint Lonigan she would blot out all improper thoughts. She was no longer a silly young girl with a head full of romantic dreams. She was a woman with serious responsibilities.

When Eve tiptoed into the adjoining nursery rooms, she found both children awake in their beds. Their little faces were unwashed, their clothes lying in rumpled heaps on the floor.

"Where have you been, Aunt Eve?" Thomas's brown eyes were dark pools in the lamplight. "We were worried. Did that man hurt you?"

Lonigan's searing kiss flashed through her mind. She forced the memory away. "No, he only scared me. I've been on an adventure, but everything's all right. I'm here now." Eve brushed his rumpled curls back from his face. "Did you get yourselves ready for bed?"

"Uh-huh." Rose looked as if she'd been crying. "Papa was cross and Alice's knees hurt too much to climb the stairs. Will you tuck us in, Aunt Eve?"

"That's why I'm here." With cloths wrung from the basin, Eve washed Rose's face and let Thomas wash his own. "Did you brush your teeth? No? Come on then, up you go." Eve made sure the children were properly ready for bed. Then she heard their prayers, tucked them in and kissed them good-night.

By the time she left them, they were already settling into sleep. Thomas wouldn't need tucking in much longer, she reflected as she crossed the hallway to her bedroom. In a few years he would be a young man. But with his mother so recently gone, he seemed to welcome a touch of tenderness. Eve would enjoy mothering him while she could. After that she would take on the task of making sure Margaret's son didn't grow up to be like his father.

Eve had always hoped to have children of her own. But it hadn't happened with the earl. Now, at thirty-one, she had to face the likelihood that it wouldn't happen at all. These sweet children of Margaret's were heaven's answer to her prayers for a family—perhaps the only answer. But they weren't really hers, she reminded herself. They could be snatched away from her at Roderick's whim. How could she ensure that she would always be there to nurture and protect them?

Become their mother.

The answer slammed her with the force of a steam hammer. Marriage to Roderick—and Eve had little doubt that was what he had in mind— would secure her place in the home and in the children's lives. She'd be there to protect them from their father's temper and from the chance that he'd remarry a woman who wouldn't care for them, a stepmother who would eject Eve from their lives.

She'd married once out of duty, to save her father from ruin. Could she do it again to save Margaret's children?

The bedroom was stuffy from the heat of the day. Striding to the window, Eve flung it open and leaned over the sill. As she filled her lungs with the rain-freshened air, conflicting thoughts warred in her head. Marriage to their father would provide Rose and Thomas with the love and security they needed. But life with Roderick would be as stifling as an airless room. No freedom. No joy. Only shame, perhaps even fear. As for the thought of his touching her, touching her intimately...

A shudder passed through her body. How could she make such a sacrifice when she could scarcely abide being in the same room with the man?

She inhaled deeply, filling her lungs with the sweetness of mountain air. There was no call for a fast decision. She could let events take their natural course. Maybe in time she would warm to Roderick. But she doubted that would happen—especially while, somewhere out there in the darkness, an unsuitable man was galloping away from her on his tall buckskin horse.

A man she had to forget.

Chapter Eight

Clint rubbed down his horse and left it in the barn with some oats and water. Inside the dark house he found Gideon Potter snoring with his shaggy head on the kitchen table. One skinny hand rested on his Colt .45.

"Gideon, wake up." Clint spoke softly to the young man, not wanting to spook him and risk a shot.

"Wha…?" Gideon sat bolt upright, his eyes staring, his hand groping for his pistol in the darkness. Clint slid the weapon out of reach.

"It's just me." He stepped into full view. "What the devil are you doing here? Didn't I tell you to stay put on the mountain?"

"We got worried about our place." Gideon rubbed the sleep from his eyes. "Came down to have a look, figured to go back afore sunup.

When we rode over here to ask you how things stood, you was gone. So Newt went home and I stayed here to keep a lookout."

"Thanks, I'm beholden to you." It had been a kind gesture on Gideon's part...but a foolish one, as well. Clint couldn't help imagining what would've happened to the boy if the ranch had been raided in his absence. Buildings and stock could be replaced. Friends couldn't. "Long as you're back, you might as well stay," he said. "I talked to the sheriff. He's not looking to arrest you boys. But just in case, keep away from town for a spell."

"Ever find out about that cash from the Cattlemen's Association?" Gideon stood up, stretched and scratched his side.

"No. But I may have found somebody who'll keep us informed."

He glanced up with interest. "Who's that?"

"The countess."

"What?" Gideon blinked. "Holy Hannah, man, how'd you manage that?"

"Long story. I'll tell you later." It dawned on Clint that he was weary to the bone. He yawned.

"But ain't the lady all cozied up with Hanford? Her livin' with him and all."

"That's just what makes her useful."

Gideon shook his head. "I got a bad feelin' about this, Clint. Can we trust her?"

"That part may take some time. But if she turns out to be reliable—and willing—her help could make all the difference."

"But *her*? You're playin' with dynamite, Clint."

"I know." That was how it had felt kissing Eve—like playing with sweet, warm dynamite, knowing it could explode in his arms. "We'll just have to be careful—watch what we let her see and hear, double-check anything she tells us."

"Not that I'm one to give advice, you bein' older and all, but you'd better watch yourself. A looker like her could turn a man's head and make a fool of him."

Wise words, Clint knew. He'd be smart to remember them. "Thanks. You can head home now, Gideon. Tell Newt what I said—no going into town until things cool down. I'll come by and tell you if there's any news."

Gideon's horse was waiting behind the house. Clint stood in the doorway and watched him set off for home. The Potter boys were brave and good-hearted, as their parents had been. But they could be reckless, especially Newt.

If a showdown came with the cattlemen—and sooner or later it would—making sure they survived wouldn't be easy. But Clint was determined to keep them safe if he could.

Over the past few years, especially since Corrie's murder, he'd come to feel responsible for all the settler families in the valley. He would give his life to protect them. But in a violent confrontation with the cattlemen and their hired killers, simple folk like the Potters and the Yosts would be slaughtered. Clint's only chance of saving them would be to keep that ultimate bloodbath from happening. That was why he needed Eve, and the information she could provide.

The night was silent now except for the drone of crickets and the faint chorus of frogs from the creek. Even the wind had gone still. Clint lingered in the darkness, remembering the hunger that had coursed through his body when he'd held her in his arms—a hunger that had nothing to do with the reason she *should* be so important to him.

Lives depended on his winning her loyalty. But making love to her wasn't the answer to winning her over. If things went sour, a wounded lover could turn on a man in a heartbeat, making a shambles of all he held dear. There was too much at stake to risk such a tragedy. That aside, Eve may have caught fire in the heat of a reckless moment; but if she learned about his past, she would spit on him and walk away.

Eve had been right. So had Gideon. This shaky arrangement would work only if they suppressed their natural urges and kept apart.

But as he stepped into the house and locked the door behind him, Clint knew that when his eyes closed in sleep tonight, her lovely, moonlit face would be the last image in his mind.

A girl showed up the next morning, perched on the tailgate of a mule-drawn buckboard that dropped her off at the ranch gate. Tall, with an ample figure and thick, tawny braids, she strode up the long drive with a vigor that was almost masculine, yet graceful in its way.

Stepping out onto the porch, Eve was puzzled for a moment; but then she remembered. This would be the girl Etta Simpkins recommended to help Alice with the housework. That had been just yesterday—a day that seemed like a lifetime ago.

"Mrs. Townsend, I'm Beth Ann." At least

she'd gotten the name right. She stood at the foot of the steps, her belongings slung over one shoulder in a feed sack. Up close, even in her ragged, outgrown gingham dress, she was surprisingly pretty. Her hazel eyes were framed by golden lashes. Her features were strong and regular, her sun-kissed complexion flawless. She looked to be about nineteen.

Was she some poor farmer's daughter? But surely, with such enmity between farmers and cattle ranchers, Mrs. Simpkins would have known better than to send someone from a farm family.

"Come in, Beth Ann. Let's get acquainted and discuss your duties." Eve was accustomed to hiring servants. She ushered the girl to a seat in the parlor. "You'll be on probation for two weeks. If things are going well by then, you'll have a permanent position." She paused to assess Beth Ann's appearance. Her strong, work-worn hands attested to her capability. "Tell me about your family. Do they live around here?"

She shook her head. "My parents died of diphtheria three winters ago. I went to work for the family of the man who ran the land office. His wife was crippled and needed help. But now they're moving away…and here I am." Her smile held the glimmer of a tear.

"You'll report to Alice and do whatever she tells you," Eve said. "She's been handling it all for a long time, so she might be a little resistant to your help. You may have to step in—"

"Oh, I understand."

"You'll meet the children. I'll be looking after them myself, but if I'm not available for some reason, you're to see to their needs, as well." Eve rose. "Let's go back to the kitchen and find Alice. She'll show you to your room and get you started." She eyed the girl's undersized dress. The faded gingham stretched tight enough across her breasts to show the outline of her nipples. "Uh…do you have other clothes you can work in till I find a seamstress to make you some uniforms?"

"Uniforms?" The girl looked startled, then quickly recovered. "I have some old clothes that'll do for now. But I can sew just fine. Get me some cloth and I'll make whatever you want me to wear."

"Oh—excellent! I found some sewing supplies in my sister's chest. I'll pick up some fabric and trim next time I'm in town."

The girl was a gem, Eve thought as she

guided Beth Ann toward the hallway leading back to the kitchen. If she was a skilled seamstress, she might even be pressed into service making clothes for the children. They'd soon be outgrowing the garments they had. So many things to attend to. And Eve hadn't forgotten her promise to get information for Lonigan. But that would have to wait for the right time.

Lonigan...

She blotted his image from her mind.

As they passed into the hallway, Roderick came down the stairs dressed for a day in town. As he paused midway to pull on his gloves, his glance fell on Beth Ann's golden head. One eyebrow slithered upward.

"You, girl, look at me," he ordered.

Beth Ann raised her pretty face.

"So you're the new hired help." He gave her a cursory inspection, then nodded. "You'll do."

If Eve had expected the girl to blush and lower her gaze, she'd misjudged her. Meeting his eyes boldly, Beth Ann gave him a slow, sly smile. "Why, thank you, Mr. Hanford," she said.

Roderick made no reply, but exited the front door with an added swagger to his step. Was it her imagination, Eve wondered, or was Beth Ann flirting with the master of the house?

Never mind. For now Eve had more pressing concerns.

Escorting her back to the kitchen, she introduced her to Alice, who eyed the girl as if she were an interloper who'd come to steal her job. "Looks like this one might eat a lot," the old woman said, frowning.

"Then we'd best give her a lot of work so she can earn her keep, hadn't we," Eve said. "Come with me, Beth Ann, I'll show you to your room. When you've changed, Alice can send you upstairs to get the rugs, carry them outside to the line and give them a good beating."

Eve led her upstairs, feeling as if she'd just refereed a territorial dispute between two cats. She could only hope time would ease them into a smooth working relationship—maybe even a friendship.

Meanwhile, it was time she started the children on their lessons.

Thomas and Rose were already at the table, waiting for her. They opened up their books, Rose practicing her sums while Thomas did a lesson about George Washington. The children were bright and quick and seemed to enjoy learning. What a shame it was so far for them to go to school in town with other children. Maybe she could talk Roderick into building a school here on the ranch, so the children who lived close by could attend. Rose and Thomas were growing up in isolation. They needed friends their own age to learn and play with.

But sadly, Eve recalled, most of the neighboring children lived on homesteads. Roderick would never allow Rose and Thomas to mingle with them.

What would their mother have done? At times like this, Eve would have given anything to hear her sister's calm voice and steady advice. But Margaret was gone. Now it was up to her to stand up for Margaret's children and be their champion.

Her opportunity came after Roderick had returned from town. By then the children had finished their lessons and their lunch and gone upstairs—Rose to play with her dolls and Thomas to work on the model train set he was putting together.

Eve was seated in the parlor, finishing the stitch work on the black mourning bands she'd fashioned for herself and for Roderick. She glanced up as he walked into the room.

"Put your sewing down and walk with me, Eve. We need to talk."

"Yes, we do." Leaving her project on the arm of the chair, she rose and allowed him to usher her outside. The afternoon sun was too warm for walking, but she preferred open air to the trapped feeling when he loomed over her inside the house.

"I need to speak to you about the children," she said.

"Fine." He was steering her toward the back of the house—and the kennels. "I thought while we were out, I'd give the dogs another exposure to your scent. They should be much calmer this time."

"About the children," she persisted.

"Yes? Is there something they need? New clothes? New schoolbooks?"

"What they need," Eve said, "is to be around other children. It's far too lonely for them here on the ranch. Their mother taught them good manners, but they need to socialize. They need to play."

"Play?" Roderick snorted. "But they do play. They're playing now, upstairs."

"But they're playing alone. If we could open a little school here on the ranch and invite other children to come, I'd even volunteer to teach—"

"Out of the question! The children who live

around here are trash. Most can't even speak proper English. I won't have Thomas and Rose associating with their kind."

Eve sighed. "I feared that's what you'd say. So I have another suggestion. Why not rent a house in town? I could stay there with the children during the school year. You could visit them all you like, and they could spend holidays and summers with you on the ranch."

"No. That wouldn't do. It wouldn't do at all."

"And why not? Surely you wouldn't mind their sharing a classroom with the town children."

"Perhaps not. But there are no suitable houses for rent in Lodgepole. And even if there were, a young, single widow like you, living alone in town, would be a scandal. The men—"

"Oh, for heaven's sake, I'm hardly a naive girl—"

"No, listen." He gripped her hand tightly— too tightly for her to pull away. "What I'm saying is, I need you here on the ranch. I have plans—and you're an important part of them."

Eve's stomach clenched. It was as if the trapped sensation she'd felt indoors had followed her outside and was threatening to surround her like the bars of an invisible cage.

"Roderick, I've barely arrived here. I don't know what I'll be doing from one day to the next."

He appeared to ignore her protest. They'd passed the big cottonwood where Margaret was buried and were coming up on the stockade that surrounded the dog kennel.

"We'll talk more on the way back to the house," he said, opening the gate.

Eve willed herself not to recoil as the odors of rancid meat and dog waste assailed her nostrils. These animals were God's creatures, she reminded herself, as was the strange hulk of a man who tended them. None of them had chosen to be where they were or to live the life they lived.

As Roderick had predicted, the huge brindled creatures no longer snarled and lunged at her through the wire mesh. Some bristled, others whined or displayed their teeth; but even when Roderick forced her to stand very close to give them her scent, they made no move to attack.

Hans stood at the side of the cage, one hand fondling the steel whistle on its leather thong. Behind the shaggy locks that screened his blunt features, his blue eyes gazed shyly at her. Remembering Lonigan's story of the man's torture by the Pawnee and the loss of his tongue, she gave him a friendly smile. He flushed and turned away.

"That's enough. We can go now." With his hand at the small of her back, Roderick ushered her out through the gate in the high wooden fence. As it closed behind them she gulped in the fresh air. No matter how long she lived here, she would never get used to that wretched kennel.

"One of these days I'll take you hunting," Roderick said. "Watching those dogs pull down a deer—it's pure poetry."

Eve paused to stare at him. "Killing as poetry? What an odd comparison."

"Death has a beauty all its own," Roderick said. "Seeing a noble animal fight for its life, then bringing it down—the experience is spiritual, like playing God."

"And the death of a man?" Eve asked, repelled by his words.

"The same. But men tend to be less noble in death than their fellow creatures. Maybe because they know what's coming. That knowledge is enough to turn them into begging cowards."

Eve shuddered, just wanting to end the conversation and get back to the house. But something told her he wasn't going to let her off so easily.

They were passing Margaret's grave. Watered by the storm, weeds were already sprouting on the lonely mound. Soon there'd be no trace of where the children's mother lay.

Margaret deserved better than this, Eve vowed. As soon as time allowed, she would come out and pull the weeds. And if she could find any seeds in town, she would let the children help her plant flowers, and hunt for pretty rocks to make a border. She would also see to it that a proper headstone was ordered and put in place—as well as a wrought-iron fence to mark the grave and keep out roaming animals. Surely Roderick could spare the money.

As for now... Roderick strolled past without a glance at his wife's burial spot. "Back to what we were discussing earlier," he said. "I have a dream, Eve. A dream of making this house, and this ranch, a showplace of elegance and culture, comparable to the great estates in England. I've got a good start on the money. And once I get those vermin homesteaders cleared out, I'll have room to grow my cattle herds. All I need to complete the picture is the perfect woman at my side. And the minute you stepped off that stage, I knew I'd found her."

A lump, like a leaden fist, clenched in the pit of Eve's stomach. Heaven save her, was the man proposing? She'd only half believed Lonigan when he'd told her how quickly available women were snapped up after losing their husbands. Now she knew better.

She kept her eyes on the ground, her steps rapid in a vain effort to escape. "This is happening too fast, Roderick. How can you think of such things with your wife barely in the ground? You're in mourning. So am I."

"This is Wyoming, Eve. If I don't stake my claim, somebody else will. Don't tell me that Irish ex-convict Lonigan didn't try a thing or two."

Hot color flooded Eve's face. "He wouldn't dare!" she sputtered.

Roderick gave a knowing chuckle. "Never mind that. You're mine and I want the whole county to know it. This coming Tuesday night I'm giving a dinner for the local cattle ranchers and their wives. You'll be my hostess. I want to show you off, dressed like the countess you are."

"Oh, but I didn't bring—"

"You'll find some suitable gowns in Margaret's closet, not that she ever wore them. She disliked entertaining. But she was about your size before the baby. The styles may be a little dated, but this is Lodgepole, not London."

"I'm sure they'll do nicely." Eve squelched the urge to protest. A gathering of ranchers could provide just the opportunity she needed to learn about their plan to hire gunfighters. All she'd need to do was keep her ears open and get word to Lonigan.

"I'll plan the meal with Alice and pick up whatever we need in town. Beth Ann can help me. May I assume you'll take care of inviting your friends?"

"Of course." Roderick sounded distracted. Following the line of his gaze, Eve saw Beth Ann by the backyard clothesline, beating the rug from one of the upstairs bedrooms. The maid was putting her all into the task, perhaps because she knew she had an audience. Beneath her faded chambray shirt, her ample breasts quivered with each blow.

"I say, that new girl seems very energetic," Roderick commented.

"Yes, she appears to be a willing worker." All very true, Eve mused. But there was something unsettling about Beth Ann. For one thing, in a town where wives were snapped up quick as a blink, why was such a pretty girl, with the kind of buxom body that could keep a husband happy and birth a brood of strapping babies, still unmarried?

At the next opportunity, Eve resolved, she would get some answers.

Eve got her chance three days later when she and Beth Ann took the buggy into town to get supplies for Roderick's dinner party. They'd be shopping for dress fabric, as well. Since Beth Ann would be helping serve, Eve was anxious to get her into something more presentable than the chambray shirt and shabby dirndl she wore for work around the house.

"You aren't going to fix me up like one of those fancy English maids with a black dress and a little cap, are you?" Beth Ann asked as they rounded the last bend and started the descent into town.

Eve laughed, easing back on the reins to slow the horse. "This is Wyoming. People would think we were putting on airs. Anyway, didn't I promise you could choose the cloth?"

"As long as it's something sensible, you said."

"Of course. You'll want a dress you can work in. One that will wash up nicely." Eve had decided not to mention what she'd discovered last night. When she went into Margaret's old room and opened the wardrobe to choose a dress for the dinner, she'd found the doors ajar, the beautiful silk and lace gowns crooked on their hangers and unfastened down the back as if they'd been tried on and put away hastily, perhaps because someone was coming upstairs.

The dresses would have been too small through the body for Beth Ann. But she could have tried them on and admired her reflection from the front without fastening them, imagining herself dressed like Cinderella for a party or ball.

Eve couldn't blame the girl for wanting pretty things. And since nothing had been taken or damaged, she'd decided to let the matter slide for now. But the incident did give her pause.

"There's something I've been wondering, Beth Ann," she said. "A pretty, hardworking girl like you would make some man a fine wife. You must've had offers. Why is it you're not married?"

Beth Ann gazed ahead at the road, then down at her work-roughened hands. "Oh, I've had of-

fers, all right. Plenty of them. But I don't want
to spend the rest of my life sleeping with a man
who smells like horses, and raising his snot-
nosed brats in some dirt-floor cabin. I want
something better—a man with manners and
money, who'll give me a decent life. I want to
be a lady—like you."

"Well, this being America, I suppose you can
become whatever you set your mind to," Eve
said. "But being a lady and having a wealthy
man take care of you is no guarantee of happiness."

"Were you happy with your husband? Alice
says he was older."

Eve sighed, remembering another time, another world, and the pliant young woman she
would never be again. "He was a good man.
He gave me every material thing I could want.
I was grateful and I cared for him, but I wasn't
in love with him—at least not in the romantic
way a girl dreams about."

"Well, I mean to have it all. And I don't plan
to settle for less."

"Then I wish you the best of luck." Eve
couldn't help admiring the girl's determina-
tion. But she'd seen enough of life to fear that
Beth Ann was headed for disappointment—

or worse. And something about the girl's cold-blooded ambition made her ill at ease, in a way she couldn't quite explain. She just had a sense that Beth Ann wouldn't let anyone get in the way of her achieving her dreams, no matter what it took.

Clint had checked the buck fence every night and early morning. So far he'd found nothing from Eve. Had she changed her mind about helping him, or was it just that she had no news to pass on?

Either way, he didn't like it. Things had been too quiet since the incident with Yost and his calves. Something was in the wind.

With the tension growing every day, he decided to pay another visit to town. Maybe Smitty had overheard new rumors in the saloon. Or maybe Mrs. Simpkins had some gossip to pass on. As things stood right now, Clint was a bundle of raw nerves, just waiting for something to bust loose.

Leaving his horse at the livery stable, he set off toward the main part of town. The muddy street was drying under the summer sun. Gnats swarmed above a shrinking puddle, scattering when a ragged boy lobbed a rock into the water.

Lodgepole was bustling this morning. Shoppers strolled along the boardwalk. Buggies and wagons were pulled up along the street. Clint's throat jerked tight as he recognized the Hanford buggy hitched to the rail in front of the general store. Was Roderick Hanford in town, or—the thought caused his pulse to skip—was *she* here, someplace close by?

He shrugged off the rush of anticipation. If Eve was here at all she was probably with Hanford. Even if he saw her, they couldn't so much as exchange a glance. For safety's sake, and for even more personal reasons, they'd agreed to treat each other as strangers.

The Three-legged Dog was open for business, but it was early and the place was quiet. Two men with their hats pulled low, and a bottle between them, were playing cards at a corner table. With no more than a passing glance at them, Clint ambled to the far end of the empty bar and ordered a whiskey.

Smitty, who'd lost his lower leg in a railroad accident, stumped over to Clint with a bottle and a clean glass. A wiry, balding man in his sixties, he was friendly to everyone in the valley. But Clint was aware that he favored the homesteaders over the wealthy ranchers.

"Might have some news about that money for the cattlemen," he muttered, pouring three fingers of good whiskey into Clint's glass. "Don't look now, but see those two fellers at the table?"

Clint knew better than to turn his head. He sipped his whiskey in silence.

"They come in here this morning, said they heard somebody was payin' good money for hired guns. Asked what I knew about it."

Clint waited, his eyes asking the questions.

"Not much I could say," Smitty continued. "But I told 'em they could hang around and wait. Figured sooner or later somebody might come in."

"So the money must've arrived." Clint whispered the words.

"Looks that way. But there ain't been another stage since the one you and that countess come in on."

So the money must have been on the stage, after all. That, or it had been carried in privately. "Notice any strangers in town who might've brought it?"

Smitty shook his head. "Not lately. Just these two galoots."

Turning ever so slightly, Clint gave the pair a sidelong glance. Rough, hardened men, they were both armed with heavy six-shooters. As one of them turned in profile, Clint's throat jerked. He would know that hooked nose and scarred face anywhere—Ned Canaday, last seen doing ten years at Lansing for attempted murder. Clint had watched him beat another convict almost to death with his bare fists. The guards had looked the other way because even they were afraid of him.

If Canaday was here, there could be no more doubt. The money had to be here, too. And the Cattlemen's Association was planning to use it to wipe out the homesteaders for good.

Chapter Nine

While the clerk at the general store was filling her order, Eve set off to the bakery. According to Alice, Etta made excellent pies. Buying several from her would save Alice the work of baking them before the dinner party.

Beth Ann trailed after Eve down the boardwalk, clutching the paper-wrapped bundle that contained her new clothes. In the back of the dressmaker's shop they'd discovered a rack of finished dresses. One of them, a flattering blue calico, had been a perfect fit. With the white ruffled apron Eve had bought, the girl would be more than presentable to serve at the dinner party.

Beth Ann had offered to sew her own dresses, but she had other work and an urgent need for suitable clothes. Eve had ordered two more dresses made to the same pattern—a green gingham and a more subdued twill in a gray stripe, along with two more aprons. Beth Ann, she suspected, would have preferred something more glamorous. But these would do nicely for her service in the house. Even though she'd been hired on probation Eve felt comfortable spending the money. So far, despite her bold nature, the girl had proved herself capable and willing. Even Alice had begun to accept her.

The bakery door opened with the jingle of a bell, summoning Etta from the back room. She had specks of flour on her apron and a cheery smile on her face.

"Well, look who's here!" she said. "Since the two of you came in together, can I assume the job's going well?"

"Quite well, thank you. We just bought Beth Ann some new clothes." Eve glanced down at the glass-fronted display case. "I was hoping you'd have some fresh pies today, but I don't see even one."

"The hotel buys most of my pies on Friday. But you're in luck. I have four extras in the back room—two apple, one cherry and one mince-meat, still warm. I was about to bring them out front. Which would you like?"

"If no one else has spoken for them, I'll take all four."

"Fine. I'll bring them right out for you."

As Etta disappeared behind the wall, another customer entered the bakery. From behind her, Eve heard the jingle of the bell on the door, the tread of a footstep, a breath. Knowing better than to turn around, she stood rigid, sensing his presence as if he'd reached out and brushed her shoulder. It had to be Lonigan.

Lonigan the train robber, the ex-convict. The man she'd agreed to help—before she'd learned the truth about him.

The man who'd kissed her as she'd never been kissed in her life.

Don't look at him. Don't speak to him. That was what they'd agreed on. But this might be her best chance to let him know about the dinner, and alert him to watch for a message.

Etta was still in the back, boxing up the pies, but Beth Ann was right here, standing next to her. Eve didn't know whose side the girl was on, but she'd be a fool to make assumptions.

"Here we are." Etta had come back with four neatly stacked cardboard boxes tied with string. "Don't jostle them, now. The filling tends to run when they're warm."

"We'll be careful." Eve raised her voice slightly as she laid the boxes in her basket. "The pies are for a dinner party Roderick's giving Tuesday night. Some of the other cattlemen will be there with their wives. I'm looking forward to meeting them and hearing what they have to say."

"Well, I'm sure it will be very grand, dearie." Etta counted the bills Eve had handed her and gave back some coins. "Your sister wasn't much of a one for entertaining, especially when she was expecting her babies. It's nice to know some things will be different now."

Beth Ann hadn't uttered a word during this exchange, but Eve could sense her restlessness in the way she shifted from one foot to the other. Had she heard something she didn't like, or was she just getting tired?

Eve picked up the basket with the pies, taking care not to tip them. "It's time we were getting back," she said. "Let's hope the clerks at the general store have finished loading the buggy. We'll have a lot of work to do when we get home."

She turned, knowing Lonigan was still behind her. He moved aside with a tip of his battered Stetson. "Mrs. Townsend." His gray eyes were as cold as his voice.

"Mr. Lonigan." She swept past him, hoping to hide the way her knees were quivering beneath her skirts. Even with what she knew about him, his gaze could turn her rigid self-control to warm, pulsing jelly. Had he heard her comment about the dinner party? Did he understand that she'd meant it for his ears?

Beth Ann followed her, clutching her bundled dress. Half a block up the street, the buggy was loaded and waiting. Eve let the girl climb in first, and handed her the basket of pies to protect. Then she unhitched the reins, mounted the driver's seat and pulled into the street.

As they passed the bakery, she couldn't resist a sidelong glance. There was no sign of Lonigan. He hadn't come outside to watch her leave.

"So, Etta, have you heard any good rumors?" Clint asked.

She reached into the display case, found a molasses cookie and thrust it toward him. "On the house."

"Thanks." He chewed a bite. The cookie was stale but still tasty.

"What kind of rumors? I take it you're not

interested in what the preacher's wife did after she caught her husband fooling around with the church organist."

"That might make an entertaining story. But, no, I'm wondering about that alleged money that's supposed to have come in. I've been wondering about it since those two young fools held up the stage."

"Oh, yes, those two hooligans." She gave him a wink, leaving no doubt she'd recognized the Potter boys. Clint was grateful she hadn't told on them. "I haven't heard a thing," she said. "I can't imagine how that silly rumor got started in the first place."

"So you don't know if the alleged money has anything to do with those two gunslingers sitting in the saloon?"

"How would I know—unless they got a hankering for sweets and paid me a visit? This is the first I've heard of them."

"And you haven't heard anything about the money or the men?"

"Not yet. Why? Is there something going on?"

Clint hesitated, then decided to tell her. "Smitty says the pair had heard somebody was hiring."

A frown flickered across Etta's plump face. "I don't know what to tell you. But I'll keep my ears open. Stop back in the next couple of days. Maybe I'll have heard something by then."

"Thanks, I'll do that." Clint turned to go, but she wasn't finished with him yet.

"The countess seems to be settling nicely into ranch life, doesn't she?"

"I wouldn't know."

"Hmm." Etta gave him a knowing look. "I did notice the two of you weren't too friendly."

"The countess is out of my class."

"Maybe that's just as well. I'll tell you something I did hear. Roderick told some friends he means to marry the lady. He's planning to announce their engagement at the dinner he's giving."

Clint tried to ignore the gnawing sensation in his gut. "He didn't waste much time, did he?"

"Can you blame him? Margaret was a nice looking woman, but this one…" Etta punctuated the sentence with the lift of an eyebrow. "A man would have to be crazy not to claim her if he could."

Feeling as if he'd been kicked by hobnailed boots, Clint groped for a different subject—one that had just occurred to him. "Does the countess know that her new hired girl is your niece?"

The older woman shrugged. "Does it matter? I kept that to myself because I didn't want it to influence her decision. But the countess does seem pleased with her. And I'm hoping Beth Ann will pick up some ladylike manners from her. Heaven knows, the girl needs them."

Yes, Beth Ann could use some lessons in how to act like a lady, Clint conceded. She had a loose reputation among the local cowboys. He knew of several who'd enjoyed her favors. Would Eve keep her on if she knew the nature of the young woman she'd hired? Didn't she have the right to know who she'd let into her house—around her niece and nephew?

But who was he to pass judgment? Everybody, even Beth Ann, deserved a second chance—and Clint knew plenty about second chances. He wouldn't be the one to ruin things for the girl.

With a muttered excuse, he thanked Etta and left. He'd spent long enough in town. It was time to pick up his horse at the livery stable and head home.

The bright summer sky did nothing to ease his black mood as he strode down the street.

Was Eve really going to marry Roderick Hanford? Was that why Clint hadn't heard from her?

Eve's private life was none of his damned business, he told himself. She could marry the devil, for all he cared. But he needed her help— needed it desperately. With gunslingers showing up, looking to be hired, something bad was about to break. The countess was his one best chance of staying ahead of the game. If she'd changed her mind about working with him, he and his friends were in trouble.

Thinking back, he went over every detail of their meeting in the bakery. True, they'd agreed not to show any familiarity in public. But she'd taken that rule too far. Except for a word and a passing glance, she'd behaved as if he wasn't there at all. Instead she'd been focused on telling Etta about the fancy dinner party she'd be hosting at Hanford's ranch. Almost as if…

Clint swore out loud, cursing his own thickheadedness. Why hadn't it sunk in at the time? Eve hadn't just been speaking to Etta. The news about the dinner had been meant for *him*. She'd wanted to let him know the cattlemen were gathering, and that she'd pass on whatever she learned.

That *was* what she'd meant, wasn't it? Lord help him, it had to be.

But what if she'd already said yes to Hanford's proposal? Clint couldn't imagine Eve was in love with the man. But her sister's children meant the world to her. He'd seen how far she'd go to protect them. If that included marrying their bloodthirsty, lying bastard of a father, all bets were off. There was no way Clint could trust her.

At the livery stable he paid the elderly attendant, saddled his horse and rode out of town at a gallop. He would make a circuit of the farms and small ranches on his way home and warn his friends to be ready for danger. After that, until he knew more, he'd be forced to do the most onerous thing of all—wait.

Tuesday was a blur of preparation for the dinner party. Alice began the day at first light, shaking down the ashes in the massive iron stove with a clatter loud enough to wake the whole house. Beth Ann was rousted out of bed to dust every visible surface on the main floor, including the mounted heads of Roderick's hunting trophies. Her orders included polishing every inch of wood and glass, beating every trace of lint and dust from the rugs and the horsehair upholstery, and helping Alice in the kitchen.

Fleeing the commotion, Roderick headed into town to have breakfast at the hotel. Eve was relieved to see him go. When he was home his dominating presence filled the house with a tension that affected everyone. Even the children seemed more subdued. When he was looming over her, Eve could barely control the urge to run out the front door and never look back. Only one thing kept her here—Margaret's children and their need for her love and protection.

Today, as usual, Thomas and Rose were her main responsibility. It would be her job to see them scrubbed, combed and dressed in their best tonight so that they could be trotted out to meet the guests before being sent upstairs. For all Roderick's lack of interest in his beautiful son and daughter, he seemed to enjoy putting them on display, as if they were trophies.

But now it was early in the day—too early for baths and party clothes. Giving the children a break from their lessons, Eve took them out to the big cottonwood to help her clear off Margaret's grave. They knelt on either side of Eve as she showed them how to pull each weed, taking care not to break off just the top and leave the root in the ground.

Watered by the recent storm, the weeds grew in thick profusion. But the soil on the grave was still loose, so the pulling was easy, even for Rose's little hands. Eve assigned her the smallest plants, while she and Thomas tackled the larger ones.

"Do you think Mama can see us pulling her weeds?" Rose asked. "Alice says she's an angel now, up in heaven, and she can look down and see us."

"I don't know if she's looking this minute," Eve said. "But if she can see us she must be smiling."

"She can't see us, and she isn't up in the sky." Thomas twisted out a stubborn burdock root. "She's dead. And dead is dead. She's right here in the ground."

Tears were welling in Rose's eyes.

"Thomas, do you really believe that?" Eve asked.

"That's what Papa told me. He said that was the truth, and I had to be a man and not cry about it."

"But what if he's wrong?" Eve laid a gentle hand on his shoulder. "Nobody knows for sure what happens after we die, not even your father. Isn't it better to hope for something happy?"

"Papa says a real man doesn't believe in fairy tales."

"Oh, Thomas!"

"But we can still make Mama's grave look nice." Setting his mouth, the boy pulled another weed. Without a word, Rose resumed helping.

Little by little they continued to clear the sad mound of earth. The work was going well, but Eve's instincts were prickling. She had the strangest feeling they were being watched.

At last the grave was clean, the weeds piled out of the way. Eve hadn't been able to find flower seeds or plants in town, but she'd thought of another idea. "There are plenty of rocks around here," she said. "Let's find some pretty ones and make a border."

This was evidently more fun than pulling weeds. The children raced over the rocky ground, picking up their choicest finds and carrying them back to form a line around the grave. Eve hadn't lost the sense that hidden eyes were watching. But she felt no threat and joined the children in their search.

By the time the border was nearly complete, all three were flagging. Only a foot-wide gap at the head of the grave remained. Something special should go there, Eve thought. But they'd already scoured the yard for rocks that were colorful or had a bit of shine to them.

They were still searching when a gate opened in the stockade that surrounded the kennel. Instinctively, Eve gathered the children close. But they showed no fear of the shaggy brown-clad figure that shuffled forward. They seemed to know that Hans wouldn't harm them.

As he came closer, one leg dragging behind the other, Eve saw that he was carrying something. It was a lumpy gray rock about the size of the ostrich egg she'd seen in a museum.

Only as he bent to place the rock at the head of Margaret's grave did she realize what it was: a geode, broken on one side to reveal a dazzling array of amethyst-hued crystals inside. A thing of rare beauty, it must have been a treasured possession.

Touched, she reached out and took his hand. His palm was as rough as horn and he reeked of the kennel. But she saw the look in his child-like blue eyes as he pulled away.

"Was my sister kind to you, Hans?" she asked.

He nodded. Then, as if even that bit of human

contact had been too much for him, he turned away and shuffled back toward the compound, entered and closed the gate behind him.

"Hans is nice." Rose spoke into the silence.

"Do you know how long he's been here?" Eve asked, hoping to learn more about the man.

"He was here before we were born," Thomas said. "And he always took care of the dogs. We don't know how he came here because he can't tell us."

"Can he write?"

Rose shook her head. "Mama said he didn't know how to read or write. She wanted to teach him but Papa wouldn't let her. He said it wasn't seemly for a lady to spend so much time with the hired help."

Eve gazed toward the gate. So Roderick had kept the poor man like one of his dogs, refusing to educate or better him. And Hans had stayed because he had nowhere else to go. Seemly or not, it wasn't right.

Much of Eve's afternoon that day was spent seeing to the dinner preparations. Roderick had insisted that she supervise everything, down to the placement of each dish, napkin, crystal glass and piece of silver cutlery on the linen tablecloth. He wanted an exact replica of a formal upper-class English dinner, complete with a real live countess at his side. Such silliness! Only her secret mission to gather information for Lonigan kept her from walking out in a huff.

Two hours before the guests were due to arrive, Eve still needed to bathe the children and get them and herself dressed. Beth Ann, who had yet to put on her new serving dress, dumped warm water into the tub in the bathing room off the kitchen. Rose would go first, since Eve would need extra time to braid her long hair.

Sitting on a wooden stool next to the tub, Eve untied the little girl's pinafore, unbuttoned her dress and slipped off her chemise and drawers. She gasped.

On the few mornings she'd been here, she'd buttoned Rose's dress up the back and tied the strings of her pinafore, but not until now had she see her small niece entirely naked. Her little buttocks and the backs of her thighs were covered with half-healed red welts and bruises. Their shape and pattern suggested they'd been inflicted with some sort of strap.

"Who did this to you, Rose? Who hit you?" she demanded in a horrified whisper.

"Papa. He spanked me with his belt."

"Why on earth…?"

"Because I was crying about Mama. He told me to stop, and I couldn't. So he spanked me and sent me to my room." Rose spoke as if the beating had been an ordinary event and she'd been justly punished.

"How often does your father spank you like this?"

"Only when I'm bad. Like when I cry. Papa says it makes his head ache."

"Does he do this to Thomas, too?"

"Sometimes. When he's bad—like when he forgets to say 'yes, sir.'"

"Oh, Rose!" Eve flung her arms around the little girl and pulled her close. "I promise you, as long as there's breath in my body, your father will never beat you or Thomas again!"

When she'd finished bathing Rose, Eve wrapped her in a towel and carried her upstairs, leaving Thomas to bathe himself. If she were to look in on him, she knew she would see the same ugly welts and bruises she'd seen on Rose. She wanted to check him over, and offer what comfort she could. But Thomas was of an age when a boy's modesty began to matter. She would spare him the embarrassment. She would confront Roderick at the next opportunity and let him know, in no uncertain terms, that she would not stand for his beating Margaret's children.

Poor, dear Margaret. Had Roderick beaten his wife, as well as his children?

Roderick was gone until late in the day. Eve was dressing for the party, in a burgundy silk frock of her sister's, when she heard his footsteps mounting the stairs and going down the hall to his room. As her fingers grappled with the row of tiny buttons up the back, Eve braced herself for the confrontation. Dinner or no dinner, what she had to say to the man couldn't wait.

She'd finished fastening herself into the gown and was sitting at the dressing table, pinning up her hair, when he opened the door and walked into her room without knocking. Seeing his reflection in the glass, she stiffened. Dressed for dinner, he was smiling, holding something between his hands.

"I must insist that you knock before entering my room," she said.

"I'll keep that in mind. But I hope you'll be forgiving when you see the surprise I have for you. Close your eyes." Still smiling, he stepped directly behind her. "I said close your eyes. No peeking."

Just wanting to get the "surprise" over with, Eve did as he asked. She felt a cold, heavy weight settle around her throat. She opened her eyes. She was wearing a double strand of lustrous pearls.

"I gave these to Margaret on our wedding day," he said. "I thought it was time I gave them to you, Eve. Your beauty does them justice."

His hands rested on her shoulders. Checking the impulse to rip Margaret's pearls from her neck and fling them in his face, Eve twisted away and rose to her feet.

"There's something we need to discuss, Roderick, and it isn't gifts. When I bathed Rose tonight I saw the marks where you beat her with your belt. She told me you did the same thing to Thomas."

His expression had gone rigid. "Are you implying I don't have the right to discipline my own son and daughter?"

"Discipline is one thing. Cruelty is quite another. I won't stand for my sister's children being whipped like animals. As long as I'm in this house, you're not to lay a hand on them. Do I make myself clear?"

Roderick's face had gone as florid as beet juice. Had she pushed him too far? What if she was about to be torn from her beloved niece and nephew and sent packing on the next stage?

Eve held her breath, bracing for an explosion of temper. But it didn't come. Roderick's shoulders sagged. His head drooped forward.

"Forgive me, Eve. I was so distraught after Margaret died, I wasn't myself. She'd always done the disciplining, and suddenly it was up to me. I took out my grief—and my anger—on my innocent children. I'm sorry."

Stunned, Eve found her voice. "I'm glad you're sorry, Roderick. But that doesn't undo what you did. It doesn't make everything all right."

"I know." He was the picture of contrition. "I need to be a better father, a better man. You can help me become that man, Eve. That's why I'm asking you to be my wife."

Eve shrank against the dresser, the heat draining from her face. She'd feared this proposal might be coming, but she hadn't expected it so soon. A paralyzing dread crept over her. It was as if she'd stumbled into a bed of quicksand and was sinking too fast to struggle.

"I've seen how much you love my children," he said. "In time you'll come to love me, as well. I know this is a bit sudden, but I want to announce our engagement tonight at dinner so our friends can celebrate with us. They'll be arriving soon. Please say yes, Eve. Make me the happiest man on earth."

She found her answer and recovered her voice. "I'm in mourning, Roderick. So are you. Neither of us is in a position to even think of getting married again just yet."

He drew himself up, frowning. "This isn't England, Eve. Here in Wyoming we don't play by the same rules."

"*I* play by *my* rules. If you really want to marry me, ask me in a year." She reached up and unfastened the clasp on the pearl necklace. "Wearing my sister's pearls will only make me sad. Put them away for Rose, perhaps for the day she marries."

Eve thrust the pearls into his hands. She feared he might argue, but the downstairs clock was chiming the dinner hour, and the first buggy had just pulled up to the house. The jingle of harness and the muffled sounds of conversation drifted up to her ears as their first guests mounted the front steps.

Roderick laid the pearls on the dresser, taking a moment to compose his features. Then, without a word, he strode out the door toward the landing. Eve could hear him greeting their guests in a jolly tone that belied what his true mood must be.

Eve's hasty fingers pinned her hair into a knot at the nape of her neck—her everyday style. In deference to her mourning she wore no jewelry; but the wine-colored silk gown, cut to display her neck and shoulders, and adorned with a gathered bustle in back, was elegant enough for a formal dinner—too elegant, perhaps for Lodgepole. But it was too late to change.

Reminding herself to keep her ears open, she hurried downstairs to greet Roderick's guests. Lives could depend on what she learned tonight.

Chapter Ten

"That was a fearful downpour we had the other day. Not at all like the gentle rains back in England. Does it always storm so violently here in Wyoming?"

Eve's attempt at conversation was met with polite murmurs and monosyllabic comments. Eating, it seemed, was serious business here in the wild American West. Apparently socializing could wait until after hungry bellies were filled with generous helpings of beef Wellington, roast potatoes, glazed carrots and fresh peas.

But then, as she reminded herself, the men hadn't really come here to socialize.

There were five ranchers at the table, not counting Roderick. Rough-edged but prosperous-looking, they were dressed in plain business suits, there evidently being no such thing as formal dinner wear in Wyoming. Judge Seth McCutcheon was the one man Eve recognized by name. He looked to be close to sixty, tall and whip-lean, his hawkish features burnished like old saddle leather. Next to him, red-haired Clive Burris appeared youthful enough to have inherited his ranch from his father.

The other three, Johnson, Prendergast and Kimball, were perhaps in their early fifties. Unlike Roderick, they clearly spent their days in the saddle. Their hands were callused and sunburned, their tanned faces moon pale above the line where their hats settled.

Eve memorized their faces. These were the cattle barons who held power in the valley—men prepared to kill women and children for their supposed right to the land.

McCutcheon, a widower, had come alone. Burris's wife, Lucy, wore a lace-trimmed periwinkle frock, the waist pulled high to accommodate her burgeoning belly. The other three women were middle-aged. They were dressed as they might have dressed for church, in subdued styles with jackets and high-collared blouses. Now Eve understood why Margaret hadn't worn the formal gowns that hung in the wardrobe. In her low-cut burgundy silk, Eve looked as out of place as a peacock in a dove-cote. Why hadn't Roderick warned her?

But no, this was just what he had wanted— to present her as The Countess, an import from the fairy-tale world he hoped to emulate on his ranch. Didn't he understand that she needed to belong here—and that the last thing she wanted was to be held apart and displayed like a freak?

As it was, the three older women were eye-ing her as if she'd just wandered out of a sa-loon. Lucy Burris, a pretty blonde, looked plain awestruck. These women had been Margaret's friends. But Eve sensed they weren't prepared to be hers. She'd felt more accepted sharing a table with Berta Yost and her family.

"So how are Margaret's children bearing up, Countess?" Sarah Kimball asked. "I felt so sorry for them when they came down ear-lier, those sad little faces. They must miss their mother terribly."

"As do I." Eve was grateful for an opening. "It's going to take time for them to heal. But I've vowed to be here for them, as my sister would have wanted." She glanced around the table at the other women—ignored by their menfolk, who were busy eating. "Do all of you have children?"

"Birthed six, buried three of them," said Sarah. "Harriet here buried four and raised five more. Mary raised two stepchildren after the mother died, and Lucy's on her first. This country's hard on little ones. Hard on women, too."

Eve thought of Berta, her two small children and her unborn baby. She thought of Margaret. What courage it must take to bring children into the world, especially in this wild country. The women at her table were brave and tough. Surely they were good-hearted, as well, with some sympathy for other mothers trying to build better lives for their children. Did they know how their husbands terrorized the homesteaders? Did they have any idea what was being planned for those poor families?

If they knew anything, Eve surmised, they'd probably chosen to ignore it. It was "men's business," beyond the realm of their concern. In any case, she couldn't count on their sympathy, let alone trust them.

Beth Ann bustled in to clear away the dinner plates. She looked demure in her calico frock and starched apron, with her tawny hair braided down her back. But whether by accident or design, the top buttons that fastened her dress in front had come undone, giving the male diners a glimpse of her ample charms when she bent past their shoulders to reach the table. The women were doing their best to look the other way, yet there was no mistaking their disapproval. The girl deserved a stern reprimand. Now wasn't the time, however. It would be undignified to make a scene in front of the others.

After the pies were eaten it was customary for the men to adjourn to Roderick's study to enjoy a smoke and a whiskey. The women gathered in the parlor for a cup of after-dinner tea.

This was what Eve had waited for, the time when plans for the upcoming raid would be voiced and shared. Somehow she had to find a way to listen.

With the women settled in for tea and easy chatter, Eve made her move. "I hope you'll excuse me for a few minutes," she said. "I really need to run upstairs and check on the children. I shan't be long."

"Take your time. We're enjoying ourselves." Sarah waved her away and took another sip of fine Darjeeling tea, a rare treat Eve had slipped into her trunk before leaving England. Beth Ann had just walked in with a fresh pot to refill the cups. Her dress was modestly buttoned to the throat—Alice must have said something. With everything under control, Eve figured it was as good a time as any to escape.

She left the parlor, crossed the entry and hurried upstairs to the nursery. A quick look into the rooms assured her that the children were both fast asleep. Moving quietly now, she stole back down the stairs.

Roderick's study was across the landing from the parlor. The double doors were closed. She would have to press her ear against the wood to listen—and risk being seen by anyone stepping out into the hall. There had to be a better way to hear what the men were saying. She thought fast.

The day had been warm, the study closed in Roderick's absence. To freshen the stale air, he would likely open a window. That would be her best chance.

Still on tiptoe, Eve darted into the kitchen. Alice was too busy to notice as she slipped past the table and out the back, easing the screen door shut behind her.

The night was pleasantly cool, the moon casting long shadows across the yard. A flash of memory surfaced—her first nighttime foray outside, the baying dogs and Lonigan dashing for his horse, barely escaping the slathering jaws.

Lonigan. She closed her eyes for a moment, remembering his powerful arms, his mouth taking hot possession of hers…

But she wasn't doing this for him. She was doing it for the families, for the women and children who would suffer if this hellish plan wasn't stopped.

And tonight was different from that first time. The place was quiet and the dogs knew her scent. She would be safe—unless someone caught her eavesdropping.

As she rounded the corner of the house, the acrid smell of cigar smoke pricked her nostrils. Yes, there was an open window. She could see it now where the lamp gleamed through the raised sash, casting a broken rectangle of light on the ground. Cursing the fragility of her silken gown, which could snarl all too easily on any unseen obstacle in the yard, she edged her way through the prickly junipers below the window until she was directly under the sill, close enough to hear every word.

"Two of the men are in town now, with three more of their pals on the way." Eve recognized

Seth McCutcheon's gravelly voice. "They should be here by tomorrow. We'll meet at my house around nine and I'll dole out the money."

"How much did you offer to pay the bastards?" The nasal twang was Sam Prendergast.

"A hundred each to start," McCutcheon said. "Fifty more for torching a house or barn, and another fifty for every man they kill. The Cattlemen's Association wanted it done right. There's enough in my safe to wipe those vermin off the earth."

"What about women and children?" Clive Burris asked.

"Not worth the money to pay out for them, though I daresay plenty will be taken care of if they get in the way. Whatever fun the gunmen want to have with the women is their own business."

Eve pressed her body against the side of the house to keep her knees from collapsing beneath her. So it was all true, every word that Lonigan had told her. She was sick with the horror and shame of it. To think she'd shared a table with these men.

"We stay out of it, of course." Roderick was speaking now. "We'll need to be somewhere in plain sight, so the law can't question our involvement."

"I'll arrange for an all-night poker game at the hotel," Johnson said. "We can keep the staff busy, give them good tips. They'll be able to swear we were there the whole time. Just let me know which night."

"Could be as soon as two nights from now," McCutcheon said. "Unless another damned storm moves in. You can't burn barns in the rain."

"So it's all set." Roderick's tone was jubilant. "When it's over that scum will be wiped out, and we'll have our open range the way it should be." There was the sound of a cork popping, the shuffle of glasses being filled. "Let's drink to victory, gentlemen."

"Hear, hear," someone echoed, followed by the clink of glasses being raised in a toast.

Knowing she had to get back in the house before Roderick discovered her missing, Eve pushed aside the spiky juniper branches. Sharp twigs scratched her skin and caught on the folds of her gown. Heart sinking, she heard the unmistakable sound of tearing silk. She could only pray the damage was slight enough to be tucked out of sight.

Free from the bushes, she brushed off her skirt and tucked a stray lock of hair into place. In the darkness, she couldn't see the tear. Hopefully, it wouldn't be noticed. But just in case, she would have to think of a story to explain the damage.

Preoccupied, she rounded the back of the house and almost collided with a massive figure. She swallowed a scream. Looming above her was Hans. He was carrying a tin plate heaped with leftover food from the dinner. Of course—the man had to eat. It made sense that he would come to the kitchen door to be fed by Alice. But for that instant Eve had almost fainted from fear.

Hans appeared as startled as she'd been. His eyes had widened beneath the thatch of his hair. He took a step backward.

"It's all right, Hans," she whispered, putting a finger to her lips. Seeming to understand, he mirrored the gesture, putting a finger to his own lips before he turned away and shuffled back toward the kennels. She could only hope it meant he wouldn't betray her—not that he could.

Seconds after she returned to the parlor, the men emerged from the study to take their wives home. Smiling, joking, murmuring gallantries as they thanked her and bade her good-night, they seemed like proper gentlemen. But they were monsters in disguise, all of them. Now that she knew their plan an even more daunting task remained—getting word to Lonigan.

The clock in the downstairs hallway struck eleven. Pacing behind the locked door of her room, Eve counted the chimes. Surely everyone in the house would be asleep by now. But she couldn't leave until she was certain.

After the party she'd made an excuse about a headache and gone straight upstairs. If Roderick had noticed the thimble-size tear in her skirt, he'd said nothing. But later in her room, as she'd reached back to unpin her hair, something small and light had fallen to the floor. Reaching down, she'd picked up a juniper berry.

Dread had sucked the breath out of her. If Roderick had seen that bright blue berry caught in her black hair, he'd have known at once what she'd been up to. Was he waiting to confront her in the morning, or had he simply failed to notice?

Either way made no difference. She couldn't leave families like the Yosts to the mercy of hired killers. Whatever the consequences, her course was set.

Late as it was, Lonigan could have already checked for a message and ridden off empty-handed. To get word to him tonight, she would have to ride to his place. If he wasn't there, she could at least leave the message she'd written and tucked into her bodice.

Outside, the wind had sprung up. Eve could hear it howling down the chimney flue and rattling the shutters. Was it blowing in another storm? But never mind, she couldn't let the weather stop her.

Dressed in the riding habit she'd brought from England, she took a moment to arrange her pillows in the shape of a sleeping body and cover them with the bedclothes, in case anyone looked in on her. Before leaving, she slipped her loose-fitting silk wrapper over her riding clothes. Anyone seeing her downstairs would hopefully believe she was getting a drink in the kitchen or headed out to the privy.

Checking the nursery, she found the children deep in slumber. Now, to reach the stairs, she would have to pass Roderick's room. As she tiptoed down the hall she saw that the door was ajar. She held her breath and listened, hoping to hear a deep, masculine snore. What she heard instead was something else—the creak of bedsprings and the unmistakable sounds of a man and woman in the wild throes of sexual intercourse.

She would have preferred not to look, but the door was cracked open the width of two fingers. As she passed, the temptation to glance into the moonlit room was too strong to resist.

As she should have suspected, it was Beth Ann, kneeling astride Roderick in the bed. Her voluptuous body was naked, her golden head flung back as her hips butted his in a driving rhythm that shook the whole bed. She was gasping and moaning in what appeared to be spasms of unbearable pleasure.

The girl had said she wanted a wealthy man. It wasn't surprising that she'd grabbed at the chance to go after one. But her boldness went beyond the bounds of decency. What if the children woke and saw such a tawdry exhibition? Something would have to be done. But what? And when?

Moving on toward the stairs, Eve was aware of the heat blazing in her cheeks. Her own experience in the marriage bed had been so circumscribed—the lifting of her nightgown, her eyes staring up into the canopy above the bed while the earl finished his business. After the first few times it hadn't been all that unpleasant. She'd accepted it, because it was her duty and because she'd wanted the children that never came. But she'd always been relieved when he gasped, rolled off her and fell asleep. The sight of Beth Ann, on top, butting away like a man, wild with the pleasure of it, was a revelation. Was this how common women behaved?

Eve remembered the rush of hunger shooting through her body as Lonigan's taut hips pressed against hers. Even the memory triggered a disturbing tingle between her thighs...

Steeling herself, she willed the thought away. This new development was something to be weighed and considered, but right now she had more urgent concerns.

Her father had taught her how to bridle and saddle a horse. In the barn, Eve chose a docile gray mare and, with some difficulty, managed to hoist the heavy Western saddle onto the animal's back and tighten the cinch. The divided skirt of her riding habit allowed her to put her left foot in the stirrup, grip the saddle horn and swing her leg over. At least it wouldn't be her first time riding astride.

The mare was easy to handle, but the open land between the barn and the ranch gate stretched like a gauntlet of terrors. Was someone on guard, watching? Were the dogs on the roam, ready to bay an alarm?

Heart pounding all the way, Eve reached the ranch gate, passed under the arch and swung the mare onto the road at a gallop. The wind was picking up. It stung her eyes and raked her hair as she rode. Shadows of blowing trees danced across the ground, making the familiar road look like some hellish place she'd never been before. Somewhere in the dark distance, a wolf howled. Eve felt as defenseless as a lost child. But she couldn't give up and go back. She could only pray that she'd find the road to Lonigan's place and that, somehow, he would be there.

Clint had passed the Hanford place earlier, as the guests were leaving the dinner party. After giving them time to get down the road, he'd returned and slipped into the shadows by the buck fence. For more than an hour he'd waited for Eve, watching the lights go out in the big house. As the minutes crawled past, the urge to see her again, perhaps even hold her in his arms and steal a kiss, had grown to a yearning ache. It had been a long, long time since he'd wanted a woman as much as he wanted Eve.

But he should have known she wouldn't come. His disreputable past was public record in Kansas. Hanford, who'd doubtless done some checking, would have told her the truth. Disgusted that she'd let Clint touch her, she would have sworn never to see him again—and had probably thrown in her lot with Hanford and those other murdering devils.

The Dowager Countess of Manderfield. Hellfire, as far as she was concerned, Clint wasn't fit to wipe her prissy little boots!

He'd ridden home and put away his horse. Now he stood on the front porch, testing the wind and wondering whether, with so much at stake, he should ride back to Hanford's to check one last time for a message.

But no, he'd given the woman every chance. He could check again in the morning. Time to give up and get some rest.

He'd turned back toward the door when he heard the sound of hoofbeats approaching at a gallop. Opening the screen, he grabbed the loaded shotgun he kept next to the door, thumbed back both hammers and slipped around the side of the house. Nobody on the road at this hour would be up to any good, and this route didn't lead to anyone's home but his.

He tensed as the sound drew closer, his ears detecting only one set of hoofbeats. The single rider was making no effort to be stealthy, but a man couldn't be too careful.

Seconds later the horse came into sight through the trees, a pale animal, its rider barely visible, clinging low to its neck like a jockey. Clint's eyes caught the flutter of coal-black hair, dark against the darkness. He eased off the hammers on the shotgun. Only his leaping pulse betrayed his emotion as he stepped into sight.

After reining the horse to a halt, Eve slid out of the saddle and dropped to the ground. For the first few seconds she stood where she'd landed, the wind whipping her hair into wild tendrils. She looked shaken and scared. How much courage had it taken for this sheltered woman to steal out of the house, saddle a horse and ride to find him in the dark of night?

When she spoke it was two whispered words. *"Thank heaven!"*

Clint checked the impulse to stride toward her and catch her close. She wasn't here for his touch and she wouldn't welcome his embrace.

If she'd taken this risk, it would be because she had urgent news.

"I'd almost given up on you," he said. "Tell me everything."

She remained where she was, one hand resting on the saddle, as if poised to spring onto the horse and gallop away at the first sign of trouble. "McCutcheon has the money," she said. "The gunfighters—five of them, if I heard right—will be meeting at his place tomorrow night to get the first payment. A hundred dollars to each man, then an extra fifty for every barn or house burned...and for every man killed. The raids could start the next night or any time after that."

Clint weighed what she'd told him. The news was even worse than he'd expected. If it came to an all-out confrontation, five well-armed, seasoned gun sharks could wipe out all the homesteaders in the valley, or send the lucky survivors fleeing from their properties. The only chance of preventing the slaughter was to derail it before it began—warn the families, maybe get the money, disarm the killers or somehow expose the bastards pulling the strings. Given time he might have a slim chance. But time was running out. He had less than forty-eight hours to stop the raids.

"What about the ranchers—Hanford and McCutcheon and the others?" he asked her. "Knowing them, they'll want to stay out of it."

"They'll be playing poker in the hotel—all night. Johnson said he'd arrange it."

"That's no surprise." The memory gnawed at Clint's gut. Roderick Hanford had been playing poker in town the night Clint had returned home to find his place burned to the ground, his wife raped and murdered.

Eve raised a boot to the stirrup. "I've told you all I know," she said. "I should be getting back."

"No, wait—please." Clint wasn't a man who shared much, but something told him he needed to share this. "Walk a little with me. There's something I want you to see."

Leaving the horse, Eve took Lonigan's arm and allowed him to lead her through the shadows. She could feel the tension in him as their path took them around the well-built log house toward the barn. He'd made no move to hold her or kiss her. Whatever he had in mind was serious business.

"I know about your prison time," she said. "Roderick told me."

A beat of silence passed before Clint spoke. "I figured somebody would tell you. But you're still here."

"Yes, I'm here."

"Since you must be wondering about it, yes, I had some bad years, did some stupid things. But I served my time, paid my debt and promised myself I'd go straight. So far, for the past six years, I have."

"That's all I need to know."

"No, it isn't, Eve. Things are going to happen—things you won't understand unless you've seen what I'm about to show you."

They'd rounded the barn. Ahead lay a grove of young apple trees, their trembling leaves soft silver in the moonlight. Sheltered in the center, where he led her, was a grave marked with a simple alabaster headstone.

"My wife," Lonigan said, and he told her the story—how he'd stood up to the cattlemen, how Roderick had called him into town for the meeting that never happened, and how Clint had returned home to find his ranch in flames and his wife brutally murdered.

"Not just her, but our baby she was carrying," he said. "She was two months from giving birth, and those brutes didn't even care."

Tears blurred Eve's vision. Emotion knotted her throat. There were no words. She could only take his work-roughened hand and press it to her cheek.

"Hard times are coming, Eve," he said. "I know you love your sister's children, but if my chance comes to kill their father, and I take it, I want you to understand why."

Still speechless, she turned away. How could she condone the taking of any life, even Roderick's?

Her gaze drifted to the lettering on the headstone.

Cora Danning Lonigan
Beloved Wife of Clinton Lonigan
1861-1885

"She must've been a wonderful woman. I can imagine how much you must have loved her," Eve said.

He made a broken sound, as if he were struggling with what to say next. "I've never told this to anyone. I met Corrie in a Kansas City brothel, fell in love with her and took her away to a new life. People would have judged her for her past, but she had the purest, truest heart of any woman I've ever known. Given the chance, she would've made a fine mother."

He stood for a moment, gazing down at the moonlit grave. Overcome by warring emotions, Eve turned away and started back toward the house. Who was she to judge this man and the wife he'd lost? How could she, who'd known so little of life, understand the depth of forgiveness, the sacrifice and the pain?

To be loved like the woman in the grave had been loved—that was more than Eve could imagine, more than she would likely ever know.

At the edge of the trees Lonigan caught up with her, stopping her with a hand on her arm. The pressure of his grip was firm through her sleeve.

"I'm offering you a choice, Eve," he said. "I know what you've risked in coming here to warn us. It's a risk I can't ask you to take again. You can walk away with my blessing, go back to your sister's children knowing that I won't expect more of you, or…"

"Or what?" She'd turned toward him, looking up into the dark wells of his eyes.

"We could still use your help," he said. "Stand with us. Talk to anybody who'll listen.

Work from your side, any way you can, to bring down those murdering devils once and for all."

She dropped her gaze, knowing that, no matter how wrenching it might be, there was only one decision she could make. She shook her head. "I made a sacred promise to be there for my sister's children. If I stand openly against Roderick, he has the power to separate me from them—forever. I can't leave Rose and Thomas to the mercy of a father who abuses them…" She drew in a painful breath. "I'm sorry."

Clint's hand dropped from her arm. His expression betrayed nothing. "I understand, Eve. It's time you were getting back. I'll walk you to your horse."

She moved beside him, feeling the tension in his silence. She had never known a man like Clint Lonigan—a man with so much strength, so much passion and courage. And yet he had a vulnerable side, as well. She'd witnessed it tonight.

This would likely be their last time alone together. Lodgepole was a small town. She might glimpse him on the road or pass him on the boardwalk. His eyes might even meet hers in a fleeting glance. But she would never feel his arms around her again or know the sweet hunger of his kisses. She would grow old, day by dreary day, without ever knowing what might have been—what she'd wanted to the depths of her woman's soul.

What if he didn't survive the dangerous time ahead? What if she never saw him again?

Her throat ached as they rounded the back of the house, where her mare was cropping grass by the fence. Lonigan was a proud man. Given her decision not to help him openly, his good-bye would be coldly formal.

"Good luck, Eve." He took her hand, in the manner of a casual acquaintance. For an instant his work-roughened fingers tightened, then slipped away. "Will you be all right? I could see you home."

"No, I'll be fine." That would mean saying goodbye to him all over again. How could she bear it? Eve turned to mount her horse. He was walking away now, back toward the house. She drank him in with her eyes, holding the picture of him to the last, almost the last...

"Lonigan!" The yearning cry tore from her throat. He turned. She flung herself off the horse and ran to his open arms.

Chapter Eleven

Lonigan's arms crushed her close. Only then, with his heart drumming against her ear, did Eve understand the hunger he'd been holding back. Behind that cold, polite mask he'd worn tonight, he wanted her as much as she wanted him.

Her fingers tangled in his hair as she pulled him down and gave herself over to being kissed, loving the burn of his stubbled jaw, the shape of his mouth—the straight, firm upper lip, the slight cleft in the lower, the teasing tip of his tongue, so intimate that it sent a tremor through her body. Sweet heaven, she wanted to be devoured by those kisses, to let him flow into her and through her like breath.

He straightened, his strong arms lifting her off her feet. Her toes hung in midair, tingling as his lips and tongue moved down her throat to brush the sensitive notch at the base of her neck. The contact of his flesh on her skin flash-flamed downward to ignite a shimmering bonfire in the depths of her body. What was happening to her? How could she, a widow, have been so unaware of the way a man could make her feel?

One big hand molded his hips to hers, so tightly that the rock-solid heat of his arousal jutted against her belly. Driven by instinct, she ground her hips against him, heightening the most delicious pleasure she had ever known. He groaned, tightening his clasp on her rump, pulling her even closer.

Wanton...wicked... The words flashed through her mind. Was this what decent women weren't supposed to feel? Or had these feelings been slumbering inside her all along, just waiting to be roused by the right man?

Whatever madness had taken possession of her, she couldn't get enough of it.

His chin was rough with stubble. She felt it brush her skin as his kisses moved lower, to the neck of her blouse. Her hand tugged at the buttons, opening the way for him. She wanted him to touch her, to kiss her, all of her. It had to be what he wanted—and he must know that she wanted it, too.

Still he paused, as if holding himself back. "I could hurt you, Eve, in so many ways."

"I know." Her hands reached up to frame his jaw. "I know and I don't care."

Even in the darkness she could read the anguish in his eyes and sense his raw need. Anything could happen tomorrow. He could die. Or they could be separated and never see each other again. He had to know that, too.

Every moment away from the house increased her risk of getting caught. But tonight could be the only time they would ever have. Eve made her decision. Her voice was an urgent whisper, a plea. "Make love to me, Clint."

Without a word he swept her up in his arms and strode toward the house. Where her ear lay against his chest she could hear the steady pounding of his heart. She could feel the answering flutter of her own. What was about to happen would change her forever.

Inside, without taking time to light a lamp, he bolted the door with his free hand. The moonlit shadows gave Eve a brief impression of sparseness and order as he carried her to the bedroom and eased her feet to the floor.

In the warm darkness his seeking hands slid beneath the hem of her blouse and camisole, stroking her breasts till the swollen nipples ached. Then he bent to kiss them. She'd left off her corset and petticoat when dressing for the ride. Had she already sensed what was going to happen?

She strained upward, pressing her hips against him to ease the burning need, but the movement only inflamed her further. Moisture slicked her thighs—an unaccustomed surprise that somehow felt right, as if her body was telling her she was ready for him.

Time was urgently short. There'd be no leisure to undress all the way—and even if there were, neither of them could wait any longer. Loosening her skirt, she let it slide off her hips and drop to the floor, along with her drawers. Then she reached for his belt buckle—a bold move her old, prim self could never have imagined. When her shaking hand fumbled he finished the task himself, but it was Eve who pushed down his drawers, freeing his erection to stand proud and hard. In the past she'd averted modest eyes when her husband happened to expose himself. But this time was different. She *wanted* to see this man. Bathed in the moonlight that fell through the window, Clint was so virile that her breath caught at the sight of him.

"Damn it but I want you," he muttered.

She gave him an impish smile. "Yes, I can tell."

Somehow she managed to kick her boots off before he seized her in his arms again. They fell onto the bed in a glorious tangle of limbs and bodies. Her senses were singing with the feel of him, the taste, smell and texture of his skin. As for the things he was doing to her—kissing a trail from her breasts to her bare belly, then moving lower to part her thighs… Her breath stopped as he did the unthinkable.

The first brush of his tongue sent a wave of sheer rapture through her body. She closed her eyes, her gasps and moans putting Beth Ann to shame as the exquisite spasms shot through Eve like liquid lightning.

Still quivering inside, she opened her eyes and looked up at him. He had moved forward again and was gazing down at her, his mouth quirked in a subtle grin. "You're quite the lady. Anything else I can do for you?"

"Yes…please…" Aching for him, she arched her hips toward him.

"Please what?" he teased. "Tell me what you want."

"I want you…inside me."

With a raw laugh he entered her, his smooth hardness gliding over her sensitive membranes, his thick member filling the space that seemed to be made for him and him alone. She gasped, knowing for the first time the pure sweetness of joining with a man she loved—and she did love Clint Lonigan, now more than ever. He had set her free. For that, if nothing more, she would love him to her dying day.

He pushed hard into her, withdrew and thrust in again, then again. The delicious friction rippled through her body. Her mouth formed an O of wonder. She shuddered, her womb still pulsing as the climax ebbed.

Stopping, he withdrew partway, then bent and kissed her. "We mustn't risk getting you with child, love," he murmured.

Dizzy with loving him, she raised a hand to his cheek. "I'm not even sure that's possible. But if it were to happen, nothing could make me happier."

Without waiting for a response, she clasped his taut buttocks, arched her hips and pulled him into her. He groaned and shuddered, exploding in a burst of wet heat inside her.

Wanton...wicked...and it was glorious.

His kiss was tender, his lips clinging for precious seconds before he drew away and rose from the bed. "We need to get you out of here," he said.

Eve would have given anything to drift off in his arms and wake at dawn, to take up where they'd left off tonight. But she'd been away too long already. She sat up and reached for her clothes. They dressed hurriedly, saying little. Eve knew better than to mention the future. Who could say when they would meet again, or if so, whether they would meet as friends or enemies?

"Check the fence for messages," she said as he walked her to her horse. "If I have any news, I'll leave word there."

"Thanks, I will." His voice was flat, without emotion. But she knew what he was hiding. She was hiding the same thing.

"Be safe, Eve." He placed his hands on her shoulders. His lips brushed her forehead in a tender caress. "Don't take any chances. If you want, I'll ride back with you as far as Hanford's gate."

"No, I'll be fine. If there's trouble waiting at the ranch, I'll be better off alone."

While she still could, she mounted up, swung toward the road and nudged the mare to a gallop. She kept her eyes straight ahead, letting the wind dry her tears.

Clint stood where she'd left him, the sound of hoofbeats fading from his ears. Eve had been right about going back alone. If Hanford had men out looking for her, or even if she happened to pass a late traveler on the road, it wouldn't do for the two of them to be seen together. Clint could only pray she'd get home safely.

His body burned with the memory of her warm skin against his. Making love to Eve had been a reckless act, one that, in the long run, would likely do them both more harm than good. But he had no regrets. Kissing that eager mouth, burying himself in the satin honey between her thighs and hearing her little pleasure cries as he brought her to her peak had been worth whatever price had to be paid. He could only hope that she wouldn't be the one to pay it.

Eve wasn't just a countess. She was a magnificent woman—as strong, compassionate and brave as she was beautiful. But the thought of having her for his own was like a wish to own the moon. He was a poor rancher and an ex-convict, a former criminal who'd loved and married a prostitute. Eve was living in the house of his bitterest enemy, bound by her devotion to his children. But if their circumstances were different, he would fall on his knees and beg her to be his wife.

After Corrie, he'd believed that he would never love again. Now he knew he'd been wrong. Eve was in his blood, in his breath, in the beat of his heart. Even if he never saw her again, he would never stop loving her.

But right now he had other concerns. Wheeling back toward the barn, he raced to saddle his horse. The news Eve had brought would need to be shared and discussed, the alarm spread among his friends, who depended on him for leadership and protection.

He had to find a way to stop this tragedy in the making.

In the barn Eve put away the mare and replaced the saddle and bridle in the tack room. Her silk wrapper lay where she'd tossed it over the side of the stall. Slipping it on to cover her riding clothes, she made her way back into the house and tiptoed upstairs.

She'd been lucky. Everything was quiet. The children were slumbering, and Roderick's snores vibrated through the closed door of his bedroom. Was Beth Ann still in his bed? But what did that matter? As far as Eve was concerned, the girl was welcome to him.

Entering her own room, Eve bolted her door and began undressing. Unaccustomed aches and twinges, souvenirs of Clint's vigorous lovemaking, triggered a pleasant rush of warmth. She'd returned from tonight's adventure a changed woman—a woman who'd awakened to herself in her lover's arms. Even at the price of a broken heart—a price she was sure to pay—she would never regret what she'd done.

But other concerns were crowding in on her thoughts—the hired gunmen, the planned raid. And now there was the question of Beth Ann, and what to do about her. Should she confront Roderick, confront the girl, dismiss her on some other pretext, or just look the other way?

Early on, Beth Ann had voiced her ambition to snare a rich husband. Climbing into Roderick's bed was no way to guarantee he'd wed the foolish girl, not even if he got her with child.

But what if her scheme worked? What if Roderick actually married her?

Beth Ann could have the man with Eve's blessing. But what about the children?

Lost in thought, Eve hung away her riding clothes, pulled on her muslin nightgown, rearranged her pillow dummy and sank into bed. She was exhausted. All she really wanted was to close her eyes and drift into dreams. But sleep was impossible tonight. She lay awake, staring up at the ceiling.

In her time here, Beth Ann had shown no fondness for children. She'd spoken disdainfully of raising some farmer's snot-nosed brats. And when ordered to help in some way with Rose and Thomas, she treated them so brusquely that little Rose shrank away from her. Otherwise she ignored them. At her best, she'd make an indifferent stepmother. At her worst, she could be neglectful or even abusive. She certainly wouldn't interfere with any so-called discipline that Roderick saw fit to inflict on the children.

As for Eve's own position here... She rolled over, punching her pillow into shape. If Beth Ann were to marry Roderick, the girl would become the mistress of the house. Eve would be little more than a glorified governess, subject to dismissal at the slightest whim. The possibility was very real that she could lose her darlings.

How could she leave Rose and Thomas to be raised by Roderick, who not only beat his children, but was capable of sending his minions to murder an innocent woman and her unborn child? Roderick Hanford wasn't just an unpleasant, arrogant fool. He was a monster.

Only one solution offered a glimmer of hope. Eve would beg Roderick to let her move with the children into town. He'd refused her once. But now that he had Beth Ann to share his bed, he might be more willing. She would ask him again tomorrow.

For now she was beyond tired. At long last she felt herself sinking into slumber. The tension eased as the dark fog closed around her.

But even in sleep she found no rest. Her dreams were swirling nightmares filled with gunfire, mounted men riding down women and children, blazing barns, stampeding cattle— and in the midst of it all, Clint. Clint in danger.

Clint found the Potter boys at home. The barking of their two dogs brought the brothers stumbling around the house in their underwear, shotguns ready. As they recognized Clint, they lowered their weapons and welcomed him inside. Over rewarmed coffee he gave them Eve's news.

"The countess told you all that?" Gideon blinked himself fully awake. "What makes you think we can trust her?"

Clint knew better than to share the true answer. "She's all we've got. We don't have much choice. Besides, her information matches up with what we already expected. I'll need you boys to saddle up and help me spread the word to be ready. But first we need to come up with a plan to stop those hired gunslingers."

"They won't fight without money," Newt said. "If we could get our hands on the cash—"

"For that we'd have to break into McCutcheon's house and steal the safe," Clint said. "But if we could find out who brought it in, maybe put some pressure on them…"

"Smitty was positive the money was comin' in on that stage," Gideon said. "I'd still bet that the countess brung it."

"The countess is on our side," Clint insisted.

"You just believe that 'cause you're sweet on her." Newt's mouth twitched in a lopsided grin.

Clint ignored the jab. "Whoever carried that

money might be able to tell us more—if we can find out who it was."

"What about the five gunslingers?" Gideon leaned forward across the table. "They're the ones we have to stop."

"I've been thinking about that." Clint sipped the bitter, black coffee, which was none too warm. "Together the five of them are more than a match for all of us. But break them up, isolate one here and one there, and we might have a chance."

"Do they hang together?" Newt asked. "Are they friends?"

"I doubt it," Clint said. "Men like that tend to be loners. But they'd stay together for protection, if they had to, or to get a job done. They'll be going to McCutcheon's tomorrow night."

"At least that's what the countess told you," Gideon said. "I still don't trust any woman who's livin' with Hanford."

"Have you got a better idea?" Clint set his tin mug down hard, sloshing coffee on the rough wooden table. "Right now we've no choice except to trust her. Let's get going. I'll take the homesteads above the road. You two split up the rest. Tell the men we'll meet here at first light to work out a plan."

He strode outside and mounted his buckskin, leaving the brothers to dress and to saddle their horses. The Potters were stubborn and hotheaded, but at heart they were good boys who deserved to grow up and build their lives. He would do everything in his power to give them that chance.

Neither of them trusted Eve. Clint could understand why. They'd met her only briefly, during their botched stage robbery. They'd never seen her courage or her tenderness.

But what if they were right and he was wrong?

What if he'd been so bewitched by the woman that he was ready to believe anything she told him?

Half-angry at himself, he spurred the horse toward the road. If he let himself think like that, he could be paralyzed by doubt. He had to act on the best information he had—act swiftly and boldly.

But Lord help him, what would happen if he'd been misled?

Eve caught Roderick at breakfast the next morning. He was alone at the head of the dining table, the children having their usual morning meal in the kitchen with Alice.

Setting down her tea and the bowl of porridge she'd dished up for herself, Eve took the seat on his left. So far this morning there'd been no sign of Beth Ann. But that was fine for Eve's present purpose.

"Good morning, Roderick." Her smile was cordial, her stomach clenching. Had he noticed the juniper berry caught in her hair last night? Was he about to demand an explanation?

He returned her smile over his plate of bacon, eggs and flapjacks. "Good morning, Eve. How's your headache?"

It took a moment to remember her excuse for fleeing upstairs last night. "Much better, thank you."

"I'm the one who should be thanking you. The dinner last night was a grand success. You were a magnificent hostess."

Was he holding back, waiting to pounce like a cat on a bird? Eve steeled herself for whatever was to come. Roderick was being entirely too jovial this morning.

"My pleasure," she lied. "I enjoyed meeting your friends."

"I can tell you made quite an impression on

the wives," he said. "You showed them what it means to be a real lady."

"But that wasn't what I wanted, Roderick. I wanted to make friends. I wanted them to like me. And I'm not at all sure they did."

"Give them time. They were friends with Margaret. They'll be friends with you, too." He continued eating, unconcerned. Maybe she hadn't been caught, after all.

"You should compliment the children, as well," she said. "Their manners with the guests were perfect. Margaret did a fine job with them."

"Yes, of course." He appeared disinterested, as if Rose and Thomas were none of his concern.

Eve took a sip of tea and put down her cup. "I hope you won't mind my asking one more time, but I truly believe the children need schooling and friends in town. If you'd allow me to take them—"

"No." He dashed her hopes with a scowl. "As I told you before, it's out of the question."

"But I was hoping that after last night... things would be different." Now she'd done it—opened Pandora's box. It was too late to slam it shut again.

"Last night?" His eyebrows shot upward. "Please explain yourself."

She glanced down into her empty teacup, composing herself before she met his gaze. "I needed to get up in the night. When I passed your room the door was ajar. I could tell you weren't alone."

"Oh, that." Color tinged his face. "I'm sorry you had to be privy to that, Eve. As you know, a man has his needs. The girl showed up willing, and I took what she was offering, that's all. It meant nothing."

"Does Beth Ann know it meant nothing?" Eve glanced around to make sure she wasn't nearby, listening.

"What does it matter? It's no secret she's a common slut. It's not as if I'd marry such a creature." He gave Eve a sly smile. "I'm saving that honor for you, my dear countess. But if you insist on our waiting a year, you can hardly expect me to live like a monk."

Eve pushed back her chair and rose, quivering. "You're using that poor, foolish girl!"

"Only as she enjoys being used. Marry me, or join me in my bed, and I'll send her packing. Until then, she stays."

"In that case, you shouldn't mind my moving into town with the children."

His expression hardened. "You have no income, Eve. You're dependent on me for support. I can't stop you from leaving, but I won't give you a penny if you're not living under my roof. And I certainly won't allow you to take my children."

Eve had run out of words. White-faced and trembling, she turned, walked out into the hall and fled to the front porch. Sinking onto the top step, she stared numbly toward the distant gate. If only she could walk out that gate and never look back. She would do whatever it took to survive and support the children—scrub floors, wash dishes, work as a servant. But the children would never be permitted to leave, so she was trapped here—and not even Clint could set her free. There was no way she could desert Margaret's children.

Eve needed someone to talk to, someone who would know the situation and understand. Alice was here, but the old woman didn't seem to care about other people's problems. Only one person could offer Eve the sympathy and insight she needed—the woman who'd recommended Beth Ann in the first place.

Eve rose and brushed off her skirt. She would spend the morning hours with the children and their lessons. In the afternoon she'd find an excuse to go into town and pay a visit to Etta.

Clint had met with the other homesteaders that morning at the Potter place. Although most were hunters and fair shots, there were no seasoned fighters among them. They wouldn't stand a chance against five hired guns.

Their best hope lay in knowing where the enemy would strike so they could get their families into hiding and ride to each other's aid. Newt and Gideon Potter, along with a couple of the teenage farm boys, would serve as lookouts and messengers.

It was a flimsy plan at best, and liable to get some people killed. Clint hoped to hell it wouldn't need to be put into action. That would be his job, to try and keep the raids from happening—which meant somehow persuading five ruthless, well-paid gunfighters to back off and leave town.

His plan was evolving in steps—the first and only clear one to get a look at the quintet, fix their identities in his mind and learn where and how they were spending their time. After that it would be a matter of catching them one at a time, hopefully alone and vulnerable. If they all were as tough as Ned Canaday that would be a dangerous proposition. Back in his wild years, Clint had never gone so far as killing a man. But now, if it came to that, he was prepared to kill for the sake of his friends.

Just as he was prepared to kill Roderick Hanford if the chance arose.

The sun was climbing the peak of the sky as Clint rode into town. He was fully armed with a loaded Colt Peacemaker on his hip and a well-sharpened knife in his boot. But after a sleepless night he was nothing but raw nerves braced with a lake of coffee, more dependent on reflex than on reason.

He forced himself to think ahead. What would he do if Ned Canaday recognized him? What about the other men? Would any of them know him from prison or even from the old days?

Would they be friendly? Or would there be an immediate challenge? He had to be ready for anything.

In town, he tied his horse to the hitching rail outside the saloon. If the gunfighters were in

Lodgepole and needed to pass time this was where he'd find them.

He paused outside the swinging doors. From the tavern's shadowed interior he heard the low mutter of voices. But the place was too dark to make out the customers. For that he would need to walk through those swinging doors. Once inside, he'd be in plain view.

He checked the big pistol to make sure it would clear the holster without jamming. In his younger days, he'd been known as a fast draw. But that was before his time in prison. These days he was out of practice.

Steeling his nerves for whatever he was about to face, Clint pushed through the doors and strode into the saloon.

Chapter Twelve

"By gawd, if it ain't Lonigan!" Canaday was hatless today. His scraggly hair was grayer than Clint remembered, and his grin showed a missing front tooth. "Thought I recollected that purty-boy face when you come in before. Get yourself a drink and sit down!"

So Canaday was feeling friendly—for now. But Clint knew the man's mood could change with the speed of a rattler's strike. There was something out of kilter about Ned Canaday. In prison, Clint had stayed out of the big convict's way. But he'd seen enough of his vicious temper to remember and be wary.

He got a whiskey from the bar and put down his coins. He could only hope the glance he gave Smitty would be taken as a warning to keep quiet. Ambling over to the round table,

Clint took the chair on Canaday's right. Only now did he realize there were just four gunmen at the table. He was curious about the reason one man was missing. But he knew better than to ask. He wasn't supposed to know there were meant to be five.

As he sipped his whiskey, Clint's gaze took in the other three gunslingers. One he recognized as Black Bart Grogan, who'd been part of the old train holdup gang. The remaining two men were strangers, but they had the slit-eyed look of seasoned desperados.

"So, you live 'round here, Lonigan? Got you a sweet little wife and young'uns tucked away somewhere?" Canaday appeared to be the leader and spokesman.

"No family. But I've got a nice ranch a few miles south of town." Clint knew he was walking a tightrope. If Canaday mentioned his name to Hanford or McCutcheon and learned the truth, his back would be one big target. But while these men still seemed to trust him, he had to learn as much as he could.

"What about you boys?" Clint asked. "You fixing to settle in these parts?"

"Just passin' through. Doin' a little job— some big ranchers payin' us to wipe out nesters on their range." Canaday's eyes narrowed in his pockmarked face. "Don't suppose you'd consider lendin' a hand? Jake Button was plannin' to show up here, but he got hisself shot—by me, truth be told." The ex-con chuckled. "Bart tells me you're a good hand with a gun."

Hair prickled on the back of Clint's neck. What if he could really do this—join the gunmen, pass on their plans, maybe divert them or even lead them into an ambush?

The risk was enough to trigger a cold sweat. "How much are the ranchers paying?" he asked.

"Hundred each to start. The rest depends on how much damage we to do them nesters. We can do more damage with five men than with four—more than enough to make up for the extra split."

Eve had told Clint the kind of "damage" the ranchers had in mind. He willed his emotions to freeze. "I could use the cash," he said. "Trouble is, I live here. Folks will recognize my face. They mustn't know it's me, not even the ranchers. After you boys are gone, they could get it into their heads to shut me up about this—for good."

"We'll all be wearin' masks." Bart Grogan spoke up. "You could wear one, too. An' when the four of us meet the ranchers, we could tell 'em Jake Button's comin' later. They'd never have to see your face."

"So what d'you say, Lonigan?" Canaday leaned so close that his pitted faced looked like a shell-scarred battlefield. "Are you in or out?"

Clint thought fast. He knew what they wanted—somebody who knew the country and where to find the homesteads. When the raids—and his usefulness to them—were at an end they likely meant to kill him and split his share of the money among themselves. Although he didn't plan on that outcome, things could get out of hand in the blink of an eye.

But he couldn't let that worry stop him. For the sake of his friends, he had to take this chance.

He drained his whiskey glass. "I'm in," he said.

Armed with Alice's shopping list, Eve drove the buggy into town alone. Beth Ann had asked to come with her—in fact she'd been rather demanding about it. But Eve had ordered her to stay and help Alice. Then she'd simply driven off, leaving the girl pouting on the porch. Was Beth Ann already planning for when she'd marry Roderick and take charge? If so, she had a few things to learn about life's realities.

The day was pleasantly cool, with wispy clouds drifting over the peaks. Gazing at the sky, Eve sent up a silent prayer for a storm that would delay the planned attack on the homesteaders, buying Clint more time.

Would she see him today? Was that the real reason she'd chosen to risk Roderick's disapproval by coming alone? The memory of last night's lovemaking lingered in every part of her body. There were times when the yearning to be in his arms again was like physical pain. But her selfish wishes couldn't be allowed to matter now. Not when there were life and death concerns driving them both.

As she pulled up to the general store, she noticed the rangy buckskin tied to the rail outside the saloon. Was it Clint's horse? Her pulse skipped as she noticed the familiar-looking underlined *L* brand on its haunch.

Never mind, she cautioned herself. Even if Clint was nearby, they'd agreed to treat each other like polite acquaintances. Since she had no news for him, it might be less of a strain on their self-control if they didn't meet at all.

Tearing away her gaze and refocusing her

thoughts, she climbed down from the buggy, secured the horse and strode into the general store with the list Alice had made. The young clerk was busy with customers, but he acknowledged her arrival with a friendly nod. Eve waited a few minutes, then left the list on the counter, trusting he'd fill it for her as soon as he was free to do so.

When she stepped onto the boardwalk again the buckskin horse was still tied outside the saloon. If Clint was inside he wouldn't be there just to drink or gamble. Not today. With so much at stake, he had to be involved in some dangerous business. Right now, all she could do was leave him alone, go about her errands and pray for his safety. Meanwhile, maybe Etta would have time to talk with her about Beth Ann.

Etta was bent over, arranging a fresh batch of raisin-filled cookies on the display shelves when Eve walked in. She straightened, a smile on her plump, rosy face. "What a nice surprise to see you again, dearie. How did your dinner party turn out?"

"Fine. Everyone enjoyed your pies. Roderick seemed quite pleased."

"I'm happy to hear that. And happy that

you've met the other ranchers and their wives. Having the right friends can make all the difference in this country."

"Yes, I suppose so." Eve checked the impulse to confide how out of place she'd felt with those stoic women. Etta Simpkins wasn't exactly known for keeping secrets. But since she'd been the one to recommend Beth Ann, maybe she would at least keep this one.

"I'm hoping you can advise me about something else," Eve said. "It's Beth Ann. She's competent and a willing worker, but I've discovered that she, uh…"

"That she has a certain weakness for men." Etta finished the sentence, and not as a question. "Oh, dear, I was hoping that wouldn't be a problem."

"You knew?"

"Beth Ann is my niece. My late sister Madge's girl. Didn't she mention that?"

"I'm afraid she didn't." Eve had been prepared to ask whether she should dismiss the girl and hire someone else. But she could hardly expect a balanced answer from Beth Ann's aunt.

"Who was it this time, one of the cowboys?" Etta asked.

"I'd…rather not say," Eve hedged. It might

not be wise to tell the woman she'd caught her niece in bed with Roderick, or that he'd excused his behavior by calling the girl a common slut. The last thing Eve wanted was for Roderick's misdeeds to become known and reflect on his children's future reputation.

Etta sighed, her ample bosom rising and falling beneath her white apron. "You say Beth Ann's a good worker?"

"Yes. I can't fault her in that respect."

"Then I hope you'll indulge me and keep her on for now. Beth Ann isn't a bad girl. She just needs a good example to follow. That's one reason I sent her to you. I was hoping she'd learn to be a lady."

"I see." Eve sighed in surrender. "All right, I'll give her a little more time. But this behavior of hers needs to stop."

"Of course it does. Bring her along the next time you come to town. I'll give her a good talking to. Don't worry, I'm sure I can persuade her to change her ways."

"I sincerely hope so. Otherwise I'll be forced to dismiss the girl. I can't have the children exposed to such goings-on."

Deciding to change the subject, Eve turned to the display case. "Those raisin-filled cookies look delicious. As long as I'm here, I'll take a dozen. And thank you, Etta. Life here is so different from what I knew in England. It helps to have a friend I can talk to."

"Anytime, dearie." Etta reached across the counter and patted her arm. "Don't worry. Lodgepole won't always be the rough-and-tumble backwater it is now. Once we get rid of those squatters and their lice-infested broods, we can welcome people of quality. People like us."

"Get rid of the homesteaders, you say?" Eve was too shocked to conceal her surprise.

"Yes indeed, dearie. There's a plan afoot—a plan to drive those vermin off our land. Once their ramshackle farms are disposed of, you'll never know they were here." Etta scooped raisin cookies into a paper bag. "This valley will be the beautiful spot God meant it to be."

Eve paid for the cookies and took the bag, hoping Etta wouldn't notice her shaking hands. As she walked out of the bakery, her mind reeled with what had become a certainty.

It was Etta Simpkins who'd carried the money from the Cattlemen's Association— money that would pay the hired gunmen for their hellish work.

Eve had to get word to Clint. His horse was

still tied across the street where he'd left it. But she could hardly go rushing into the saloon to find him, especially since she didn't know who else might be there.

She could write a note and tuck it partway under his saddle where he'd be sure to see it. She didn't have a pencil or paper in her reticule, but surely she could borrow or buy them in the general store.

A frayed-looking immigrant woman trailing two small children was coming up the boardwalk. Eve thrust the bag of cookies into the woman's hand, then wheeled and dashed into the store.

The clerk was still busy with customers. The list she'd left for him lay untouched on the counter next to a tin can with several used pencils in it. Grabbing the sharpest one, Eve glanced at the list, committed the items to memory, then turned it over and scrawled a brief message on the back.

"Etta carried the money. She knows the plan. Don't trust her. E."

After dropping the pencil on the counter, Eve folded the paper and hurried back outside— only to halt on the boardwalk with a groan of dismay.

Clint's horse was gone.

* * *

Clint planned to stop by the Potter place on his way home. His friends would need to know he was pretending to throw his lot in with the hired guns. He could trust Newt and Gideon to spread the word to the right people.

It was a stroke of luck that the gunslingers had been missing a man, and that they'd recognized him from the old days. If he could set up an ambush and lead them into it, the danger could be ended in a single gunfight, with the homesteaders having the advantage of surprise and cover.

The thought of the risk involved was enough to make him sweat. If Canaday and the others discovered which side he was on, all hell could break loose.

But that was a chance Clint would have to take.

He found Gideon Potter outside the cabin chopping wood. Newt joined them from the barn. In a few brief words, Clint brought them up to date on his plans.

"Holy hell!" Newt swore. "If we could get those buzzards surrounded, in one place, we could pick 'em off like a flock of fool hens."

"I know just the place for that." Gideon used

a stick to sketch in the dirt. "This spot here, where the old wagon road cuts through the gully. We'd have plenty of cover on both sides, and if we cut them off they'd have no way out."

"That should work, as long as they keep trusting me," Clint said. "We should be safe tonight. The bastards won't fire a shot till they get their money. After that, when they want to strike will be anybody's guess. I'll be meeting them tonight in town, after they get their down payment from McCutcheon. That'll be when they make their plans. When I know, I'll find a way to get word to you."

Leaving the brothers to contact their friends, Clint headed home to get a few hours of badly needed rest. Before he'd left town, he'd noticed the Hanford buggy outside the general store, but he'd kept his distance. Even if Eve was nearby, and even if she was alone, he couldn't run the risk of being seen with her—as much for her sake as for his.

Now, as he rode, the memory of last night swept over him—her pale arms twining around him, pulling him down to her, the eager sweetness of her loving…

But he had to stop thinking of her that way. He would continue to check the fence for messages. He'd welcome any help she could offer for his cause. But he had to remember to think of her as an ally—not a lover. He knew better than to believe one night could lead to a happy ending. Eve was a lady, a countess. He was nothing but a poor rancher with a prison record. And she'd already made her choice. She had chosen to stay with her sister's children—and with Roderick Hanford.

On the approach to the ranch gate, Eve pulled the buggy up to the clump of willows that screened the buck fence. Leaving a message by daylight posed the risk of being seen from the house. But now that she'd missed Clint in town, this was the most likely way to reach him. She could only hope he was still coming by to check.

After folding the shopping list she'd used to write the message, she slipped it into the chosen spot, leaving an inch of the paper in sight to make sure it would be seen. Then she found the fallen branch and, stretching on tiptoe, laid it in the fork of a limb as a signal. Her news was important, but riding out in search of him would be dangerous for them both. This was the safest way to get word to him.

That done, she drove the buggy through the gate and back to the barn, where she left the rig for one of the hired men to put away.

Beth Ann was standing on the porch, a smug expression on her pretty face. "I saw you come in," she said. "What were you doing out there in those trees?"

Eve checked the impulse to rebuke the girl, which would only make the incident more memorable. She drew herself up. "If you must know, I wasn't sure whether I could make it back to the privy in time. Now, shouldn't you be helping Alice in the kitchen?"

Beth Ann giggled and sauntered back into the house. The girl was becoming impossibly bold, flaunting what she saw as her new power as Roderick's mistress. Back in England Eve would have sent her packing with no letter of reference. But here…her heart sank as the truth dawned. She needed Beth Ann to distract Roderick's advances. It was a delicate balance, sure to tip and shatter. But for now Eve had little choice except to keep it in place.

She found the children upstairs, Rose playing with her dolls and Thomas working a puzzle. The boy was too pale and too thin. He needed time outdoors with companions to encourage him to roughhouse, play and explore. And he was old enough for riding lessons. Even Rose would enjoy a small pony of her own. Once more, Eve decided to speak to Roderick. If nothing else, maybe he'd consider building a small house on the ranch and hiring a married man with a growing family to live and work here. But knowing Roderick, he would only put her off with some excuse and press her, once more, to marry him. How could a father care so little for his offspring?

The future was beyond Eve's control. But today, on this beautiful afternoon, she could at least get the children out of the house for some fun. Forcing her other worries to the back of her mind, she gave them her brightest smile. "I have an idea," she said. "Let's make a little picnic and take it down to the creek. On the way back, we can stop and see the barn cat's kittens. They have their eyes open now. Maybe, if nobody's looking, we can even slide down the haystack. Would you like that?"

Dropping their toys, the children ran to her. Eve hugged them close. Her precious darlings. She would sacrifice anything to protect them and give them happy lives.

But could she make the one sacrifice that might be demanded of her?

Mounted on a fresh horse, Clint waited in the shadow of an alder thicket that overhung the road. The hour was late, the sky clouding over to veil the moon and stars. The air carried the fresh scent of rain.

Half a mile off the road, a glowing light marked the location of Judge Seth McCutcheon's house, with its ornate gingerbread trim. The four gunslingers were there now, getting their blood money and their instructions. Any minute now they should be leaving, mounting up and heading back to the road that would take them into town.

Dismounting, Clint led his horse back into the trees and tethered it to a sapling. Slung from the saddle was the long leather scabbard that held his Henry repeating rifle. He drew out the gun and made his way back to the roadside.

A storm was moving in, the approaching thunder no more than a murmur above the faraway peaks. Crouching low in the brush, Clint cocked the rifle and settled back to wait. This new plan hadn't come to him until after he'd left the Potters' place. Leading the gunmen into an ambush might work fine, but things could go wrong, and innocent people could die or get hurt. The gunfighters were already down one man. If he could kill or disable more of them, or even give them a good scare, they might decide the job wasn't worth the risk, so that they'd call off their planned attack and leave town. It wasn't foolproof, but it was at least worth a chance.

And the only life at risk here would be his own.

Sheet lightning danced across the sky. The storm was moving closer. Rain would be a good thing, Clint thought. True, it would make hitting his targets more difficult. But a heavy downpour would hamper the gunslingers, making it harder for them to return fire. It would also cover his getaway.

But even a fast-moving storm might not arrive in time to be of much help. He couldn't count on the rain—especially now. A glimmer of movement against the distant light, and the faint sound of horses, told him the four men had left McCutcheon's house and were moving in his direction at a brisk trot. They were probably anxious to get back to town before the storm broke.

Clint shifted forward, feeling the bowstring tautness of his nerves and muscles. Lying in ambush with the intent to kill was a first for him. Only the thought of the helpless women and children he was protecting steeled his resolve.

The riders were getting closer. Clint had chosen his spot for the deep shadow and also for its position at the cutoff to McCutcheon's ranch. To head back to town the men would turn left, exposing their backs to him. He would aim for Canaday if he could pick him out. Without their leader the other three desperados would be more likely to give up and leave.

Clint would be lucky to get more than one or two shots off before they turned on him. Once he'd done all he could, he'd race to his horse and take a shortcut back to town. He'd be waiting in the saloon when the others arrived. At least that was the plan.

The night air was cool and heavy with moisture. A bead of cold sweat trickled down Clint's cheek—or was it a raindrop? As the four riders turned onto the road, a lightning bolt cracked across the sky, splitting the clouds and sending down a torrent so dense that it was like standing under a waterfall. The riders were thrown into a melee of confusion. Horses reared and bucked. Men cursed.

Picking out Canaday was impossible. Clint aimed his rifle at the closest moving body and pulled the trigger. As the report echoed through the storm, the man slumped in the saddle, clutching his shoulder. Wounded most likely, but not fatally hit.

Clint got off one more shot before the gunmen drew their pistols and began firing in his direction. But they couldn't see him through the brush and the downpour. Without taking time to see if his second shot had struck home, Clint raced back through the trees, sprang onto his horse and headed for the wooded shortcut back to town.

By the time the four men stumbled into the saloon he was seated at the bar sipping a whiskey, his horse under the eave and his rifle stashed out of sight in a back room. At that late hour there were no other customers, but Clint had alerted Smitty that the men were coming.

Canaday, wild-eyed and dripping but unhurt, staggered in first. Behind him, the two men Clint hadn't recognized were supporting a white-faced Bart Grogan. Grogan was clutching his wounded shoulder, blood seeping through his shirt and between his fingers. The men lowered him to a chair.

His second shot, Clint surmised, must have missed.

"Damn fool!" Canaday was cursing Grogan. "With your shootin' arm bunged up, you ain't no more use than a three-legged mule. Hell, along with the other trouble you been givin' me, you ain't even worth the price of a doc." He raised his pistol and pointed it at the wounded man's head. Grogan's bloodshot eyes widened. Clint forgot to breathe as Canaday's finger tightened on the trigger. Lord, the man couldn't be meaning to...

The gunshot echoed like a dynamite blast in the small space. Grogan slumped over and slid sideways off the chair, a neat bullet hole in the side of his head.

The only sound in the room was Canaday's cackling laughter. Clint forced himself to keep still. If the man was capable of this, he was capable of anything.

Smitty's grizzled face had gone ashen. Whatever happened, Clint vowed, he wasn't going to walk out and leave his friend to the mercy of this maniac who killed at the slightest whim. Clint waited.

Canaday holstered his pistol. "Let's go back to the hotel and turn in, boys. We can't burn barns in the rain." He glanced toward Clint. "What about you, Lonigan?"

"Somebody ought to stay here and help Smitty clean up this mess. Looks like that somebody's gonna be me. After that I'll be headed home till the rain lets up. That suit you, Canaday?"

"Long as you show up here soon as the weather clears. I'll hang on to your cash to make sure you do." He ambled through the swinging doors into the rainy night. His two remaining cohorts followed, slinking after him like beaten dogs.

Clint helped Smitty drag Grogan onto the back stoop and scrub the worst of the bloodstains off the floor. No use bothering the sheriff at this hour. An outlaw had murdered one of his own. Score settled. The undertaker could pick up the body in the morning.

After Smitty had closed up, Clint rode out of town through the pouring rain. He'd planned on going straight home to dry off and get some rest; but as he reached the turnoff to his ranch he remembered that he hadn't checked for a message from Eve.

Not that he expected to hear from her. She'd stepped away from the conflict to be there for her sister's children. And it wasn't as if he needed her help anymore. Now that the hired gunmen had accepted him, he had his own access to their plans.

But something—if only the need to hear from her—compelled him to ride on down the road toward the Hanford ranch. At least a message from Eve would let him know she was all right.

His pulse quickened when he saw the stick in the fork of the tree—their private signal. Rain streamed off his hat and wet clothes as he splashed through the mud toward the fence. Now he could see the end of a white paper, which he drew out from between the protecting logs. The sheet was barely damp, but it was too dark to read Eve's message here. Without unfolding it, he tucked it beneath his vest and rode for home.

By the time he'd put away the horse and lit a fire in the iron stove he was shivering with cold and fatigue. After sinking into a chair and sliding the lantern closer, he unfolded the paper and smoothed it out on the table.

Clint had never seen Eve's handwriting. He'd

imagined her script to be flowing and feminine. But this message was printed in blocky grammar school letters.

GOOD NEWS. THE GUNMEN WANTED MORE MONEY THAN THE RANCHERS WERE WILLING TO PAY THEM. THEY HAVE PACKED UP AND LEFT THE VALLEY. YOU AND YOUR FRIENDS ARE SAFE FOR NOW. EVE

Clint reread the message, his bewilderment darkening to anger. The whole message was a lie, of course. He'd been with Canaday and his men tonight. He knew full well they planned to raid the homesteads as soon as the weather cleared. But Eve wouldn't be aware that he knew the truth. She'd spun this tale to lull him and his friends into a false sense of security, leaving them unprepared for the coming attack.

She'd turned against him. Damn the woman to hell.

Chapter Thirteen

Eve was helping Rose and Thomas with their morning schoolwork when Roderick walked into the dining room. "Come into my study, Eve," he said. "I want a word with you."

"Can it wait until we're finished here?"

"I'm afraid it can't. Please excuse yourself from the children and come with me."

What now? Eve rose from her chair, sensing yet another withering confrontation. Roderick's expression revealed nothing. But she was learning that when her brother-in-law was at his most impassive, he was at his most dangerous.

He ushered her out of the dining room and down the hall to his study. Outside, water drummed on the roof and streamed down the windows, its cadence like a dirge, or the drum roll that preceded a hanging. The steady drone of the rain, which had come in the night and showed no sign of letting up, had set everyone on edge. Even the children were fretful.

Eve had hoped to sneak away later and check to see if Clint had found the message she'd left at the fence. But with rain battering the house and making a quagmire of the yard, that wasn't going to happen. She could only hope that sometime before the storm broke, Clint had come by and found her note.

The study door closed behind her with an ominous click. Eve felt like a school girl summoned to the headmaster's office for punishment. "What is it now, Roderick?" she asked. "Have I done something wrong?"

"Sit down, Eve." He indicated the chair that faced the desk. As she sat, nervously arranging her skirts, he walked around the desk and took a seat opposite her, in his high-backed leather banker's chair.

"Have you been happy here?" he asked.

"I've found happiness in caring for Margaret's children," she replied.

"Have I been generous with you? Have I given you everything you needed?"

"Every material thing? Yes, of course."

"And the rest? Your situation here?"

"I'm learning to make adjustments."

"Then perhaps you can explain the meaning of this note."

He slid a creased slip of paper across the desk toward her. Eve's heart dropped. It was the message she'd written for Lonigan and left at the fence.

"Well, what have you got to say for yourself?" Roderick's voice was stern but his eyes were gloating. How could she answer him? Lying would be useless.

"Where did you get this?" she demanded, though she knew the answer to that question. Beth Ann had seen her come out of the willows. The girl must have gone out to investigate, found the message and turned it over to Roderick.

"I'm the one asking the questions here," he said. "Since you're not denying you left it, suppose you tell me who it was meant for—not that I can't guess."

"Who it was meant for doesn't matter." Eve rose from the chair to face him. "What does matter is that you and your rancher friends have hired professional killers to wipe out the homesteaders—not just the men but innocent women and children whose blood will be on your hands. I overheard you the night of the party, and I knew I had to stop it."

Roderick leaned back in his chair, a half-amused expression on his face. He was letting her talk, listening as she dug herself deeper with every word.

"You've treated me well enough, and I've learned to love your children. It would break my heart to be separated from them. But I can't close my eyes and pretend this isn't happening. I can't condone cold-blooded murder. Call those men off, Roderick! Settle your fight some other way!"

"Believe me, we've given those vermin every chance to pack up and leave peacefully." Rising as he spoke, Roderick moved around the desk toward her. "This is the final solution—the only solution. And I'm not about to let you… interfere."

His powerful hand closed like a vise around her upper arm. "You're coming with me," he murmured in her ear. "And I trust you not to make a fuss and upset the children. It won't help."

Gripping hard enough to send a dart of pain up her arm, he guided her out into the hallway. As they mounted the stairs, she glimpsed Beth

Ann watching from the entrance to the kitchen. Her pretty face wore a triumphant smirk.

From the landing he propelled Eve down the hall to her room. Did he mean to force himself on her? To assert his dominance in such a cruel, violent way? She was prepared to fight him off if need be, but he only shoved her inside, stepped back and closed the door. She heard the click of his key, locking her in.

"You can plan to stay here until this business is finished." His voice filtered through the thick wooden door. "Beth Ann will bring your meals and carry out your chamber pot. If you try to escape you'll be caught. And there are less pleasant places I can put you, like the granary or the root cellar. So don't test my patience."

"The children…" She pressed against the door.

"They'll be fine. We'll tell them you're sick and need to be quarantined. Your betrayal will be dealt with later."

There was a moment of silence. Eve held her breath, listening, wondering if he was still outside the door. Just when she'd begun to believe he'd gone, Roderick spoke again. "By the way, in case your so-called friend was expecting to pick up a message, I left one for him. It might be somewhat misleading, but at least he'll know you were thinking of him."

Eve bit back a cry as Roderick's footfalls died away down the hall. What message had he written and left for Clint to find? Something to trap him, or maybe to lull his friends into a false sense of security?

There was always the chance the storm or some other delay had kept Clint from coming by and collecting the note. But she couldn't count on that. She had to assume he had read the message. And unless she could get out of here, there was no way to let him know it wasn't from her.

If she tried to escape while Beth Ann had her door unlocked, Eve had little doubt Roderick would carry out his threat. She'd be shoved into some dark, rat-infested hole with no hope of getting out until it was too late. She would have to find another way.

Walking to the window, she stared out at the rain, thinking. Beyond the house she could see the cottonwood that sheltered Margaret's grave; and far beyond that the stockade that surrounded the kennels. From where she stood she could make out Hans's massive head and shoulders moving back and forth, heedless of the downpour. He was probably feeding the dogs or caring for them in some way. Was he a prisoner, too—held captive by the torment that isolated him from the world? Opening the window a few inches Eve inhaled the fresh, damp air. Raindrops, blown by the wind, spattered her face. She'd hoped, even prayed for a storm like this to delay the raids on the homesteads. But the weather was bound to clear—and with that clearing the terror would begin.

Where was Clint? Somehow she had to get away from here and find him.

Climbing down from the second floor with no hand or footholds was out of the question. And the old trick of tying bedsheets together would work only with plenty of sheets and the arm strength to climb to the ground. Even if she could do it, she was liable to be seen and caught.

That left only one option—a long shot to be sure, but she had to make it work.

Opening a dresser drawer, she lifted her ruby ring from its hiding place. For a moment she hesitated, torn. If her escape plan worked, she'd be leaving the children here. And there was always the heartrending chance that Roderick wouldn't let her return to them. But she'd already taken a step across that bridge, and right now families' lives were at stake. She could only hope Rose and Thomas could persuade their father to let her come back. If not, she would have to find other ways to be there for them.

Decision made, she changed into her riding habit and slipped the ring into her pocket. If she found herself cast out into the world, she would need it.

Hours seemed to pass before Beth Ann showed up with Eve's lunch. Unlocking the door, she walked in with a tray that held a dry sandwich and a glass of water. Food for a prisoner. Was the paltry meal the girl's idea or Roderick's?

"I'm glad to see you, Beth Ann," Eve said, ignoring the unspoken insult. "I've been wanting to talk to you."

"What about?" Her eyes narrowed with suspicion. "You don't have any reason to like me now."

"True." Eve kept her tone and expression pleasant. "But even though we may never be friends there's no need for us to be enemies— especially if we can help each other."

"I...don't understand." Beth Ann's brash

manner seemed to evaporate in a haze of un-certainty.

"Don't you see, my dear? You've won. You wanted Roderick, and now he can be yours. All you need to do is leave the door unlocked and let me walk out of here."

Beth Ann hesitated. "Roderick wouldn't like me to do that."

"He doesn't have to know. Make up a story, say I tricked you somehow. You're a clever girl—you'll think of something."

Beth Ann was silent, a frown creeping over her face.

"I know you see me as a rival, standing in the way of your happiness," Eve pressed. "But it doesn't have to be that way. Once I'm out of the house you'll have him all to yourself."

The girl shook her head. "Roderick's already mad at you for writing the note. Why should I make him mad at me by letting you go when I don't need to?"

At the point of desperation, Eve played her last ace—it was all she had, but people were liable to die if she couldn't get away to warn Clint. Snatching the ruby ring out of her pocket, she held it up. "See this? Solid gold and a gen-uine ruby, worth more money than you'll ever see in your life. Get me out of the house and it's yours."

Beth Ann scowled at the ring. "It looks more like a man's than a woman's. Roderick's promised to buy me some pretty things, prettier than that clunky old ring." Turning away, she strode out of the room, closed the door behind her and locked it.

Seething with frustration, Eve sagged against the door. She'd thought she might have a chance with Beth Ann. But she hadn't counted on the girl being so stubborn—or so foolish. Now, with her last hope gone, Eve was trapped.

She forced herself to eat the sandwich—dry bread and the tough heel of a beef roast. She could barely chew it, but she finished it all and washed it down with the water. There was no telling when she'd get to eat again.

Time crawled at a leaden pace. Downstairs, the grandfather clock in the entry struck six. The mouthwatering smells of cooked meat and fresh hot rolls filtered up from the kitchen below. It was dinnertime for the family, but no one brought Eve anything to eat. Had they forgotten her, or was Beth Ann deliberately ignoring an order to serve her meals?

Outside, the wind had ebbed, but the rain was

still falling in a cheerless, gray drizzle. Gazing through water-streaked glass, Eve watched the clouds fade to mud-colored twilight. Shadows flooded the room, but there was no reason to light a lamp. Seeing outside was easier through darkened windows.

Carrying a lantern and wearing a black oil-skin slicker, Roderick left the house and sloshed across the yard to the barn. He emerged a few minutes later mounted on his big piebald horse. Eve watched him disappear into the rainy darkness. Was he going to town to meet with the other ranchers? Were they already finalizing arrangements for the poker game that would give them an alibi during the raids?

Frantic to get out, Eve seized the doorknob and twisted it with all her strength. The lock held fast. In a fit of despair, she pounded on the door, bruising her fists against the unyielding wood. Nothing.

Slumping onto the chest that had carried her scant belongings from England, she buried her face in her hands. She was dry-eyed, spent beyond tears. Terrible things were about to happen and she was helpless to try and stop them.

As the darkness deepened, rain pattered on the windows.

Eve could hear the tiny settling creaks as the house cooled in the night air. It was so quiet that the turn of a key in the lock was enough to startle her. She sprang to her feet as the door swung open a few inches and two small, nightgown-clad figures slipped into the room.

"Why aren't you in bed, Aunt Eve?" Rose's voice piped. "Papa said you were sick."

"Beth Ann said we mustn't bother you," Thomas added, closing the door behind them. "But we were worried. We took the key off the hook in the kitchen."

"Shh! I'm fine. Come here." Eve dropped to her knees and gathered them close. How dear they were, so soft and loving in her arms. She embraced them as if she might never see them again, filling her senses with their warmth and the clean, sweet smell of their hair. How could she leave them?

But she knew what she had to do.

Releasing them, she sat back and gazed into their solemn little faces. "I'm not sick, but I'm in trouble," she said. "I need to leave for a while. There's someone I have to help."

"When will you be back?" Thomas asked.

"I don't know." Eve stumbled over the words, choking on her unshed tears. "I love you and I promised I'd never leave you. I'll do my best to keep that promise. But sometimes things happen that can't be helped. Right now I have to go."

"No!" Rose flung her arms around Eve's neck. "Please don't go, Aunt Eve!"

Heart aching, she eased the child away from her. "I need you to be a big girl and do what I tell you, Rose. Can you do that?"

Rose wiped away a tear with the back of her hand. "Yes," she whispered.

"Listen to me now," Eve said. "Put the key back where you got it, Thomas. Then both of you go to bed. Don't tell anybody you were here tonight. Let them think I got out by myself. Understand?"

The children nodded, their eyes huge in the darkness.

"Then understand this. Whatever happens, remember that I love you more than my life. I will do whatever it takes to come back to you. Now go, before somebody hears you—quietly now, like two little mice."

Before her resolve could shatter into tears, she nudged the children back to the hall and watched them tiptoe downstairs to replace the key. With the door closed, she arranged the bed and rummaged through the trunk for her dark blue woolen cloak. By the time she came out again, ready to ride, Rose and Thomas were nowhere in sight.

As Eve stole down the stairs and out the front door, her thoughts flew ahead to Clint. She had to find him.

Clint had given up trying to sleep. He stood on the porch, watching the drizzle slide off the eave. By turns he blessed the rain and cursed it. The wetness had delayed the raids and was soaking into roofs and haystacks, making them less likely to burn. But the waiting was a hell of uncertainty, like sitting atop a keg of black powder with a sputtering fuse.

He had read and reread the message from Eve, hoping to discover some hidden meaning between the lines. In the end he'd crumpled the paper and stuffed it into the unlit stove. The only truth in it was that Eve had attempted to deceive him and his friends. If he hadn't been in touch with the gunmen himself, she might have succeeded.

Taken in by her beauty, he'd allowed himself to trust her. All the while she was gaining his confidence, she'd been reeling him in, priming him for betrayal. He had no doubt she'd carried the cash from the Cattlemen's Association under her fancy silken petticoats, or in her trunk. He didn't understand why she'd told him the truth about the number of gunmen and what they were being paid, but no doubt she had some devious reason for her one moment of honesty. And who knew what else she'd done to damage his cause? If he ever saw the cursed woman again he would tell her exactly what he thought of her.

At the sound of a horse approaching fast through the rain, he snapped to alertness. Grabbing the double-barreled shotgun, he thumbed back the hammers and flattened himself against the inside wall, next to the open doorway.

The horse pulled up a few paces from the porch. Standing out of direct sight, he didn't recognize the rider until he heard her voice.

"Clint! Are you there?"

A knot jerked tight in his stomach. With the gun still cocked, he moved into the doorway and stepped out onto the porch.

Rain-soaked and mud-spattered, she looked ready to fall out of the saddle. The hood of her cloak had fallen back. Tendrils of dripping hair framed her pale face. Clint steeled himself against the urge to lift her down and gather her chilled body into his arms.

"What are you doing here?" he demanded.

"I came to find you—to warn you…" Her voice trailed off as she reacted to his cold anger.

"I don't trust warnings from traitors. Get out of here, *Countess*." The word hissed off his tongue. "Go back to Hanford and tell him your ploy didn't work."

She straightened in the saddle, her gaze defiant. "I know what you must be thinking, but—"

"Then you know why I'm not interested in anything you have to say."

If he'd expected her to grovel or burst into tears, he'd underestimated the woman. She sat her horse like a queen, muddy and bedraggled, but no less regal. "Be that as it may, I'm not leaving until you've heard me out. The sooner you stop interrupting me and start listening, the sooner I'll be finished."

"Fine, go ahead." A gentleman would have invited her to dismount and come inside to dry off, but this was no time for fine manners. Besides, he didn't want to give her an opening to work her wiles on him. Lowering the gun, he set it back inside the door.

"You called me a traitor. But when I was in

town earlier, I discovered who the real traitor was. Etta Simpkins pretends to be helping you. But she's hand in glove with the cattlemen. I'm certain she was the one who carried the money to pay the gunfighters. And I'm equally sure that, if given the chance, she'd betray you in a heartbeat. That was the message I left you at the fence."

"Well, it damned well wasn't the one I read."

Etta Simpkins—that made some sense now that he thought of it. She'd put on a good show of swooning during the stagecoach robbery. But he still wasn't ready to believe Eve's story.

"Be still and listen." She spoke as if chastising an unruly schoolboy. "Beth Ann found my message and gave it to Roderick. He replaced it with one of his own. Since it was gone when I checked on my way here, I'm guessing you must've picked it up."

"So the gunmen haven't left? The raids are still in the plans?" He wasn't ready to tell her the truth about his own involvement.

"Whatever Roderick's message said, it's a lie. That's what I came to tell you."

A chilly breeze rippled through the trees. Eve shivered as it lifted the edge of her cloak. She was cold and wet and looked exhausted. But pride was keeping her upright in the saddle. Surely Hanford wouldn't have sent her out in this condition—especially since, if her story was true, she'd be in deep trouble at home.

"So you've escaped and run away, have you, Eve?" he asked.

"Roderick locked me in my room." Clint could hear the strain in her voice. She was beginning to crumble. "The children let me out."

"And you left them to ride here and warn me. I'm sorry, Eve. That couldn't have been an easy decision."

She shivered as a gust of wind whipped her cloak back from her body. "Roderick might try to keep me from seeing them again. I knew that was a risk, but then I thought about other children, families like Anders and Berta Yost and their little ones, who could die if I didn't find you and tell you what I knew…"

Her words ended in a sob. She sagged, swaying in the saddle. Lunging from the porch, Clint caught her as she slid sideways off the horse. Holding her in his arms, he led the mare around the back of the house, under the shelter of the low, overhanging roof.

Eve buried her face against his chest as he returned to the front, mounted the steps and carried her into the house, bolting the door behind them. She was so small and cold, yet so brave and honorable. How could he have ever believed her capable of betraying him?

"It's all right, love," he murmured against her damp hair. "There are things going on you don't know about. As soon as I read the message, I knew it wasn't true. You could've stayed with your sister's children."

"But I didn't know that."

"Hush. It doesn't matter now." His mouth brushed hers in a tender kiss, warming her rain-chilled lips. She responded with a hungry little whimper, pulling his head down to her. Heat flashed to his loins as her eager tongue flicked along his lower lip in open invitation. Lord help him, but she was so desirable and so needy. All Clint could think of was how much he wanted to sweep her into his bed, plunge his sex into her sweet body and ravish her till she moaned with pleasure.

But this was a dangerous time, with lives at stake. He'd be a fool to lower his guard long enough to make love to her.

"We've got to get you warm," he said, easing her away from him and lowering her to one of his two chairs. Her woolen cloak was soaked through. Lifting it away from her, he hung it over the back of the other chair and turned it toward the potbellied stove, which was already stoked with dry wood and tinder, and needed only a match, touched to Hanford's crumpled note, to kindle a cheery blaze.

Until now Clint had avoided making a fire. Why let the wrong people know he was in the house? A man couldn't be too careful. But Eve was shivering with cold. Before he sent her back he needed to get her warm and find her a slicker for the ride home.

She would demand to go, he knew. Eve would risk anything to return to her sister's children. But how could he let her go back to Hanford, knowing how he'd made her a prisoner? What else would the man do to her if he caught her coming home after a visit to his enemy?

Roderick Hanford was capable of anything.

Forcing the thought aside, he left her long enough to step into the bedroom and strip the faded patchwork quilt off the bed. After helping her stand, he wrapped the quilt around her, took a seat and pulled her onto his lap. With a sigh she relaxed against him, her head nesting beneath his chin as the fire's warmth filled the room.

"Thank you," she murmured. "This feels much better than having you angry with me."

The fire crackled in the darkness, glowing through the mica panes of the stove. Clint trailed a path of kisses across her forehead. "What am I going to do with you, Eve?"

"Isn't that up to me?"

"Not entirely." He forced a chuckle. "If this was a different time and place, I'd carry you to bed and spend the night making love to you. Then in the morning I'd get up, bring you breakfast and start building a palace to keep you safe and happy."

"I don't need a palace to be happy. Bed and breakfast would be enough..." Eve's words trailed off into silence. She shook her head. "You know I have to leave."

"Don't go back to him." The words escaped Clint's lips before common sense could stop them. "I know the man. I don't even want to think about what he could do to you."

"I can't stay here. When Roderick discovers I've gone, this is the first place he'll look for me."

"I can take you into town and get you a room at the hotel."

She shook her head. "You know I have to go back for the children's sake."

"Damn it, Eve…" Clint knew better than to argue, but the urge was almost impossible to deny. His arms tightened around her, cradling her close. He'd once thought desire was the most powerful emotion he could feel for this woman. But now the need to protect her was eating him alive.

And short of murdering Roderick Hanford there was nothing he could do.

The thump of a heavy fist on the bolted door froze his blood. Rising, he shoved Eve toward the bedroom. "Hide!" he whispered, reaching for his rifle. "Don't make a sound till I tell you it's safe."

The pounding on the door continued. "Get a move on, Lonigan!" a familiar voice growled. "Open up! It's colder than a witch's tit out here!"

Clint felt his heart go leaden. He muttered a curse. The voice outside the door was the last one he'd have chosen to hear tonight.

It was Ned Canaday.

Chapter Fourteen

Clint faced an excruciating choice. Canaday sounded friendly enough for the moment, but refusing to open the door was bound to rouse his suspicion and ignite his temper. A locked door wouldn't keep the gunmen out for long. But letting them inside would put Eve in terrible peril.

The pounding continued. "We know you're in there, Lonigan!" Canaday bellowed. "We can see the smoke. Open the door before we kick it in!"

"Hang on—just getting decent." Clint grabbed Eve's cloak off the chair and strode into the bedroom, where she had flattened herself behind the door. Her eyes were wide with questions, but she seemed to understand the danger. She didn't speak as he opened the single window, boosted her over the sill and passed her the cloak. "Stay out of sight till they're inside, then go for your horse," he whispered. "Get away from here as fast as you can. Whatever happens, don't look back."

Her eyes flashed in the darkness, her gaze holding his for a precious instant. Then she ducked into the shadows, covering her white blouse with her cloak.

"Open the damn door, Lonigan!" Canaday's voice bawled.

"Coming." Clint closed the window. Every instinct told him the gunmen were up to no good, but his best chance of getting Eve safely away would be to let them inside and keep them occupied. Balancing the rifle, he loosened his belt as he strode toward the door and threw back the bolt. As the door swung open, he made a show of fumbling with the buckle.

Canaday stepped across the threshold, his hat, clothes and boots dripping muddy water. One hand rested on the butt of his holstered pistol. He was alone, but before the door swung closed behind him, Clint glimpsed two horses beyond the porch. Dread tightened his throat. Somewhere outside in the darkness was at least one more man. Clint sent up a silent prayer that Eve would get away without being stopped.

"Where are your pals, Canaday?" he asked, feigning friendliness.

"Curly hightailed it after I put ol' Bart out of his misery," Canaday said. "Pete's takin' a piss. He'll be in shortly. Sure could use some hot coffee."

"Have a chair. I'll put some on." Nerves screaming, Clint willed himself to move slowly and purposefully as he leaned the shotgun against the counter, filled the enameled coffeepot and set it on the stove. The task bought him a little time to size up the situation. It didn't look good. Canaday wouldn't have dropped by for a casual visit. He'd ridden here through the storm for a reason. And the man had known exactly where Clint could be found. Somebody must have told him.

As he remembered Eve's lost message of warning, Clint could guess who that somebody was. Etta Simpkins had unmasked her true loyalty.

Too late, Clint realized his big mistake had been not shooting Canaday the second he'd opened the door. He might have done it if he'd foreseen that the man would walk in alone. Instead Clint had tried to bluff, feigning innocence—not the best move.

Canaday had come to kill him—no doubt about that. But the man would take his time, playing with his intended victim like a cat playing with a mouse, drawing out the suspense until the death blow. For now the outlaw, known to be a lightning draw, had his hand resting on his pistol. Clint had set the shotgun close by to make the coffee. He could go for the weapon, but he'd likely be dead before he could raise and fire it.

His ears strained for the sound of hoofbeats that would tell him Eve had made her getaway. Nothing—but she could still be hiding from the man outside. If gunfire could provide the diversion she needed to reach her horse, going for the rifle might be worth the risk. At least if he died, it would be for a good reason.

Canaday was watching him from the seat he'd taken near the door. His pale eyes followed Clint's every move. The man hadn't lived this long by lowering his guard. His hair-trigger nerves were on full alert. For Clint to gain any advantage he would need some kind of distraction.

That distraction came an instant later in the

form of a shout from the man outside, the one called Pete. "Hey, Canaday! I got a surprise for you!"

For a split second Canaday glanced toward the sound. Clint grabbed the shotgun and cocked it. But before he could fire, the door, kicked by Pete's heavy boot, flew open.

Clutched in front of the man, her arm twisted behind her back and a pistol shoved hard against her temple, was Eve.

The man's grip sent pain ripping up Eve's arm and into her neck. But the pain was the least of her worries now. It was Clint's expression, as he saw her, that tore at her heart.

The big, dirty-looking man in the chair laughed. "Quite a prize you caught there, Pete. Put that shotgun down easy, Lonigan, and kick it over here. It would be a damned shame to have this purty lady's brains splattered all over your wall, wouldn't it now?"

Clint did as he was told, lowering the rifle to the floor and sliding it away with his boot. In his eyes, Eve read helpless fury. He would risk his own life, but he would not risk hers.

Her father's lessons in courage flashed through her mind. *Never give up*, he'd told her time and time again. At some point it would be up to her to act. Otherwise Clint might not take action to save himself.

The man in the chair grinned. "Hell, Pete, you look like you been clawed up by a wildcat."

"She got me good, Canaday," the man muttered. And she had. Eve had kicked, bitten and clawed the man with the strength of terror, gouging skin and drawing blood, before he got her arm twisted behind her.

"I'd have killed your man if I'd had a weapon." Eve spoke up boldly. "My name is Eve Townsend, Dowager Countess of Manderfield, and I order you to release me at once."

The man named Canaday rose, leering down at her. He was huge and ugly, with the glint of madness in his eye. "Uppity little bitch, ain't you? Well, your highness, let's see how fancy you look on your back, with your petticoats up and your royal knees in the air."

A snarl of rage rose in Clint's throat. Sliding his pistol out of its holster, Canaday swung toward him. "You got somethin' to say 'bout this, Lonigan? Is this little tart your woman?"

"Not mine. She belongs to Roderick Hanford. Lay a finger on her and Hanford will have you thrown to his dogs."

Canaday frowned. "Heard about them dogs. Meaner than hellhounds, they say. But I ain't worried about Hanford. By the time he gits what's left of his woman back I'll be long gone."

"Don't be a fool, Canaday. Hanford will pay anything to get her back—a lot more than you could make raiding homesteads, which won't be easy with just two men. You could collect the ransom, return the countess and ride out of here a rich man."

"Maybe. But it won't hurt to have a little fun with the lady first. 'Specially since I already got the itch for her."

Replacing the gun in its holster, he loosed a small coil of rope from his belt. "Turn around, Lonigan, hands behind your back. Behave yourself and I'll even let you watch."

Eve caught the flash of rage in Clint's eyes as he turned to one side. He was like a coiled spring, ready to strike. Even so, he'd be hesitant to risk her life. She had to make her move soon. Whatever happened, she couldn't let Canaday tie Clint's hands.

She could feel the cold steel muzzle against her temple. But surely Pete wouldn't risk Canaday's anger by shooting a valuable captive, especially a woman Canaday was about to enjoy raping. She had to take that chance.

Canaday yanked a tangle out of the rope and reached for Clint's wrists. "How 'bout you, Pete?" he asked, without glancing around. "You want a poke at the lady when I'm done?"

"Sure. Why not?" Pete chuckled. "Ain't had one this purty in a 'coon's age."

With his thoughts elsewhere, Pete's grip on her arm slackened. Sensing his distraction, Eve made her move. With an attention-getting moan, she went completely limp, slumping forward in her best imitation of a dead faint.

Caught off guard, Pete wasn't prepared to hold her weight. Eve felt the wrenching pain as her twisted arm pulled free. Eyes closed, body inert, she fell across the gunman's boots.

"What the hell—" Pete lurched forward, stumbling as she caught his leg and yanked him off balance. His pistol crashed to the floor and spun out of reach.

In a lightning-fast move, Clint dived for the shotgun, swung it upward and fired point-blank at Canaday's chest. The shot rang like a thunderclap in the small space of the cabin. Canaday staggered backward, eyes wild, hand clawing for his pistol. As he went down, he yanked it free and pulled the trigger.

The shot should have gone wild, but it didn't. Eve heard the roar of the big .45 and saw Clint spin sideways, crimson staining his shoulder, spreading fast.

"No!" The cry left her throat as she seized the pistol Pete had dropped. Clutching the weapon, she sat up. She'd meant to finish off Canaday if she had to, but a glance showed the outlaw lying sprawled on the pine floor, blank eyes staring upward and blood spreading beneath his body.

Pete had clambered upright and was cowering against the door frame with his hands raised. "For the love of God, don't shoot me, lady," he whimpered. "All I want is to get the hell out of here."

"Then go!" Eve kept the pistol aimed as the gunslinger backed out the door, pulling it shut behind him. The sound of departing hooves mingled with the drizzling rain as she rose and lunged toward Clint.

He was slumped against a table leg, where he'd gone down. One hand clutched his wounded shoulder. Blood was streaming between his fingers. So much blood.

Eve had never tended a wound in her life. But

she was the only help he had. "Tell me what to do," she said.

"Get something to stop the blood," he muttered between clenched teeth. "A sheet, a pillowcase…"

The quilt he'd wrapped her in earlier had fallen under the table. She pulled it next to him. "Lie down. I'll get something."

He sagged onto the quilt while she raced into the bedroom, returning with a pillow and a flannel sheet from the bed. In her absence, he'd managed to roll onto his back. He lay on the quilt, his face ashen in the flickering light of the stove.

Eve's hands shook as she bent over him, but this was no time for weakness. Nothing mattered but saving this man's life.

Wadding one end of the sheet, she pressed it against the wound.

"Harder…" His voice was gritty with pain. "Put your weight into it…"

Eve feared hurting him worse, but she did as he'd asked, leaning hard to put pressure on the wound.

"That's my girl." His attempt at a smile was more like a grimace. "Now listen. The bullet went through, so you'll need to put something underneath."

"Don't try to talk. I understand." After wadding the other end of the sheet she stuffed it under his shoulder and pressed hard. If she couldn't stop the bleeding, Clint would die—and her world would be empty without him. If she hadn't known it before, she knew it now.

Pressing down hard with her hands, she sent up a silent prayer. She would give anything to keep this man alive. But what was there for her to give?

"What about Canaday?" He spoke as if every word cost him strength.

"He's dead. And Pete ran off. We're all alone here." She knew she ought to drag Canaday's foul body onto the porch. But for now she couldn't leave Clint's side. If only somebody would show up to help—somebody with the knowledge to treat his wound and save his life.

He was shivering on the cold floor, but she was afraid to move him even as far as his bed. Freeing one hand, she pulled the sides of the quilt over and around his body and worked the pillow beneath his head. Her thick woolen cloak was damp but still warm. She spread it over him to anchor the quilt and hold in the meager heat.

"Thanks," he murmured, sounding weaker.

"Don't talk, my love." Leaning down, she brushed a kiss across his cool, pale lips. Crimson blood was still seeping into the worn flannel sheet. Maybe she should check the wound. But that would mean removing the pressure.

Time crawled past. By now the fire in the stove had burned down to coals. The rain had stopped, and the sky outside the kitchen window was streaked with dawn's first gray light.

Eve lay with her hand on the bloodied sheet and her head on Clint's chest. His eyes were closed, his breathing shallow. Only the slow, steady pulse of his heart told Eve that his body was still fighting for life. She'd gotten up twice to get him water, but he'd been almost too weak to swallow.

If only someone would come—maybe Anders Yost or one of his other neighbors. Her lips moved in a silent plea to heaven. *Please send someone...anyone...before it's too late.*

As if in answer to her prayer, she heard the faint jingle of harness and the snort of a horse as a buggy approached from the direction of the road. Her heart leaped. She could only pray that the driver was friend not foe—and that help hadn't arrived too late.

Moments later, the buggy pulled up to the house and the tread of heavy footfalls rang across the porch. From where she sat near the foot of the table, Eve could see just the lower part of the door. She forgot to breathe as it swung open and a pair of shiny calfskin riding boots, lightly spattered with mud, stepped through.

Her stomach twisted. She recognized those boots, and she knew who'd be wearing them.

"Hello, Eve," Roderick said. "I've come to take you home."

Eve remained where she was, crouching over Clint like a falcon protecting its wounded mate. Roderick took another step toward her. Now Eve saw that someone else had come in behind him. Hans's shaggy, hulking figure filled the doorway.

Stepping over Canaday's body, Roderick glanced down at Clint. "Is he alive?"

"For the moment, yes, but he was wounded saving me," Eve said. "I'm not going anywhere without him." Her defiance melted as she caught the hard glint in her brother-in-law's eye. "Please, Roderick. If you leave him here, he'll die. I'll come willingly, but only if you save him."

Roderick scowled, brushing a fleck off the sleeve of his tweed jacket. Eve held her breath, knowing her brother-in-law was capable of walking away, leaving Clint to bleed to death.

Like a Roman emperor weighing the fate of a downed gladiator, he let the suspense drag out before he spoke. "Very well. Carry him to the buggy and do what you can for him, Hans. If he survives, the man may yet prove useful to me."

Light-headed with relief, Eve moved aside as the giant man approached. Hans worked his arms under the blanket and lifted Clint as if he were no bigger than a child. With Roderick's grip firm on her arm, she followed them outside to a gray morning.

Two mounted cowboys, whom Eve recognized as Roderick's hands, had rounded up her horse and Canaday's and tethered them to a lead rope. Only as she climbed onto the front seat of the buggy did she remember Canaday's dead body, still lying where the outlaw had fallen.

Roderick had taken his seat beside her and picked up the reins. Turning toward him, she touched his sleeve. "That dead man in the house—he needs to be buried."

"Not worth the time and sweat." Roderick gave her a sour look, then motioned to one of the cowhands. "Burn the house," he ordered as the buggy pulled away. "What the hell, run the animals out and burn the barn, too. Burn it all!"

Clint woke to warm darkness and the rank smell of dog. For the first few moments he was confused. Ghosts of memory drifted through his mind—Canaday's gunshot and the burn of lead, Eve bending over him as his thoughts spiraled into darkness, then the odd sensation of being carried in a giant's powerful arms. How much of what he remembered had been real?

As the fog began to clear, he became aware that he was lying on his back on what felt like an old buffalo robe. Above him he could make out what looked like log rafters overlaid with rough-sawn planks. So he was in some kind of cabin—but not his own.

Pushing an arm beneath him, he tried to sit up. The effort triggered a tearing pain in his right shoulder. So he'd been wounded—that memory, at least, had been real. Sinking onto his back again he explored the injury with his left hand. The wound had been dressed, the shoulder wrapped in strips of cloth. Under the wrappings he could feel a damp, spongy lump—some kind of poultice, he guessed, most likely an Indian remedy. Whatever it was, it seemed to be doing its work. As long as he remained still, there was little pain—just a tingling sensation that told him the wound was already starting to heal.

But where in hell's name was he?

That question was answered a moment later when light from a lantern, held high, fell across the bed where he lay. As a hulking form bent over him, he recognized Roderick Hanford's socalled master of the hounds. So this dark, odiferous place must be where the man lived. And that meant Clint was on Hanford's property.

"What in blazes is going on?" Clint demanded, before he remembered that the man was mute. Hans—that was the name he had heard him called.

Hanging the lantern on a hook, Hans placed a finger to his lips. Now Clint noticed that he'd set a small pottery bowl, with a spoon in it, on the upright log that served as a bedside table. With surprising care, he raised Clint's shoulders and bunched a pillow underneath, so that he was half sitting. When the giant picked up the bowl again and stirred its contents, Clint realized he was about to be spoon-fed. The brown mixture in the bowl smelled like skunk cabbage or some other noxious weed, and he'd wager the spoon was none too clean. But he was too weak to fight off a man even half Hans's size. When the spoon was lifted to his lips, Clint opened his mouth and took his medicine. It tasted as bad as it smelled, but Hans showed him no mercy until the bowl was empty.

"Do you have water?" The lingering taste of the medicine was foul in Clint's throat.

Hans left the room with the bowl and returned with a battered tin canteen. Compared to the food, the water was sweet and clean and cool. Clint drank all he could hold, then settled back onto the pillow. "Thank you, Hans," he murmured.

As if unaccustomed to gratitude, the big man averted his eyes and shuffled out of the room.

The fog was lifting from Clint's mind. He forced himself to think. He had only vague memories of what had happened after the gunshot, but if Hans was taking care of him, he must be at Hanford's place by the man's orders—as much a prisoner as a patient. To get up and go outside would be to alarm Hanford's dogs—as effective a deterrent to trying to leave as if Clint were in a locked cell. For the moment he had little choice except to remain here and gather his strength until the time came to use it.

Questions swarmed in his mind. Why had Hanford brought him here instead of killing him on the spot? What did the bastard have in mind for him—and where was Eve? If Hanford had taken him, he would have taken her, too. She would be somewhere close by, a prisoner just as he was, locked in her room, perhaps, and forbidden to see her beloved niece and nephew.

Clint wasn't worried about Hanford hurting her physically—the man wanted her too much for that. Clint had seen the hungry looks he gave her, and the possessive way he walked beside her in town. But there were other ways to hurt, other ways to punish, and Roderick Hanford was the sadistic master of them all.

Eve stood at the bedroom window staring out at the dawn. She'd been locked in her room for nearly twenty-four hours, more than time enough to change her wet clothes for a simple cotton dress and pace the carpet in endless anxiety. She was exhausted, but sleep had been impossible. The meals Beth Ann had brought her had gone untouched, and she'd seen nothing of the children. For all she knew, their part in her escape had been discovered and they were locked away, too.

What would she do if Roderick had beaten them again? But that thought was too painful to pursue.

From the back window she could see the compound where the dogs were kenneled. She could see the roof of the cabin and the top of Han's shaggy head as he moved among the dogs, shoveling their waste and dousing the graveled floors of their pens with buckets of water.

She hadn't seen Clint since Hans carried him into the kennel compound. The big man had handled him as gently as one might move a sleeping child to bed. But Hans was Roderick's man. He would follow the orders the cattleman gave him. By now Clint could be dead, his body thrown to the dogs.

As the morning sun crawled up the sky, Eve grew even more agitated. From the front of the house she could hear the sounds of an arriving buggy, accompanied by mounted men. Something, she sensed, was about to happen. Something unthinkable.

She was pacing the rug in helpless fury when she heard the sound of a key in the lock. Roderick walked into the room, dressed in a suit and wearing a holstered pistol at his hip. The sight of the gun chilled Eve's blood. What was happening?

"Fix your hair and put on a pretty gown, Eve," he said. "You'll want to look your best this morning."

"This will have to do." Her gesture took in her everyday hairstyle and plain lilac dress. She was through dressing up like a doll for the man to show off.

"Suit yourself." He dismissed the matter as if he had more urgent things on his mind. "I'll be back for you in fifteen minutes."

He was about to close the door when she spoke his name. He paused, one eyebrow sliding upward.

"Where are Rose and Thomas?" she asked. "Are they all right?"

"The children are fine. Beth Ann is taking care of them. When you're ready to behave as a loyal member of our family, I'll consider letting you see them again."

The door closed with a click, the key turning in the lock.

Nerves screaming, Eve forced herself to eat the cold oatmeal and dry bread Beth Ann had left her for breakfast. Whatever was about to happen downstairs, she was going to need her strength.

A few minutes later Roderick was back, unlocking the door and offering his arm to escort her downstairs. She moved beside him like a sleepwalker, feeling as if she were on her way to an execution.

An execution...

Her pulse lurched as the realization struck home. Was that what she was about to see? Was that why Roderick had ordered Hans to save Clint—to make a spectacle of killing him later?

Stepping out of the dim entry into the sunlight, she was blinded for a moment by the glare. As her eyes adjusted, she saw Judge McCutcheon, dressed in a suit and standing next to his buggy. A few paces to his left, four armed men, their horses waiting behind them, flanked a standing figure whose hands were bound behind his back. Eve stifled a cry. It was Clint.

His bloodshot eyes met hers through the sunlit haze. His skin was pale, his mouth covered by a tightly bound bandanna. At least he was alive. But for how long?

Mounting the porch steps, Judge McCutcheon turned to face the prisoner. Only then did

Eve realize what she was witnessing. It was the end of a trial—a mocking travesty of a trial in which the defendant was gagged and the verdict was a foregone conclusion. Only the judge was legitimate.

McCutcheon cleared his throat. "Clint Lonigan, having been found guilty of kidnapping Countess Eve Townsend and murdering Mr. Edward Canaday, I hereby sentence you to be taken to the place of execution and hanged by the neck until dead, sentence to be carried out immediately."

Chapter Fifteen

"No!" The cry burst from Eve's throat as she flung herself in front of the judge. "Clint didn't kidnap me! I went with him willingly! And he shot Canaday in self-defense. Look at his wound! Canaday did that!"

"Control yourself, Eve." With an iron grip on her forearms, Roderick yanked her back to stand beside him. "His Honor isn't finished. Be still and listen to what he has to say."

"However..." McCutcheon's gaze circuited the watchers, lingering on Eve before returning to Clint. "However grave the nature your crimes, Mr. Lonigan, Roderick Hanford has spoken up on your behalf. Mr. Hanford has persuaded this court to be merciful—on one condition."

In the silence, Eve's gaze locked with Clint's.

Even with his mouth gagged, his eyes were defiant. Beneath the crude bandage that wrapped his shoulder he was still wearing his blood-stained denim shirt. But he stood tall, his back straight, his head high and proud. He had saved his friends and neighbors from a deadly threat. If the price to be paid was his life, she could see that he would meet his fate like a man. But *she* was not willing to see him pay that price.

Heaven help her, she would do anything to save him.

After a dramatic pause, McCutcheon turned toward Eve. "Mrs. Townsend, as a judge, I'm legally authorized to perform marriages, and I've taken the liberty of having the necessary papers drawn up. You can absolve this man of the charges against him by consenting to become Mrs. Roderick Hanford here and now."

Eve sucked in air, strangling in her tightly laced corset. Her knees had gone liquid, threatening to collapse beneath her. Seeing her sway, Roderick took her arm and patted her hand. "Think of the children, Eve, dear," he said. "Think of the life we could have here together. You know I'm doing the right thing. One day you'll thank me."

You're a monster! Part of her wanted to fly

at him and claw his face. But there was no way out of this. Roderick had won. If her marrying him could save Clint's life there was no way she could refuse.

Sick with dismay, Clint watched Eve's resolve crumble. He had no doubt what her answer would be. He wanted to call out to her, but the gag, and the wadded handkerchief stuffed in his mouth beneath it, kept him from uttering a word.

No! he wanted to shout at her. *Don't do it! There's more going on here than you know!*

His beautiful, brave, tender Eve was about to give herself to an evil man—a man who couldn't be trusted. She thought she was saving his life, but he knew better. She was only sacrificing her own. And there was nothing he could do to stop her.

"We're waiting for your answer, Mrs. Townsend," McCutcheon said.

Eve's face had gone moon pale. The eyes that held Clint's across the distance pleaded for understanding. When she spoke it was scarcely above a whisper.

"My answer is yes, I will consent to marry Mr. Hanford."

Roderick's smile was as broad and as wicked as a crocodile's. "Then please proceed with the ceremony, Seth," he said.

"Wait." Eve's head was up, her gaze determined. Only her shaking voice betrayed her emotions. "Before we go any further, I want your promise that Mr. Lonigan will be cleared of all charges and released."

The judge nodded. "Mr. Lonigan has been charged with kidnapping and murder. For the record, in the presence of these witnesses, I declare those charges dismissed."

"And his release?" Eve demanded.

"In due course. After the ceremony. So let us proceed."

She lowered her gaze as the judge began reading the vows. "Dearly beloved, we are gathered here before God and these witnesses to join this man and this woman in holy matrimony…"

Glancing up at a movement in an upstairs window, Clint saw Roderick's two children watching, with Beth Ann behind them. The girl's expression was as sour as vinegar. She'd probably hoped to snag Hanford for herself—which was why she'd gone to him with Eve's message. But her scheme had come to nothing.

"Do you, Roderick Hanford, take this

woman…" the judge droned. Clint willed his ears to block the words and Roderick's sonorous *I do*. Behind his back, his hands twisted and pulled at the strip of rawhide that Hans, on Roderick's orders, had used to bind his wrists. To his surprise, Clint felt the slightest loosening. The rawhide, he realized, was damp enough to stretch, as if it had been left in the rain and not fully dried.

Had Hans failed to notice the rawhide's condition, or had the mute giant, who'd treated Clint with kindness, tried to help him in the only way he could?

Keeping his arms still, Clint continued to stretch the rawhide with his wrists, feeling its tightness slowly begin to yield. Working it loose enough to free his hands would take precious minutes—too much time to save Eve from her tragic mistake. Clint wasn't even sure he could save himself. But he'd been given one small chance—a chance he couldn't afford to waste.

"Do you, Eve Townsend, take this man to be your lawfully wedded husband…"

As the judge's voice rumbled on, Eve's gaze rose to the upstairs window, where Rose and Thomas stood watching with Beth Ann. She had married once to save her father from debt and disgrace. Now she was marrying to free her lover and to ensure that she would always be there for Margaret's children. As for Roderick, much as she despised him, she would bear her misery, knowing her sacrifice had saved the man she loved. But she would give ten years of her life to have had things turn out differently.

Her eyes lingered on him for one last, loving moment. Clint had shown her the sweetness that could bind a man and a woman—something she would never know again. But wherever life took him, her heart would go—a heart she could never give to another man.

"Do you, Mrs. Townsend?" Seth McCutcheon's voice prompted her. Eve willed her emotions to freeze.

"I do." She spoke the bitter words and it was done. She stood like a winter icicle as Roderick slipped a ring on her finger. Then she took the pen with a shaking hand and bent to sign the marriage document.

She could feel Clint's eyes on her, but she couldn't bear to return his gaze. The unthinkable had come to pass. She was Mrs. Roderick Hanford.

Roderick slipped a controlling hand around

her waist. "Come, Eve, dear, let's go inside and introduce the children to their new mother."

"No! Wait!" She pulled away from him to face the judge again. "I want to know you'll keep your promise!"

McCutcheon regarded her with a cold stare. "But I already have. Lonigan's been cleared of kidnapping and murder."

"Then let him go!"

"I can't do that, Mrs. Hanford. The prisoner has yet to be tried on a third charge—cattle rustling, a hanging offense in these parts."

"Cattle rustling!" Eve bridled. "That's ridiculous! And how can you hold a trial if the defendant can't even speak for himself?"

"That's enough, Eve. Come on inside." Roderick tugged at her arm.

Still confronting the judge, she ignored her new husband. "At least let him speak in his own defense," she insisted.

"All right." McCutcheon nodded to one of his men. "Let's hear what he has to say for himself. Remove the gag."

The bandanna was untied and pulled away, revealing Clint's grimly set mouth. To Eve, he looked as defiant as a captive eagle.

The judge cleared his throat. "Clint Lonigan, to the charge of cattle rustling, how do you plead?"

"The only cattle I've ever rustled were the ones you stole from me and my neighbors."

"Then you plead guilty."

"If you say so, you conniving bastard."

"Then I sentence you to be hanged, sentence to be carried out immediately." McCutcheon signaled his men. "Take him away."

"Liar!" Eve lunged toward the judge. In her fury she might have attacked him if Roderick hadn't seized her shoulders and pulled her back.

"You're my wife now, Eve," he said. "I order you to stop making a scene and come into the house this minute."

"No!" She hurled the word at him. "You tricked me into this marriage! Don't you ever come near me again!"

Roderick's big hand shot up and cracked across her face, hard enough to explode stars in her brain. As she reeled to one side, she saw that Clint's hands were free. He was bolting for one of the horses that stood behind his guards. But the four men were already after him, closing in to pull him down. If they caught him, he'd be too weak to fight them off.

Twisting toward Roderick, she whipped his

pistol out of its holster and jammed the muzzle into her husband's back.

"Let him go," she said. "Don't tempt me to make myself a widow—believe me, I'd pull this trigger in a heartbeat."

The guards froze. "Don't do this, Eve," the judge said. "You're already guilty of aiding a criminal. Shoot your husband and I'll see that you hang for murder."

Eve willed herself to ignore him. Clint had reached a horse and managed to clamber into the saddle. But he'd opened up his wound again. Fresh blood seeped into the wrappings on his shoulder.

For an instant he hesitated, his gaze seeking out Eve as if to make sure she was safe.

Go! Her mouth shaped the word. He swung the bay horse toward the gate and spurred it to a gallop. Clint had made his escape, but he was weak and bleeding, with no place to take refuge. His home was gone and soon he'd have armed men on his trail. Alone, what were his chances?

In a flash Eve made up her mind. "Bring me a horse—that roan," she ordered. When the guards hesitated she jammed the gun harder into Roderick's back, hard enough to hurt. "Tell them to do it!"

"Bring the damned horse," Roderick snarled. "The woman's crazy enough to kill me."

The horse was led to the foot of the steps. As Eve turned to mount, Roderick took advantage of the vulnerable instant. His powerful hand seized her wrist and twisted it. Pain shot up her arm. The pistol dropped from her hand and clattered to the ground. She could try to get it or she could run.

Roderick was reaching for the fallen weapon when she broke free and sprang into the saddle. Did he have the gun? Would he shoot at her? There was no time to look back. Crouching low over the horse's neck, she dug her heels into its flanks and thundered toward the gate.

Where would Clint go? He might not be aware that his ranch was ashes. Even so, he wouldn't go where he could easily be found. Nor would he endanger his friends by seeking shelter with them. She realized he would likely head for the mountains, where the trails were as familiar to him as his own face.

Acting on a hunch, she galloped the big roan down the road toward Crow Hollow, where she and the children had picnicked. If he'd gone this way, she had a chance of catching him. Her horse was carrying the lighter load, and Clint's injury might force him to a slower pace.

She would no doubt be followed, as would Clint. The last thing she wanted was to lead their pursuers right to him. But if she didn't find him he could pass out and bleed to death.

All she could do was keep moving—and pray for a miracle.

By the time he swung off the road at Crow Hollow and headed up the canyon toward the ridge, Clint's vision had begun to blur. He'd felt his wound open up when he'd sprung for the horse, and the seepage had already soaked through the bandages. If he didn't pack the wound with something, grass or leaves if nothing else, he would soon pass out from blood loss.

He needed to stop, and soon. The trouble was, someone was on his trail. From down the slope he could hear the horse breaking through the thicket—the crackle of brush, the snort of a straining animal. Startled by the sound, a raven flapped upward, croaking an alarm.

His ears told him it was a single rider. Was it Hanford, hot on his trail and primed for the kill? If so, the pursuit wouldn't end until one of them was dead. If he had a gun, Clint groused, he could lie in wait and hope for a lucky shot. But he was weaponless and as weak as a newborn calf. His only chance was to get away or hide.

Dizzy, he rested his head against the horse's warm neck. This wouldn't do. He had to get off the trail before he lost consciousness. Sliding out of the saddle, he led the horse back in the aspens and tethered it where it wasn't likely to be seen. Then, hidden by undergrowth, he belly-crawled forward to where he could see the trail through the brush. If the other rider passed without spotting him, maybe then he could do something about his shoulder.

His pursuer was coming closer. Clint could see flashes of a roan coat through the green leaves. As the horse came into view, Clint flattened himself against the earth. Let Roderick Hanford spot him now, and he was a dead man.

He held his breath. Then he saw her, leaning forward in the saddle, her gaze on the ground.

"Eve..." Struggling to stay conscious, he rasped out her name.

Eve had been following the splotches of crimson on the leaves and on the ground. At least she knew she was on Lonigan's trail. But he had to be losing blood fast. He couldn't be far ahead. But she didn't dare call out to him. Someone following behind her might hear her voice.

Her ears caught the sound of her name. Had it been the wind? She turned in the saddle, seeing nothing at first but dense green thicket. Then her eyes caught a slight movement. The silhouette of a man's prone body took shape behind the screen of undergrowth.

With a muffled cry, she was off the horse, running to him, parting the prickly brush. He raised his head, even that small movement costing him effort. "Get the horse out of sight," he said.

"Yes. I'll be right back." Finding Clint had erased practical thought from her mind. Thank heavens he was still thinking clearly. She'd almost forgotten that others would be on their trail, perhaps close behind her. She led the roan off into the trees and tethered it near the bay horse Clint had ridden. Taking the canteen she'd found slung over the saddle horn, she hurried back to him.

In her short absence he'd managed to roll onto his back.

Dropping to the ground, she cradled his

head on her knees and tipped the canteen to his mouth. He took several swallows, then motioned her hand away. "What are you doing here?" he demanded, keeping his voice low.

"Hush, don't try to talk," she whispered. "You've lost a lot of blood."

"I asked you a question." His callused fingers gripped her arm, almost hurting. "You were safe. You'd gained legal access to your sister's children. Damn it, Eve, you'd married the rich bastard. All you had to do was put up with him and you were set for life. So I'm asking you again, what in hell's name are you doing here?"

"What do you think?" Pulling away from him, Eve scooped dry leaves to pillow his head, then rose to step out of her white cotton petticoat. "You were bleeding, and I knew they'd be after you." She tore at the ruffled hem, yanking it off in one long strip, then ripped the rest of the petticoat in half. "How could I let you ride off alone?"

Eve examined the old, blood-soaked dressing that covered the wound and decided that for now, peeling it away would do more harm than good. But she had to stanch the bleeding. He mouthed a silent curse as she wadded a piece of the petticoat against his wound and pressed down with all her strength, just as he'd told her to do before. It had to hurt, but she remembered his admonition to put as much pressure on it as she could to slow the bleeding.

"Hanford won't forgive you for this." He spoke through pain-clenched teeth. "He'll have you arrested for stealing a horse and aiding a criminal. And that crooked judge will back him all the way. You won't stand a chance against them."

"Hush. Don't try to talk." Helping him sit up, she began wrapping the wound with the long fabric strip she'd torn from her petticoat ruffle, looping it around his neck to keep the bandage from slipping down his arm.

"Damn it, Eve, you're not thinking. What about the children? All you wanted was to be there for them."

Eve split the ends of the wrapping and tied a tight knot. From the remaining piece of petticoat she fashioned a triangular sling to support the arm and help keep the wound from opening up again. But even as she kept her hands busy, her mind turned over his words. True, leaving Rose and Thomas had been a heartbreaking choice. The children would be safe and decently cared for, but they'd counted on her to be there for them. She refused to believe they were lost to her forever. Somehow she would find a way. As their stepmother, surely she would have some right to see them. But that would have to wait. With the future yawning before her like a black pit of uncertainty, all she could do was deal with the here and now. And the here and now was Clint.

The only thing that could matter was that she loved him.

Positioning his arm, she knotted the sling at the back of his neck. "Can you get to your horse?"

He nodded, his mouth set in a line of pain. After pushing himself to his feet he declined her proffered arm and made his way back to where the horses were tied.

Facing her, he took her hand. "Eve, you've done all you can for me. Now I want you to take the horse and go back. Circle around so you won't meet anybody coming up the trail. Tell Hanford you got lost, or that you changed your mind and decided to come home."

She stared up at him, knowing this wasn't what she wanted. "But where will you go? You must know that Roderick had your ranch burned."

"Yes. He laughed when he told me. But there's an old line shack in the mountains. My friends know about it. I can stay there till my shoulder heals. After that…" He shrugged. "I don't know. I may have to leave the territory. But one thing I do know, my love, is that you can't come with me. The life I'm looking at is no life for a lady."

"Please, Clint." She knew he was right, knew that no argument she could offer would make any sense, but the thought that she might never see him again was tearing her apart.

"Listen to me." He clasped her hand tighter. "I love you, Eve. If things were different, I'd fall on my knees and beg you to be my wife. But that's not possible. Right now, the most loving thing I can do for you is let you go."

Giving in at last, she flung an arm around his neck and felt him pull her close. "I'm not making this easy for you," she whispered. "But know that I'll never stop loving you. Wherever you go, a part of me will be with you. And when you come back—if you come back—I'll be here, waiting."

Foolish words from a woman married to another man, but she wanted him to hear them and remember.

"Forget me, Eve." His mouth found hers. He kissed her long and deep, then pulled away. "Now go. Be safe, my love."

He mounted with effort, gripping the saddle horn with his free hand and swinging his leg over. Determined not to cry in front of him, Eve hitched up her skirt and climbed onto the roan. She was waiting for him to wheel away and head up the ridge when the breeze carried a sound up the slope to her ears—a faint howling, baying sound that chilled her to the marrow of her bones.

Clint glanced at her with questioning eyes. But something told Eve he already knew.

"The dogs," she said. "Roderick's coming after us with his hounds."

Chapter Sixteen

Clint listened in silence, gauging the direction, distance and speed of the pack. They were following his blood trail up the canyon, coming fast. Cold sweat formed a bead on his cheek. Even with the fresh bandage, he was still bleeding. Lord help him, he would rather face an armed posse with a rope than be torn to pieces by Hanford's dogs. But he had run out of choices. Right now, what mattered most was getting Eve to safety.

"Go!" he urged her. "Circle south along the ridge and cut down the next canyon. Go through the creek to cover your scent. If you get away now you should be safe enough. It's me the dogs are after."

"No." She lifted her chin defiantly. "I'm not leaving you."

Clint cursed under his breath. "This is no time to be stubborn. Get going!"

"Listen to me!" she said. "Those dogs won't stop till they find you and bring you down. But they know my scent, and they're less liable to attack me. I might be able to distract them while you get away. Or if Roderick's there—as he surely will be—I may be able to bargain for your life. You won't have a chance without me. You've got to keep me with you."

Clint would have chosen to face his end with her safely gone. But there was no time to argue. The hellish baying told him the dogs were racing up the slope toward them, minutes away.

"Come on then!" He urged the horse forward. Eve followed close behind on the roan. But they had no hope of outdistancing the pack. Here, where the narrow trail zigzagged across the slope to mount the ridge, there was no way a horse could run without risking a fall. They'd have to climb slowly, carefully. The sure-footed hounds would have no such problem. They could head straight uphill.

It seemed a lifetime before Clint and Eve reached the top of the ridge. Here the trail leveled out above the outcrop where they'd taken shelter from the storm. Below them, the face of the steep limestone cliff was honeycombed with caves. Given the chance, they might be able to climb down to a spot where the dogs couldn't reach them. But that would be wasted effort. Even if they found a secure cave, Hanford could bide his time and starve them into the open.

The horses could hear the pack, and likely smell them, too. They were dancing in terror, snorting and rolling their eyes, making the climb even more dangerous for their riders.

Eve was struggling to control the roan. Clint had one last chance to get her out of here. "Go," he insisted. "If you head down into the trees you could still get away."

"Not unless you come with me. If—" Her words ended in a shriek as her horse reared and bucked, arching high like a wild bronc. Eve flew out of the saddle, lost the reins and landed with a thud on the hard ground. She lay on her back, eyes closed, as the roan bolted off the ridge and down the steep, wooded hill on the far side.

Was she hurt, even dead? Clint only knew that he couldn't leave her. With what little remained of his strength he slid out of the saddle and dragged himself to her side. He could hear the sliding rocks and breaking brush as his horse fled, thundering off the ridge in a panic. Now, with no horses and no weapons, they were truly out of options. If need be, he would die right here, protecting Eve as best he could.

Sick with dread, he laid a finger alongside her throat to feel for her pulse. At his touch she stirred and opened her eyes.

"Are you all right?" She stared up at him.

He grinned in relief. "Since you just got bucked off a horse, I should be asking you that question."

She shifted, flexed her arms and legs and managed to sit up. "I seem to be fine," she said. "Just stunned, I think—and lucky."

"Then let's get the hell out of here." Rising with effort, he pulled her up beside him. Still unsteady, she clung to his arm as they made their way across the outcrop above the cliff.

"Maybe we can still climb down into one of the caves," he said, trying to offer a thread of hope. "At least it would buy us a chance to rest."

Eve's clasp tightened on his arm. She shook her head, knowing, as he did, that they'd run out of time, with no place left to go. For better or for worse, this was where they'd make their last stand. "I love you, Clint Lonigan," she said.

"And I love you, my beautiful countess," he

said. "But if you have a chance to save yourself, for God's sake, don't think twice. Just do it."

Eve didn't reply. Once, there might have been a chance that Roderick would take her back. But she had crossed the line and wounded his manly pride. He would no more forgive her than he would Clint.

The hideous baying had risen to a nightmarish din. Clint pulled her against him as the dogs came pouring over the ridge, yellow teeth flashing, wet tongues lolling from their long run up the hill. Only two men had come with them. Roderick rode at their heels, still dressed in his wedding suit, with his pistol at his hip. Behind him, mounted on the biggest mule Eve had ever seen, came Hans.

Clint stepped up to protect her. "No," she said, moving in front of him. "They know me."

Still barreling toward them, the dogs were an easy stone's toss away when Hans raised his steel whistle and blew two short, earsplitting blasts. The pack halted as if hitting an invisible wall.

So two blasts on the whistle means stop. Eve remembered that fearful night when *three* short blasts had sent the hounds rushing back to their kennels. Brutish as they looked, these animals were intelligent and superbly trained. No wonder Roderick had had so many offers to buy them.

The dogs milled in a restless knot, growling and whining, but none of them made an aggressive move as Roderick dismounted, dropped the reins and strode to the front of the pack. Eve's eyes met Hans's across the distance. What was the man thinking? How deep was his devotion to Roderick? Had his torture by the Pawnee so inured him to pain and death that he could watch a pack of dogs rip a helpless man and woman to pieces?

Pistol drawn, Roderick stopped a half dozen paces from where Eve and Clint stood. "Would you beg me on your knees, Eve?" he asked. "Would you vow to be a faithful and proper wife if I agreed to pardon you?"

"Only if you promised to pardon Clint, too." Her voice was flat and cold. "But that's what you promised me before, wasn't it? That was the only reason I married you. And you betrayed me. Maybe you should be the one on your knees, begging my forgiveness."

His expression darkened. "You're in no position to dictate to me, woman," he growled. "To tell you the truth, I never meant to forgive you. You're going to die right here, with your lover."

"Let her go, Hanford," Clint said. "If she won't beg you, I will. I'm the one you want. She's done nothing to harm you."

"Did I give you permission to speak?" Roderick snapped. "You're nothing but a criminal and a convict, and your wife was a whore. The men I paid to burn your ranch told me how they all took a turn at her—not like it was anything new to a woman like that."

Clint lunged for the cattleman's throat, but was too weak to do anything more than stumble forward. Stepping to one side, Roderick cracked him across the side of the head with the butt of his pistol. Clint collapsed facedown on the ground.

"No!" Eve flung herself over his unconscious body. "Haven't you done enough, Roderick? Do you really want to go home to your children with blood on your hands?"

Roderick spat on the ground, turned his back and walked away along the rim of the outcrop. Eve saw him signal Hans with a nod. "Set the dogs loose," he ordered.

The giant shook his massive, shaggy head.

"Are you deaf as well as dumb?" Roderick shrilled. "I said set them loose! Blow your whistle!"

Again that silent refusal, that shake of the head. The dogs, restless but obedient, remained where they were. What was the attack signal? Most likely a single long blast, Eve surmised. Otherwise the first short blast would confuse the animals.

Livid with fury, Roderick raised his pistol. "Do it now, damn it!" he screamed. "Blow your whistle or I'll shoot you dead!"

Hans raised the whistle. He was close enough for Eve to catch a glint of defiance in his gentle blue eyes, and suddenly she knew what he meant to have happen.

Hans's signal, three short blasts of the whistle, would send the pack racing for home.

Roderick must have guessed Hans's intent. With a scream of rage he fired the pistol, once, then twice into the big man's chest.

The first shot sent Hans reeling backward. As the second shot struck he pitched sideways, tumbling off the mule to sprawl on the ground.

Seized by sudden confusion, the dogs began to howl and keen, lunging at anything within reach, including each other. Headed back along the rim of the cliff to his horse, Roderick side-stepped the melee, lost his footing and staggered backward into thin air.

For the space of a heartbeat he seemed to hang in space. Then, arms flailing like chicken wings, he vanished over the cliff. His scream echoed all the way to the rocky bottom a hundred feet below, where it abruptly stopped.

There was no time to see what had happened to him. With their master down, the agitated dogs were nearing the brink of panic, snapping and snarling, widening their circle. The largest, fiercest animal moved to stand guard over Hans's inert body. As if following the leader, two others joined him. The other three dogs were edging toward her and Clint, growling as they closed in.

The whistle. She had to get Hans's steel whistle.

Clint moaned and opened his eyes. "What—?" he muttered, seeing the dogs. "Where's Hanford?"

"Hush," she whispered. "Roderick's dead but we're still in danger. Lie still and keep your face protected. I know what I have to do."

She gazed past the dogs, trying to gauge the safest route to where Hans lay. Without the big man to control them, the beasts were becoming more agitated by the minute. Before long one of them was bound to attack and the rest would follow. There was no time to lose.

Eve rose slowly, willing herself not to make any sudden moves. The pack had been exposed to her scent, but here, in this unfamiliar place, would they remember her as family, or would they tear her apart before she could reach the whistle?

A memory stirred—walking with her father and their docile retrievers while he taught her to whistle bird calls and simple tunes. The dogs had always seemed soothed by the music. Now, fueled by nervousness, she began to whistle.

If a body meets a body comin' through the rye...

The hounds swung their golden eyes toward her, ears pricking. Had Hans whistled for them? It struck her as possible, since they seemed to recognize it as a friendly sound. Moving forward across the top of the outcrop, into their midst, she kept on whistling. Hackles stiffening, they growled and sniffed warily at her skirt, but they let her pass.

Only one dog remained to challenge her— the biggest brute of all, standing guard over his fallen master. As Eve approached he snarled, pulling back his black lips to display fangs as long as her little finger.

Again, she remembered her father's advice. *Don't challenge a dominant animal. Lower your eyes, be submissive. Don't make him think he has to prove he's the boss.*

The dogs were stirring again, growling and snapping as they edged toward Clint. Whistling softly, Eve lowered her head and dropped to a crouch. If the big hound meant to kill her he had every chance now. A growl rumbled in his throat, but he held his place as she reached forward with one trembling hand and clasped the whistle.

That was when she felt it—the rise and fall of the broad chest, the pulsing of a heart beneath her fist. No wonder the dog was so protective.

Hans was alive.

With the dogs closing in on Clint there was no time left. Eve put the whistle to her lips and blew three sharp, quick blasts.

The effect on the pack was stunning. The superbly trained beasts wheeled as one and headed down the slope toward home. The hound guarding Hans hesitated; then, as if knowing his master was in good hands, loped off to join his brothers.

Hans had opened his eyes. His face was pale through the tangle of his hair.

"Where are you hit?" she asked. He pointed to his ribs and his shoulder. He didn't appear to be bleeding much but his massive body had taken some serious punishment. He needed more help than she had the means or the knowledge to give him.

"Can you lie still and rest while I figure out what to do?"

He nodded and closed his eyes again. As a man who'd been brutally tortured, Hans would know how to endure pain.

Eve rose, her legs quivering beneath her. Roderick was dead. The dogs were gone. But her troubles were far from over. She was stranded on a mountain ridge with no medical supplies, no food or water, and no way to move two badly wounded men who could die without urgent care. Roderick's horse and the mule had wandered off, and even if she knew where to get help, she couldn't leave Hans and Clint long enough to walk off the mountain and find someone.

"Eve, come here." Clint's voice beckoned her. He was sitting up, holding out his arms. She sank down beside him, burying her face against his chest. He held her close, his lips grazing her hair. "I know a lot of things happened while I was out," he said. "You can tell me after you've had a chance to rest."

"I can't rest," she said, pulling to her feet again. "Roderick shot Hans for trying to save us. His pulse is strong, but he needs help, and I can't move him. Neither can you, in your condition—and it looks like you're still losing blood." She shook her head. "What we need is a miracle."

Clint stiffened as a sound reached their ears—the approaching clip-clop of horses' hooves coming up the trail. He grinned as two lanky, mounted figures appeared over the ridgetop, leading the mule and Roderick's horse. "Eve, sweetheart, I think our miracle just arrived," he said.

"Lonigan! We was roundin' up your stock and heard the gunshots! What the devil happened here?" The youthful voice had a familiar ring to it. For a moment Eve was puzzled. Then she realized that their rescuers were the two inept stagecoach bandits.

The younger one spoke. "Countess, somethin' tells me you remember us. I want to apologize if we scared you that day at the stage."

Eve gave them a smile. "You've earned my forgiveness, boys. And you needn't call me Countess. It's Mrs., uh..." Her voice trailed off. She was not about to say "Mrs. Hanford."

Clint's arm slid around her waist. "Get used to calling her Mrs. Lonigan. That's what it'll be from here on out if this widow lady will have me."

Turning, Eve treated the two young men to the sight of one spectacular kiss.

Epilogue

Two years later...

Eve stood on the porch of the home her husband had built, watching the sun set in a glorious blaze above the mountains. Many things had changed in the past two years—her name, her family and the happy, modest life they enjoyed. Most days she barely remembered that she'd once been a countess. But she would never forget that day on the mountain when her life—and Clint's—had changed forever.

Clint, with Eve sitting behind him, had been strong enough to ride Roderick's horse down the trail. Hans had been transported on a makeshift Indian travois drawn behind his mule. Where the going was rough, the Potter brothers had lifted the foot of the travois and carried it to keep from jarring his wound. At the Potter place they'd waited while Gideon rode into town to summon the doctor. Both wounded men had made a full recovery.

The hounds had returned safely to their kennels. A few weeks later Eve had sold the lot of them, along with the whistle, to a Montana man who ran a hunting resort for wealthy Easterners and Europeans. The man had also carted away Roderick's stuffed trophies to decorate the walls of his lodge. He'd made an offer for Hans, as well, but Eve had informed him curtly that she didn't sell human beings—and Hans had chosen to stay where he was known and appreciated.

Roderick's body had been retrieved and buried. As his legal wife, Eve had inherited the ranch and all his worldly goods, but all that had really mattered was keeping her promise to Margaret's children. Rose and Thomas had taken their father's death hard. But Eve had been there to mother and comfort them through their loss. Now, with Clint as their stepfather, they were truly a family.

Other players in the drama were gone from town, as well. Once Judge McCutcheon's part in hiring the gunfighters was made known, he'd been kicked out of office. He'd died of heart failure a few months later. Etta Simpkins and her niece, Beth Ann, had left on the stage and were never heard from again. A new family had taken over the bakery in town.

As for the range war...memories were long and bitter, but things were slowly changing. With more homesteaders moving into the valley, building farms and businesses, voting in elections, the big cattle ranchers were bowing to the inevitable, and conceding that violence was no solution. As a man able to see both sides of the conflict, Clint had become a valued peacemaker. He'd even been asked to run for political office, but he valued his privacy and his family over the chance to make a public name for himself, so he had wisely declined.

The monstrous house that Roderick built had been demolished log by log, the lumber used to build fences and homes—and, for Eve, the most precious thing of all, a school. With part of the ranch land opened up to families, Rose and Thomas now had schoolmates. Eve taught part-time at the school herself. The children in her class were a joy. But her prize pupil had his own oversize desk and chair.

Learning to read and write had opened up a new life for Hans. Now that he could communicate his thoughts to others, he had come out of his shell. Dressed in jeans and a woolen shirt, with his shaggy hair and beard trimmed, he was surprisingly handsome. To Eve's delight, the single ladies in the town had begun to take notice.

With the dogs gone, another of his gifts had come to light. Hans was a superb gardener, and the grounds around the house blossomed with his work.

Eve plucked a rose from one of the bushes he had planted by the porch. Breathing in its sweet fragrance, she thought of the new little life growing inside her. In a few more months, Rose and Thomas would have a baby brother or sister—and Clint would have one more child to nurture.

Looking across the pasture, she saw them riding home to supper—Clint on his tall buckskin, Rose and Thomas flanking him on their ponies. They'd been fishing in the creek and would be excited to show her what they'd caught.

Warm with love, she watched them come through the golden grass with the mountains and the sunset behind them. Not every moment in life was perfect. But there were some...

Oh, yes, there were some.

* * * * *

MILLS & BOON®

Want to get more from Mills & Boon?

Here's what's available to you if you join the
exclusive **Mills & Boon eBook Club** today:

✦ *Convenience – choose your books each month*
✦ *Exclusive – receive your books a month before
anywhere else*
✦ *Flexibility – change your subscription at any time*
✦ *Variety – gain access to eBook-only series*
✦ *Value – subscriptions from just £3.99 a month*

So visit **www.millsandboon.co.uk/esubs** today
to be a part of this exclusive eBook Club!